ELTING MEMORIAL LIBRARY NEW PALTZ
P9-DDG-161

A Girl's
Courage

A Girl's Courage

Mary Ellen Sinclair

A GIRL'S COURAGE

iUniverse books may be ordered through booksellers or by contacting:
www.agirlscourage.com

iUniverse
1663 Liberty Drive
Bloomington, IN 47403
www.iuniverse.com
1-800-Authors (1-800-288-4677)

ISBN: 978-1-5320-0117-8 (sc)
ISBN: 978-1-5320-0118-5 (e)

Library of Congress Control Number: 2016913594

Print information available on the last page.

iUniverse rev. date: 1/10/2017

For Michael

Yesterday a child came out to wonder
Caught a dragonfly inside a jar
Fearful when the sky was full of thunder
And tearful at the falling of a star
And the seasons they go round and round
And the painted ponies go up and down
We're captive on the carousel of time
We can't return we can only look behind
From where we came
And go round and round and round
In the circle game

Joni Mitchell
"The Circle Game"

Acknowledgments

I'd like to thank my resilient brother and sisters for being my friends as well as my family, my teachers whose positive influence helped me find my way, and my fellow survivors. By sharing our stories, we help each other learn to pass from surviving to flourishing.

1 The Garden of Eden

Providence, Rhode Island, 1958

A shrill whistle blows, hurting my ears, as my cousins and I peek through a window of the wool mill. I'm mesmerized by a giant machine standing in the middle of the factory, which pulls in clouds of white wool from the top and then spits out a rainbow of colored yarn at the bottom. Wooden looms surround it weaving tight lines of yarn in and out, creating a piece of cloth faster than my eyes can see it happen. It's noisy magic—pounding, beating, and squeaking—but as beautiful as fireworks on the Fourth of July.

A second whistle blows at three thirty, and all the machines stop.

I see Nonie in a crowd of people passing through the factory doors. She is wearing a green wool coat with a fur collar and a kerchief wrapped around her head, even though it's a warm summer day. The moment she sees us, her face lights up, and she calls out, "*Bella, bella*, my little birds. Let's go home before dark, so no getta lost."

We walk home in a line like ducklings and pass an empty lot that Nonie calls "the woods where bad boys hide." She points to scurrying noises and says, "See? Boyz, the little shitz. *Fa brutto*." She tells us to hurry. We waddle along as fast as we can until we reach our yard. Nonie counts us and then pulls the gate shut and locks it. We scatter about, playing in the yard, as she walks toward the house. I run past her, through the front door, and up the stairwell to her apartment. Although I'm only seven years old, I always beat her to the top of the second-floor landing, because her arthritis slows her down. She has to pull herself up by the handrail and rest on each step until she reaches the top.

Once inside, I sit at the kitchen table, watching Nonie put a little pot of coffee on the stove. We wait for it to percolate while she sits in her chair, rocking forward and then back, letting out an "Ah" each time. Then she says, "*Noi abbiamo café*, and we *mangare* bread."

It's hard for me to understand her because she mixes English and Italian words. She cannot read from any of my books, but she has one good story that she tells from memory. Even though it's the same story every night, I love it, because her dark eyes sparkle when she gets excited, and they grow wide when she acts afraid.

"My sitsah, Lena, and me lived in Italy as girls. One day we decide to have a picnic, so we make sanguiches and put them in a basketa. We walk to the ocean and sit on a mountain by the waves. It gets late and dark, so Lena lights a fire to keep us warm. Oh aya! The mountain moves. It was not a mountain but a big fish! A black whale! It swam so fast that the wind almost blew us away, but we hug each other until—oh aya!—the whale stopped and left us in the America. There's no way to get home." Nonie rocks back and smiles. "So we stay here. Okay?"

The coffeepot on the stove begins percolating through the little glass knob on top. Nonie gets up to lower the flame, passing by the window. She looks down and then screams out, "Mafalda!" It's my mother's name, so I rush to the window, afraid to see what's happening. Mom is lying on the grass in her swimsuit, getting a tan.

She yells back, "Mama, there's nothing wrong with this suit!"

"Mafalda!" Nonie's eyes are bulging, and her hands are clenched as she calls down, "A shame, ah, for all the men to see! Put some clothes on. Get in the house. Men are the animahlaas—to see you."

"Oh, all right, Mama." She sighs sleepily. "I have to put dinner on anyway. Send Mary Ellen downstairs. Her father will be home any minute."

I leave Nonie, who is making the sign of the cross on her chest, and bolt down the stairs, listening to her shriek something about a keister.

"Shut the door behind you!" my mom hollers over the noise she is making while clanking pots and pans at the kitchen stove. "It's after five, and I'm just starting supper. Wait with your brother, and tell me when Dad's car comes into the drive."

My brother, Ray, is only five years old, so I hold him up to the window. I see my dad's Chevy drive in, and my stomach growls because of the car's color, which is called candy-apple red. Ray and I hide, preparing to play cowboys and Indians. As soon as he walks through the door, we ambush him by jumping at him and hanging on to his feet. He laughs while trying to walk, and he begs Mommy for help. "Too late! I've been shot with an arrow!" he cries, falling to the floor and pulling an imaginary arrow from his chest. "Only a flesh wound, ma'am. It just grazed me." He stands, runs his hand through his wavy hair, and straightens out his shirt, saying, "All I need is a little rest before dinner to recover."

He heads for the bedroom and plops onto the bed.

"Larry!" my mom calls out. "I'm going next door to my sister's house. I'll take Ray with me, but watch Mary Ellen. I should be back within an hour. I've got potatoes baking in the oven. Get up and turn off the oven timer if it goes off before I get back. Don't fall asleep, Larry."

He mumbles, "I'm just resting my eyes."

I sit quietly coloring and listening to the timer ticking, when Dad calls to me, "Come into the bedroom, and take off your tired old dad's shoes, Sissy!" I don't go in, because sometimes he nods off. He calls out again. "Sissy?"

His shoes are so big and heavy that my hands can barely loosen the laces enough to pull each shoe off by the heel. They hit the floor, stinking of sweat. I hold my nose, about to run away, when he mumbles, "What about the socks? Don't forget the socks." I pull them off using only two fingers. I'm about to run away again, but he opens his eyes, looks down, and tells me to take a nap with him for a few minutes. "I'm not tired," I say. "Can I play outside until Mom gets home?"

"No," he says, pulling me alongside him. Then he

whispers, "Shush," into my ear, giving me goose bumps like the ones I get when I ride a roller coaster. "Be still. It's our secret time together." He has the same sad look as when he is about to give me medicine that is for my own good. His tongue licks me, leaving a wet trail of slop on my skin, making me angry and ashamed. I hold my breath and stiffen my body, staring at a familiar crack in the ceiling. It becomes a jagged slice of pure light that pulls me out of my body into a dream. I'm safe in a place without color; this world has only textures and shades of translucent white forming trees, rocks, and a pond with lilies floating. A horse drinks from the pond. He looks up when I call his name, Ikit. He comes to me, and we gallop timelessly until we reach the edge of luminous white. He bows to let me down. Below me are harsh colors shaping the place I came from, and the song of the universe—*Ohhhmmm*—vibrates loudly through my ears and into my head.

I'm awakened by a siren. No, it's the oven timer going off—I smell potatoes baking. Coming down, I see shiny wood floors and his dirt-streaked white socks. His words echo: "No one can see; no one can hear."

I listen to the kitchen door open and hear my mother's footsteps tapping on the linoleum floors. She calls from the kitchen, "Oh, Larry, I got here just in time! You nodded off. Dinner is ready. Wake up, you two."

At the dinner table, I feel mixed up. Now we are a happy family, and everything is back to normal. I love my father, and he loves me, but why do we have to be bad together? This secret hangs over my head, and I know my family will end if tell my mother, brother, aunts, or teachers.

Mommy asks me, "Why such a long face?" Her shiny black curls bounce around her head while her red lips beg, "Take a bite of something. You haven't touched any of your food. What is wrong?" I bite my lips and hold the secret in. "Lost in thought," she says. "Cat's got your tongue."

From the other end of the table, my father looks straight into my eyes and winks, saying, "You aren't going to grow up and leave your old dad, are you? I'm never going to let you go. You're my girl, aren't you? Let's see a smile."

I'm his girl.

Most mornings, the same things happen. The coffeepot percolates, Dad goes to work, and my little brother sleeps. I eat toast with butter and jelly at the kitchen table while Mom sits in front of a magnifying mirror. "This is a pin curl," she says, speaking through a bobby pin clenched between her teeth while she uses both hands to twirl strands of wet hair into a spring. She then flattens the curl and holds it down with two bobby pins crossed in an X. She repeats this process over and over, making a pattern of black X's all around her head.

We study her face magnified in the mirror. She plucks hair from her eyebrows. "To define their shape," she says. Her skin is soft and even, but there are some dots on it, which she calls blackheads, and she squeezes each one between two fingernails until it shoots into the air and splatters onto the mirror. I pull at her shirt, asking if it hurts. "A little," she says, "but it is part of being a woman. You have to suffer to be beautiful." She smiles and says, "I never lost my baby teeth. Odd, isn't it?" I study them, and they remind me of little pearls—like my doll's teeth but in a grown-up's smile.

My beauty routine doesn't hurt. I wash my face, and Mom combs my long blonde hair, pins it on each side with two barrettes, and then combs my short bangs down flat on my forehead. I look into her dark brown eyes, which are the same color as mine, and ask, "What can I wear today?"

"How about your birthday suit?" she replies, smiling.

"Wow! A birthday suit sounds so exciting. What does it look like?"

She laughs. "It's what God gave you when you were born—your skin. If you ran around in your birthday suit, you would be as naked as a jaybird."

What a letdown. I cross my arms over my chest and pout.

"Stop frowning," she says. "Your mouth is going to stay that way, and no one is going to like you as a sourpuss. It ruins your beautiful face. And besides, your skin is so fair you'd get terribly sunburned. Now, stop asking me questions. Get dressed, and go out and play. It's a beautiful day."

Outside, the sun is so bright that it makes everything appear magical. It's quiet except for the sound of the swing's chains softly tinkling like wind chimes. The lawn's blades of grass are streaked in shades of lime, jade, and emerald green, tempting my bare feet to run through them. Flowers burst from trellises and along pathways, filling the air with the smell of honey. Water squirts from a sprinkler in a fan shape, glittering in the sun and making a rainbow above two pink plastic flamingos that are perfect because they don't move. I feel as proud as a princess living in a magical kingdom, like the one in my favorite storybook.

A deep voice fills the air, and I run to the fence, knowing that soon the ragman will pass by. He stops in front of me, wearing shredded cloth as clothes, taking a rest from pushing his wooden wheelbarrow filled with a mountain of rags. Looking straight ahead at no one, he sings, "Rags for sale!" over and over, first in a deep voice and then higher. His voice without music is a beautiful melody as powerful as the operas Nonie plays on her record player, but no one else listens.

My mother is busy pinning sheets onto a clothesline from an open window. I shout out, "Mama, the ragman is leaving!" as if she's going to miss the ice cream truck. "Ma, hurry—he's almost gone."

She stops pushing the clothesline, dropping the pins and scolding, "I heard you. How many times do I have to tell you not to stare at him? It's a terrible thing, having nothing but rags to sell."

I'm sad because I want people to hear what I hear, an amazing song about nothing but rags. His melody gently fades as the sun casts a long shadow of him pushing his cart down the street.

My favorite tree is the cigar tree. Long green tubes grow from it, and they turn brown and fall to the ground, making it look as if the earth is littered with cigars. The tree has giant leaves the size of elephant ears that make a shady spot for the picnic table beneath it. It's easy for me to climb up its strong branches and hide at the top within its leaves, where I enjoy a bird's-eye view of the yard and all that goes on.

My mom's parents from Italy, Papa Non and Nonie, own everything: the land, gardens, and two houses, which are painted a light green like pistachio ice cream. A sparkling silver chain-link fence protects the property. My family lives on the first floor of a two-story house, and Papa Non and Nonie live in the apartment above us with their son, Frankie, who is a bachelor with lots of money because he doesn't have children to support or rent to pay.

Uncle Frankie doesn't drive his car to work because it would get dirty inside from the sooty boilers he cleans all day. It sits in the driveway with its glistening black paint reflecting a blue sky and clouds. Its chrome hubcaps gleam like rounded mirrors, capturing the world in miniature. The back has fins like a bat's wings and two red taillights that look like a Chinaman's eyes, watching everything. While in the tree, I can't seem to help looking at people below and listening to them chat. My mother calls this eavesdropping and says it's a bad habit, but adults say things to each other that they wouldn't in front of children, and listening to their conversations helps me put a puzzle together of their world. Sometimes I overhear ladies saying that my father is a looker and could be a movie star with his wavy blond hair, blue eyes, and muscles. They say nothing more. That's the outside of him. No one sees his darkness, except me.

To the right of our house, a cobblestone walkway leads to a cottage where my mom's sister Aunt Sophie, her husband, and my two cousins live. Mom's other sister,

Leah, lives up the street in her own home with her family, so it's easy for all three sisters and their children to spend summer days together in the yard.

My mother walks out the front door wearing a plaid two-piece bathing suit with her hair still in pin curls. Her olive skin and red lips glisten, and she looks like the ladies in the glossy-paged magazines she reads. She carries a towel, an alarm clock, and tanning lotion in one arm, and my little brother, Ray, is squeezed between her other arm and her waist. He looks like a plump Kewpie doll hanging from her, with wide blue eyes and blond peach fuzz on his head.

Aunt Sophie leaves her cottage in her swimsuit with her daughter, Diane, in one arm and her son, Gary, following her. Diane is the younger of the two, still in diapers and cute as a button, and Gary is tall and lanky for his age. He can outrun any of us without a sweat. Auntie calls out to my mom: "Muff!" Muff is a nickname for her Italian name, Mafalda. Nonie calls her Mafa; my dad calls her Muffy, which she likes because it sounds American.

"I'm in the backyard!" she answers. Together they let their pin curls dry as they time the perfect tan. The fifteen-minute bell rings from the alarm clock, and both of them turn around together, lying on their bellies with their behinds in the air. They undo each other's back straps and put on suntan lotion to get even tans. They have such a good time simply being together, flipping through magazines and laughing at each other's stories. Sometimes their giggling turns into out-of-control laughter, causing Aunt Sophie to beg, "Stop, Muff! Stop, or I'll pee my pants!" That makes them laugh even harder.

At the end of the day, Uncle Frankie is the first to arrive home. He walks through the gate looking like a ghost, covered in black soot except for the whites of his eyes. All the cousins laugh and point at him until Aunt Sophie yells from the blanket on which she's sunning herself, "Stop laughing! Can't you see it's your uncle?" She shakes her finger in the air at all of us while saying, "It's all right, Frankie. Don't you worry. The work is dirty, but the money is clean. You kids stop it."

I hear them mock Nonie's words about any woman he brings home: "She's no good for my Frankie. That one's *butannah*." They nod in agreement that no woman is good enough for Nonie's boy.

Then there is silence, followed by serious, hushed talk. I hear some of it: "What a tragedy it was born that way." The whispers go in and out. "It can't support its own head. It might not survive." They don't know what to do for their friend, and I hear them say what a gift from God normal, healthy children are.

I'm just about to hear more, when all conversations stop.

2

Tomatoes in the Sun

Each morning, Papa Non comes out of the house to do yard work. He is retired from the factory that Nonie still works in, yet he wears the same uniform of matching dark green pants and shirt that he wore to work. Everything about him is neat; his pants and shirt are pressed, and the top of his head is shiny, with a circle of wispy white hair left around it. He has bushy white eyebrows and black eyes. People call him Mr. Clean because he looks like the man on the label of the detergent that my mother washes floors with. He doesn't smile much and is serious about getting to the jobs to be done. He carries a can of paint in his favorite color, mint green, and looks for anything in need of a touch-up, taking out his brush and swishing it around.

The garden needs shoveling and raking, and seeds need planting.

After gardening, Papa walks to an old doghouse with a chair by it in the middle of the garden. He sits, relaxing. He then pulls out a magazine and a red box with old crows on the lid from inside the doghouse. He takes a cigar from the box, lights it, and sends puffs of smoke toward the yellow sunflowers surrounding the garden. His tomato plants are his pride and joy, and they grow tall, speckling the blue sky with dots of red. Birds swoop in to pick at them, and he jumps out of his chair, angrily shaking a rake in the air to shoo them away, screaming out Italian words. He then lights the burn barrel full of dead leaves and twigs, making a lot of smoke that blends with the smoke of his cigar.

My brother and cousin Gary ambush him from behind, hanging on to his legs as he tries to walk away. Papa yells through gritted teeth, "These goddamn kidz! Stoppa it!" His hands pull imaginary hairs from the top of his head, where the hairs are long gone, having already been pulled out.

My mother yells up from her blanket, telling us to leave Papa alone and not to make him any more nervous. "He has bleeding ulcers, for God's sake!"

My brother, Ray, and Gary are inseparable friends, but Ray is a few years younger than Gary and smaller, so he's always running next to Gary as Gary strolls along. All they want is some attention from Papa Non, and all he wants is for them to stop stampeding over his work, trampling atop his planted seeds or plopping through wet cement that's setting. A good part of Papa Non's day involves a game of trying to catch one of them. He's just about to catch Gary, who realizes his only way out of Papa Non's grasp is to run straight up a giant mountain of manure delivered for the garden. Everyone watches him reach the top of the mountain, and his feet sink slowly into the muck. He lets out the breath he's been holding in and beats his hands on his chest like Tarzan, yelling out, "King of the manure pile! No one can touch me. I dare you."

Ray has been slowly running up the back of the mountain, and he reaches the top. He tries to knock Gary down from behind to take his place as king. Instead, they roll down together, and Papa Non walks away, screaming in the language of his old country, "*Dutti basti*!"

Papa Non sits under the cigar tree at the picnic table and opens a can of olives with the pits removed to make a game of teaching his grandchildren how to count in Italian. He places an olive on the tip of each finger, and when he calls out a number, he eats one olive from a finger. "*Uno. Due. Tre. Quattro. Cinque. Sei. Sette. Otto. Nove. Dieci.*"

My mother hears this and yells out to him not to teach us Italian, because we will speak broken English, and kids will make fun of us in school, as they did her.

Papa Non continues singing and pointing to olive-tipped fingers held in the air until all the olives are gone and there's only broth remaining in the can left on the table.

A woman arrives quietly, wheeling a baby carriage, and stops to sit at the picnic table. She's looking into space at no one—as the ragman does—slowly rocking. I slide down from the tree to sit next to her. She still stares into space, rocking the carriage, not looking at me or saying anything good or bad. I go to see the new baby, as I always do when friends stop by with baby carriages. The baby has on a pink checkered dress with a matching bonnet and little white socks with lace. She is cooing and wiggling—happy like all new babies with rattles. I'm scared. Her head is twice as big as her body, and she has only one eye, in the middle of her head, and a row of bumps on her face, going under her bonnet. I am ashamed for looking, but the woman stares into space, not saying anything, rocking the carriage.

My mother and aunt call out to her from their blankets, telling her to come over and sit by them, but she stares into space, not hearing them. They whisper, and I hear some of their words: "She wants to be left alone. Just let her be." In time, she leaves. I hear my aunt say, "Tragedy, and what can we do? How can we help? Children are a gift from God."

Aunt Leah interrupts my thoughts about gifts from God, arriving with my cousins. Audrey is my age, and the twins, Cheryl and Charlene, are ten years old. We all have the same signature short cut bangs framing different hairstyles. We sit around a portable swimming pool filled with barely enough water to wiggle our toes in. The twins break a lot of shocking news to us while Aunt Leah and our moms are busy talking under the sun: there's no Santa Claus or Easter Bunny, and we can swear and not go to hell.

At the end of the afternoon, my mom and aunts wrap up their blankets, gather their things, round up their children, and head home to get dinner ready for their families.

The weekends are more fun because relatives and family visit, hugging and kissing. It's always my mother's family, and Papa Non and Nonie have a lot of long-lost relatives who came all the way from their old country to live here too. Dad never joins them because he has lots of stuff to do on the weekends. I think he feels lonely being far away from his family in Ohio, where he grew up.

Nonie plays records on an old-fashioned Victrola in her bedroom and opens her window so that scratchy Italian music flows out the window through her lace curtains. Papa Non holds up what seems like the biggest squash in the world, which he has grown. There's laughter, and we eat into the night. The adults light candles to chase away mosquitoes, and Papa Non's homemade wine comes out from the cellar.

I sit by my mother's side, listening as the adults start speaking in low voices while looking around for children, because they're talking about something only adults understand, such as a sickness or problem. If they catch me looking worried, they smile as if everything is going to be fine. I hear their whispers, though: "It's a good thing that baby died. It would have been a vegetable its whole life." I know they are speaking of the baby I saw only a few days ago. Everyone at the picnic table becomes silent.

What do I do with what I know that only adults are supposed to know?

Dad is busy in the middle of the living room floor, opening a box with the words *RCA Television* printed on it in big red letters. My mother hurries to get dinner ready so that we can all watch our first television program. In between my dad cussing at the directions and fiddling with the antennae, eventually, we hear a buzzing sound coming from our new television. My father asks my mother exactly where it's going to be in the parlor because he's not moving it once it's set up. "Right there," she says, pointing to a spot next to our artificial fireplace. She has a camera ready to take a picture of us next to our first television.

We are excited when Dad pushes a button and, like magic before our eyes, a program appears. We are mesmerized, first by the news, then by all kinds of funny shows, and then by scary shows that we watch late into the night. We fall asleep by the TV.

Falling asleep by the TV with Mom while my father works late becomes our evening routine. Tonight I wake up as Mom carries me to bed, so she reads me a story. I rub a silky piece of her nightgown, feeling its slippery softness between my fingers, as she reads *Snow White* to me: "'Mirror, mirror, on the wall, who's the fairest of them all?' the wicked queen asks into the mirror."

The pages blow soft air onto my face as she turns them. I fall asleep to the sound of her voice, like the ragman's song fading down the street.

"My lady, Queen, you are fair—'tis true—but Snow White is fairer than you."

Loud screaming awakens me. My heart pounds, but I don't move. It is dark. Mom isn't next to me, and Daddy is home. They are fighting, and I listen. My mother wants to know where he has been.

The bedroom door slams shut, but I can still hear my father's voice. "Shhh. You'll wake up Mary, your mother and father, and the whole damn neighborhood." I hear banging and crashing, and then it becomes quiet, with only the sound of the alarm clock ticking.

"Put that knife down, Muff! You hear?" My father's voice cuts into the silence.

I want to run to see, but I can't move. I'm too scared to even open my eyes, so I lie there, clenching my fists and gritting my teeth in the dark. I hear a bang, followed by some scuffling. It's quiet except for the sound of my mother crying.

I hear my father's voice say, "You don't want to do that."

In the morning, I look for my mother by the table, but she isn't there. My feet squeak as I run toward her bedroom door. The window shades are down, and the bed is made. She is lying down with her clothes on. She sits up, rocking with her hands balancing her. I watch her feet hit the floor in white socks and loafers with copper pennies in them. "Mama!" I say when I see her face and get scared, not recognizing her. Her eyes are swollen shut, and one is black and blue. Her lips are cut and swollen. There is a facecloth with ice falling out of it on the pillow. I go toward her, wanting to sit on her lap and put my arms around her.

"Outside, Mary Ellen," she whispers. I want to run to her anyway, but I run away crying.

Outside, I hide in a little garden with flowers taller than I am and giant leaves to hide under. There are clear round dots on the leaves, glistening like my mother's diamond ring. I touch them, and they turn into water trickling down the long leaves. I'm safe in a corner behind rows of plants if Papa Non doesn't see me. I cry to myself, digging up dirt from around a flower stem, watching all the bugs run away.

I bury my face within a bush of pink bellflowers. It smells sweet, and the warmth of the sun dries my tears. I hear a tiny buzzing sound and then feel puffs of air on my cheek. Right in front of my eyes is a tiny bird the size of a bumblebee, sipping from a flower. It has a long snout like a black trumpet and an emerald-green and ruby-red body. It floats from flower to flower before my eyes and then comes close to my cheek, tickling me with its wings. I watch it hovering and whirling its black lace wings.

It is gone, but I feel as if someone kissed me and made all the hurt inside go away.

3

Yesterday's Today

It's autumn. The leaves color the ground in bright oranges and reds. Mom gets sweaters ready and complains that our school uniforms cost too much money this year. We go to the store, and I pass pretty shoes I would like to buy as she leads me to a pile of gray suede Hush Puppies with pointed fronts under a sign marked St. Theresa's School. A salesman appears, asking Mom if she wants to buy these shoes for my school uniform. She looks at the price and complains that they are too expensive. "They last a year," the man squawks. He measures my foot and asks if she wants the regulation gray knee socks. My mother tells him she can get the same thing for half the price at Atlantic Mills.

I'm going to be in the third grade. Each new school year, I forget how big the school building is and how different the nuns are from my family. They are holy women married to God, and I am not sure if nuns are real people or saints. I don't see hair under their habits, nor can I see any feet under their long black gowns. They move as if they are floating above the floor. Sometimes they smile, but I'm sure they never laugh so hard they almost pee their pants.

All the kids are dressed in the same gray-and-green-plaid wool uniforms, running around with our new shoes squeaking along the shiny floors. "Not so fast," Sister Angelina says as she comes into the crowded hallway. "Stop all of this running wild." She pulls out the clicker, which looks like an ugly bird's head. It's wooden, and she snaps it to make it click. "When I click it once, everyone is to stop talking. After two clicks, we all say, 'Good morning, Sister Angelina.' And it's three clicks across the knuckles to anyone who forgets."

Sister Angelina divides us up into two groups, and Sister Pauline, my homeroom teacher, organizes our seats for the year, putting the smallest kids, like me, in the front desks. She asks us to sit up straight; place our hands atop the desks, folded; and wait for Father Gibbons to arrive and make his announcements.

Father Gibbons enters our room seemingly in slow motion, standing tall and straight. Everything he wears is black, from his long robe and shoes to his hat, which is shaped like a soft crown with a pom-pom at the top. He is in charge of all the other priests and nuns and can report them to his boss, God, if they make a mistake. He removes his hat, revealing pure white hair combed up in a pouf. I can't image what he used to look like because his face is so wrinkled and almost the color of chalk. His eyes hide under shaggy brows with a few wiry, long black hairs that move up and down as he speaks through thick lips. "There is enough in the school budget for two new teachers this year. While they are not nuns, please treat them with the same respect. One, an art teacher, Miss Michelle, will come once a week. The other is a mathematics teacher, Miss Karmodey. She will be full-time, as mathematics is most important."

Sister Pauline interrupts him, asking if he is tired and then offering him a chair. She continues while Father rests, explaining that Miss Karmodey has a medical condition that causes her to wear a bag at her side. Most likely, we will never see it, but if we do, we are not to stare or laugh.

We hear snores behind Sister Pauline. Father Gibbons is slouched to one side, fast asleep, with his hair still neatly shaped in a pouf. We don't dare laugh, for fear of getting hit across the knuckles with the clicker.

He wakes up, calling out, "What! Where am I?"

Sister Pauline escorts him out, and all of us start buzzing about Miss Karmodey.

Sister Pauline praises us for being on our best behavior and for not forgetting our manners over the summer. She looks serious and rolls up her sleeves, saying, "Let's get to work. I have a lot to teach." She reminds us, pointing her clicker, "With one click, we stand. With two clicks, we pledge allegiance to the flag."

We begin with hands placed over our hearts: "I pledge allegiance to the flag ..." I mix words as we end because I forgot some of it over the summer: "One nation indispensable with liberty and just ice for all."

At three clicks, we sit.

Sister Pauline pulls a pitch pipe from her pocket. Everyone ducks as she passes by, because her spit sprays into the air, bouncing off anyone below. She blows the notes, and we match their pitches, singing back to her: "Do re mi fa sol la ti do."

I wonder how many lessons I can possibly remember while looking at the clock above the blackboard, which is stuck again. A day at school is much longer than a summer day spent sitting by the sprinkler in my yard.

Sister's voice interrupts my thoughts as everyone sings the alphabet. She points to letters written perfectly along the top of the blackboard and then stops singing and says, "Today we will practice turning printed letters into penmanship." She hands out paper and Palmer pens, which are so special that she hides them in her desk drawer.

I watch her counting and examining them as she hands them out one by one, walking up and down the aisles and reminding us, "Be careful with these pens, as they are very expensive and must last."

I'm finally holding a robin's-egg-blue one. It's a ballpoint pen, round at the bottom and long and thin at the end, with a little nub at the top.

We learn the proper way to hold the pen by balancing the rounded ball between our thumb and fingers and then practice writing without putting too much pressure on the page. I concentrate hard, as Mom does at her mirror.

It's getting near lunch, and my stomach is growling. We can't open our lunch boxes until twelve o'clock, and the clock now says it's only eleven thirty. Sister Pauline floats around the room, sneaking up behind us to look at our work and catch us if we press too hard or write outside of the lines.

While admiring a capital *R* that I've finished, I push the top of the pen between my teeth, nibbling more and more into the soft blue pen. Sister Pauline tells us to hurry, finish our last letters, and hand in our pens because it's almost lunch. When I take the pen out of my mouth, I can't believe it is the same sleek pen she gave me. It's all dented with teeth marks, and the nub is half off. I feel frightened inside, as I do when my parents fight; my stomach is in a knot because of the pen.

Now the clock seems to speed up, and Sister says, "Time is up. Pass all your papers and pens to the front."

All the pens from behind me are in my hand, nice and new, and I mix my pen into them and hand the whole bunch forward. Sister Pauline picks up each bunch of pens at the first desk in each row and then drops them into her special drawer in her desk. She examines our papers and then holds up a sheet of a student's work, pointing out the smooth, even scrollwork and the way all the letters stay within the lines. Then she sits back in her desk chair, counting and examining each pen. "Ah, what is this?" she screams, flailing my pen into the air. "Who destroyed this pen? Who would do such a thing?"

No one moves or says a word.

"All right then, if no one is willing to own up to it," she says, pacing up and down the aisles, looking into each of our faces one by one, "if you are too cowardly to admit it in front of the class, I want everyone to put their heads down on their desks."

My head is down, and I sweat, listening to the floorboards creak as she passes by me.

"Now, whoever bit this pen up, lift your right hand."

I try to lift my hand, but it's stuck to the desk. Sister Pauline tells us there will be no recess after lunch. Instead, we all will sit with our heads down on our desks because of the cowardly pen destroyer who did not come forth. She gives a lecture about the person who bit the pen. He or she didn't really get away with anything because God sees everything.

Now I have God mad at me. Sister Pauline is married to him, and he will probably tell her tonight that I chewed up the pen.

My stomach stops growling because lunch is one slice of bologna between two slices of white bread with a stripe of yellow mustard. I can't eat another bite. What else is there to do but throw the sandwich back into my lunch box and snap it shut?

I feel so bad that there's no point in eating anyway. I dig holes in Papa Non's garden. My father gives me evil feelings, and now I'm the pen coward. It's the biggest mistake I've ever made in my whole life.

Before I chewed on the pen, it was easy to talk Sister Pauline after school. She would smile at me and answer my questions, such as how tigers got their stripes or why it is dark in Alaska at the same time it is light here. I hoped Sister could help me figure out a way to stop my father. But if she gets so mad over a little pen mistake, how will she react to my secret? What if this secret turns out to be a mortal sin?

Maybe Miss Karmodey, the new teacher, will be nice,

and I can talk to her after class, but now I have a scary feeling in the pit of my stomach that there is no one to tell my secret to—no one.

The clock strikes three, a loud bell clangs, and Sister Pauline dismisses us to line up around the schoolhouse. We are organized by different lines according to which streets we go home to. A loudspeaker plays band music, and we lift our hands and knees, high-marching until the line breaks; then I run as fast as I can until I get home.

The hallway at home smells of a cake baking in the oven. It's good to be home. Mom asks me how school was as she looks into my lunch box. She complains that there is only a bite out of my sandwich. I'm afraid to tell her about the pen or why it feels so bad to hide a mistake. There is nothing else to do but say that everything is good, everything is fine, so that she won't say the cat's got my tongue.

It's three thirty, and we watch Mom's favorite soap operas on TV. Ray and I get elbow burns and sore chins from staying in one spot in front of the TV for so long. Mom starts to cook, and soon Dad is home. We don't ambush him, as we used to when we were little. We pretend we aren't home, and he finds out where we are hiding.

Tonight is Friday, so instead of meat and potatoes, we have frozen fish sticks and french fried potatoes. My father complains that they taste strange, but my mother says happily, "It's the latest thing, saving mothers time preparing dinner—frozen foods that go into the oven and then onto the table."

I hope that after we eat, I can watch television. I know that after my father asks my brother and me what we learned in school, next he will bring up a subject for all of us to discuss. Tonight's topic is, today is tomorrow, and tomorrow is yesterday.

I say, "Wait a minute. No. Today is today."

"Yes, but," my father says, "don't be so sure, because yesterday it was today, and tomorrow it will be yesterday."

I am confused, wondering why today is never today, when we are in today.

My mother is trying to clean up the table, and my brother starts to fidget. My father gets angry that Ray isn't paying attention to the professor. He says it is simple if you just pay attention to your old man and try to grasp it. "I'm going to say it once more, and this time, really listen. Yesterday is today, today is tomorrow, and tomorrow is yesterday."

I listen hard, but it still sounds like the same thing. I'm sure today is today. Even in school, the nuns don't make us sit this long over one thing. My mind is on the outside and the kids playing, and my father talks on and on, almost as if he is talking to himself. It's now dark out, and my mother tries to butt in to let us go because we have homework, but my father says, "Ah, Muff, it wouldn't do you no harm to sit around the table and talk once in a while."

"Talk, talk, Larry—all you ever do is talk. No, I don't want to sit around the table and listen to you about the tomorrow that never comes," my mother answers with the disgusted tone that he gets mad at her about.

"Now, you sit here, Muffy, and listen," he commands.

My mother says, "Larry, can we please finish up and watch some television?"

It gets late into the night.

"I'm not finished yet." My father goes on and on.

Now my mother pleads, "It is time to sleep."

"Ah, go ahead," my perturbed father says. "No one wants to listen around here. The whole world is getting lazy. That television is the downfall of humanity. I'm going to make one last prediction, and then you all can go." He points his finger at me, saying, "Mark my words, Mary: in the future, people will be born with only two fingers on each hand, because we will evolve from a lazy society. No one will work hard physical labor anymore—they will use pencils, grab on to knobs, or push buttons for a living, needing only a long thumb and finger. Mark my words. Remember this day. The discussion is over."

My mother is drained. Ray and I are tired, and we race each other to the bedroom for sleep.

I hear Dad trying to get into a conversation with my mother, but she says she just wants to go to bed. He doesn't stop talking, so she heads toward the bedroom, singing over his words, "Someday my prince will come."

I hear my father's final words: "What's the use? People don't talk anymore."

4

Yes, You Can, but You May Not

Miss Karmodey is a screamer. The minute she enters the classroom, she screeches at us, "Quiet class!" as if we have already made a mistake. She points at us with her gray hair flying around her head, saying, "You listen, and you listen good, you little fat-headed Scotch-eyed lobsters. Repeat the times tables after me. No one stops. Do you hear me?" She looks exhausted as she heads to her desk and sits in her chair, looking left and then right. Sneakily, she opens her desk drawer, pulls out a little silver flask, unscrews the cap, and takes a swig. She puts the cap on and slides the flask under papers in her drawer. She puckers her lips, shakes her head, and then glares at us. "Class, repeat after me the multiplication tables."

We start with ones: "One times one is one." We go on and on and finish with "One times twelve is twelve."

"Now the twos!" she wails.

"One times two is two," we say, and we go on and on.

We memorize numbers equaling other numbers, and when I look at the clock, it's going so slowly that it seems to be going in reverse. We repeat over and over into the threes, fours, fives, sixes, and sevens.

Suddenly, Miss Karmodey's voice lowers. She slurs slowly, "One times seven is seven. Two times seven is fourteen. Three times seven is twenty-one," and then she is silent.

We carry on what we know without her: "Four times seven is twenty-eight. Five times seven is thirty-five. Six times seven is forty-two. Seven times seven is …"

We don't know what seven multiplied by seven is without her, and we don't want to say the times tables anymore anyway. With nothing to repeat, we sit quietly, not daring to wake her as we watch her head bobbing up and down.

She gives a final push to stay awake, whispering, "Six times seven is forty-two," and then her head drops to her chest.

As long as we are quiet, we don't have to say the times tables anymore. We sit silently, watching her head bobbing and then falling down to her chest while her mouth hangs open. In her sleep, she says, "Seven times seven," and her false teeth slip down from her mouth to the edge of her chin. No one can resist laughing and pointing, which wakes her up. She pushes her teeth back in place and then points to a boy giggling in the first row and scolds, "I'll teach you to laugh at me, you little fat-headed Scotch-eyed lobster! All of you!"

She grabs a vase of flowers and throws it across the room. We all duck as the vase flies past our heads, falls to the floor, and shatters into bits of glass and flowers in water.

She stands and surveys the damage under a sunny window. The light shines through her dress, revealing the bag that we aren't supposed to pay attention to. I can see it's hooked to wires and tubes. She is falling apart at the seams like a robot with batteries running out, flailing her arms to stay standing. It's why she can't make it through all the times tables without falling asleep.

Any hope I had of her being able to help me is sunk. Everyone is a fat-headed Scotch-eyed lobster to her. I'd risk having the nearest thing to her thrown at me if I told my secret to her.

My favorite teacher is the traveling art teacher. I know she would listen to me if I got a chance to talk to her, but since she is always rushing in and out to different schools, she never has the time to talk to us.

Her name is Miss Michelle, and she always holds my work up to the class, saying how beautiful my colors and ideas are. I wait to see her walk through the door carrying her brushes and watercolors, wearing an apron, and smiling with her ponytail swishing in the air. Where is she? Instead, Sister Pauline appears, announcing that the art teacher cannot make it today. We all sigh, but Sister tells us not to worry; she is going to teach art class today.

Now I can show Sister Pauline how much better my artwork is than my penmanship, and I wonder what she will teach us to create today. I can't wait much longer to begin coloring with my crayons. Sister Pauline looks at us as if she's thinking, *Yes, I can teach art*. She says, "I want each of you to draw yourself."

Hmm, this project is like getting vegetables instead of cake. Well, at least I get time to make a picture. I begin scribbling and scratching with all the energy I give to the traveling art teacher. My crayons are sprawled around my drawing, when I hear, "Time's up."

What is wrong with that clock? Whenever I want it to slow down, it speeds up!

We pass our work in one by one, row by row. Sister Pauline sits at her desk, examining our drawings, and then gets excited, stopping at a drawing and holding it up. *What? She didn't even notice mine*. Sister Pauline explains how perfect the picture is because it represents everything exactly the way it is. The hair is brown. The skin is skin toned. The uniform is green, and it's colored perfectly within the lines.

It's Palmer penmanship all over again. I know in my heart that coloring outside the lines is more beautiful, but I can't say anything. I want to fill pages and pages with red, yellow, and orange colors, scribbling outside the lines until they disappear.

Now we are on lessons about how to speak English properly.

Sister Pauline explains an example of how to ask for something, saying, "Always begin your sentence with 'May I,' not 'Can I.'"

Just because you can do something doesn't mean you have a right to do something. It is polite to ask, "May I?"

If we make a mistake and ask, "Can I?" she will correct us by answering, "Yes, you can, but you may not."

I'm not paying attention. I'm watching the clock hands move closer to lunchtime, when I hear my name coming through the fog: "Mary Ellen, come up here."

I stand in front of Sister's desk, wondering if I'm the unlucky one picked to make an example of in front of the class. She pulls open her drawer full of Palmer pens, and I see the pen I chewed on sticking out on top. My heart drops. The whole class will discover that I am the coward they gave up recess for. I'm sweating.

She reaches in the drawer, pulls out a key, and dangles it in front of my face, saying, "Ask me for this key."

"What?" I ask nervously.

She says, "Show the class the proper way to ask me for this key."

Whew. I'm relieved that her request has nothing to do with the pen.

"Well? I'm waiting," she says.

My words come out: "Can I have the key?"

Sister Pauline's tight lips answer, "Yes, you can."

I grab at the key, but she jerks it away, saying, "Yes, you can, but you may not."

Oops. I remember the proper words and say, "May I have the key?"

"Yes, you may," she answers in a satisfied tone.

As I walk to my desk, I see a relieved look on everyone's face for not being the one singled out.

I'm thankful to her husband, God, for not telling her I chewed on the pen.

Another school day passes, and we march home to band music blaring through icicles hanging from the loudspeaker on the gray school building.

At home, Ray is not happy when my father's car comes into the drive tonight, because Dad will find out that my brother can't sit still and fidgets all day in the classroom. Sister Carmelita made Ray sit beneath her chair, under her skirt, to keep him still. When my father finds out, he thinks that Ray is a normal boy and that the nun was wrong to put Ray under her skirt.

My father is tired from working overtime and weekends to save money to build a house in the country, so we get out of learning lessons about the universe tonight.

I lie awake at night, knowing that snow is falling in the darkness, because I can see it out my window, glittering around the light of the streetlamps. I listen to my mother and father talking while they drink coffee and smoke cigarettes. They laugh and make plans to change things. I love to fall asleep listening to their cups clinking on the table amid my mother's soft laughter at my father's happy stories.

Tonight all is well.

In the morning, the sound of snow shovels outside my window awakens me. "Shhh," my mother says, listening to Salty Brine on the radio station. He is announcing the schools closed because of snow. We hear his teasing voice holding back the name of each closed school: "St. Bartholomew's." My brother and I hold hands. "St. Mary's." We are still hopeful. "St. Theresa's."

Finally! "Yeah!" We cheer and jump up and down, remembering to thank God.

Outside, everything is disguised under a blanket of snow. The sky is so white that it hurts my eyes. Still, the snow keeps coming down. We run through our usual paths, which have been transformed into tunnels of snow higher than our shoulders. I stick out my tongue, catching snowflakes that taste like melted wind. Icicles hang from windows and drainpipes, and I pluck as many icicles as I want, take a bite of each, and then toss each one away. Their taste is clean and pure.

My mother comes outside, surrounded by snowflakes. The wind flutters her coattails around her like a hummingbird's wings. She points to clothes left frozen on the line; icicles hang from the clothespins. We laugh at how silly the clothes look, stiffened into the shape of the wind, and I help her rescue them.

Once inside the house, we pile the frozen laundry on the radiators to dry. My mother teaches me that if you magnify a snowflake, its pattern is like a star, and within that star are more stars, making an infinite configuration. The most amazing thing about snowflakes is that no two are alike.

She shows me how to make a snowflake by folding a piece of paper into a triangle and then cutting shapes into it with scissors. When she unfolds it, a lace snowflake appears. I try to make one exactly like hers, but I can't.

I think about all the snowflakes falling around the world and wonder how anyone would discover if there happened to be two alike, but I don't ask my mother, because she will call me a doubting Thomas, like in the Bible. That's her nickname for me—doubting Thomas—because I doubt everything.

Maybe it is true that each snowflake is unique, but I only believe in things I can see.

She makes me tomato soup in a blue bowl. As I eat my soup, more of the picture on the bowl appears of two bluebirds flying toward each other. I ask my mother if there is a story behind this picture.

"Why, yes. Those are lovebirds, and they are from a place far away called the Orient. So are the two houses." She points to a grand house with trees and a bridge leading to a smaller house in the back. "A prince lived in the magnificent house with a rich family. One day he ventured out of his house across the river, where he saw a woman sitting on the edge of the bridge by the humble little house. Upon first sight, they fell in love. He wished to marry her, and he took her across the river to meet his wealthy family. They disapproved of her because she was from a poor class, and they forbade him to ever see her again. The lovers secretly continued to send letters to each other through the birds. The birds in the picture are exchanging their letters." Mom stares into my now-empty bowl, daydreaming.

I ask, "Why did class matter to the prince's family? After all, he loved her. Didn't they want the prince to be happy?"

My mother looks as if she is the woman in the blue bowl, waiting for the love letter. "Today marriage for love happens, but it was not that way in old countries."

"Well, what class are we, Mom?" I ask.

She doesn't answer.

"Mom," I say, "we aren't poor, are we?"

"No," she finally says.

I badger her. "Well, are we middle class?"

She says, "Yes, we are middle class. Not rich and not poor. And what made you ask a question like that? Did someone ask you that?"

"No," I answer, "I wanted to know."

My mother admits that Papa Non and Nonie were poor and that, at times, they did not know where their next meal was coming from. They never wasted a scrap of food and never took anything for granted.

When they first came to this country, my mother picked dandelions on her way home from school for her grandmother to cook for dinner. Nothing went to waste. Even flour sacks were sewn into bloomers. My mother laughs. "'Pillsbury's Best' was plastered right across my behind in big red letters. You know, we didn't have a lot, but I never felt poor, not with Papa and my mother. I never felt it. On the holidays, we always had a special dinner with all the fixings and dessert. It made us feel rich indeed. We didn't need a lot of presents, although I remember one Christmas, my mom had saved coupons from the back of macaroni packages. All the coupons she saved were worth only one doll, and she gave it to all three of us sisters to share. We were all so excited, grabbing at it, unable to share it—until the doll was ripped to pieces between us." She shakes her head, still feeling a little sad, I think.

In the afternoon, we watch my mother's favorite soap operas. We eat dinner without my father. It gets later, and he still isn't home. My mother is worried about him driving in the snow. We wait for him. We watch TV, and Ray and I fall asleep.

I don't know how late it is when my mother and father's fighting awakens me. I listen in the darkness.

She screams, "You have been with another woman!"

"Oh, Muffy," I hear him say, "don't accuse me of something that isn't true. I worked overtime for extra money, and it was slow driving in this weather. It is still snowing out there, and the roads are bad."

She screams even louder at him. "I don't believe you, Larry! You always say you are working overtime, but I don't see the extra money. Where's the money? I know there is someone else, and if I find out who she is, I'll kill her."

Shivers go down my body. Aren't I his secret girl? If my mother finds out about what my father is doing to me, will she kill me?

My father's voice gets deep and threatening. "Stop that damn accusing and talking like a whore. I'm putting the money away in a special place so we can build our house. I've got a summer job lined up as an usher at the drive-in movie theater at night and on the weekend, and I've got some lawn-mowing jobs lined up."

She cries, "Damn you, Larry!"

"Quit cussing," I hear him say. "I love you."

My mother softly moans, "Damn you, Larry," giving in because she loves him too.

5 Untouchable

My catechism is my favorite book because it is mysterious and beautiful to look at, with a cross embossed on its black leather cover. The pages are thin parchment edged in gold, and they float open to a scarlet ribbon that marks the place where I left off. In the middle are glossy color pages showing pictures of saints. We can't take this book home. We must leave it inside our desks, but I sneak it out to look at the pictures whenever I can. The stories are hard to read, but Sister Pauline helps us make sense of them.

Today we read the story of Lot's wife, who is in the middle of running away from a burning town, when God tells her, "Don't look back, lest she be turned into salt." His words distracted her, and she looked back, becoming a pile of salt. Sister explains that the moral of the story is to not let anything distract you from your leap of faith once you are in it. I think she means you shouldn't turn your back on yourself.

Finally, we get to turn to the middle of the book, with

the glossy pages and colorful pictures. There are three different pictures showing God as one person—the Father, the Son, and the Holy Ghost. How will Sister Pauline explain how God can be a father, his son, and a ghost all at once?

As if reading my mind, Sister Pauline begins to explain the first picture, which shows God as a kindly old man with long white hair (the Father) watching over our souls from heaven. He is on a cloud surrounded by blue air, holding his hands outward, with gold lines radiating from him. He can't do much about our bodies because they are part of the physical world. But in the next picture, he sends his son, Jesus, down to help.

Then she explains the picture of Jesus. He looks like his father, except he has long dark hair and a beard. His work on Earth was to remind everyone that all people are part of God. Most people thought he was crazy, so they killed him, but he did get to finish his job. The picture shows a slit below his heart, with blood dripping down, but he is smiling because he forgave everyone.

The hardest picture to understand is that of the Holy Ghost, which is shown as one big eye in the middle of a triangle with golden lines spewing from it.

Sister explains, "The Holy Ghost is not scary like a Halloween ghost. It is a holy, divine spirit. Understand, children, that a spirit is your soul. We all have a soul that is part of God's spirit. Our soul is an untouchable energy within our body and the heavens. Long after our body is gone, our soul exists. It does not die. Nothing can destroy it or touch it. It is invisible to anyone else but us and is untouchable."

I repeat this word to myself: *untouchable*. There is a part of me my father can't touch. I think about the light that takes me away. It is my soul—that never hurts.

Someone interrupts. "Well, if we have a soul that rises when we die, then why do we have to be good on Earth? Why can't we do whatever we want?"

She says, "It's up to God to add up your sins to decide whether or not you get to heaven or hell. Don't get too ahead of yourselves or worry so much."

Someone asks, "If we have souls, then why can't we fly? Float around like angels and saints in the pictures?"

Sister Pauline says, "Once we die, we can, but until then, our soul is trapped in our body."

I have a soul!

Sister Pauline teaches us a prayer that we should say every night to our heavenly Father watching over our souls:

> Our Father, who art in heaven, hallowed be thy name. Thy kingdom come, thy will be done on earth as it is in heaven. Give us this day our daily bread, and forgive us our trespasses as we forgive those who trespass against us. And lead us not into temptation, but deliver us from evil. Amen.

We also have a mother in heaven, and we learn the Hail Mary:

> Hail Mary, full of grace, the Lord is with thee. Blessed art thou among women, and blessed is the fruit of thy womb, Jesus. Holy

Mary, mother of God, pray for us sinners
now and at the hour of death. Amen.

Sister tells us not to worry about hell. We will learn about penance, prayer, confession, and communion, which give God a chance to forgive us on Earth before we die. If you do all these things and are truly sorry for your sins, most likely, you will go to heaven. But you won't know God's decision until you die.

"Hell is not the kind of place to spend forever in, and once you are there, you can't get out for any reason. You burn and burn but never die. Only Catholics will get into heaven," Sister Pauline tells us.

"No, Sister Pauline. No!" everyone cries out.

"Yes, it is true," she says, nodding in certainty. "Even innocent little babies who die before they are baptized don't get to go to heaven."

"Well, where do they go?" someone asks. We all want to know.

"Limbo," she says. "Limbo is neither heaven nor hell. It's not hot or cold; it's not good or evil. It is a place they float around in forever, because the devil can't claim their soul, and God can't let them in heaven."

"Uh-oh." We all sigh.

At dinner, I look at my father, and my eyes get watery. He notices and wants to know what is upsetting me. I tell him what Sister Pauline said about him dying and going to hell.

"What? Why would she say a thing like that?"

I cry, "It's true! Please become a Catholic so you can get into heaven."

He says, looking at my mother, "Do you believe this

shit? Here I am, busting my hump, working like a dog to pay tuition for them to go to that school, and my daughter's coming home thinking I'm going to hell. Now, what kind of religion is that? I'm telling you, Muffy, we are moving away from the city into the country, where the kids can go to public school."

My mother reminds him, "We promised to bring the kids up Catholic."

He says, "That was before I knew something like this could happen—where they would be turning my own children against me."

My father looks at me and tells me not to worry. He says that he won't go to hell and that Sister Pauline had better worry about herself in saying such things to little children. He also says I can tell her what he said. This gets him going on and on, and we end up having lessons in history until late into the night. He is talking about a man named Hitler and how children turned on their own parents, getting them killed. I hear words like *Nazi* and *regime* in between fading in and out sleep, thinking about sleeping on a soft pillow in clean sheets that smell like the wind from drying on the clothesline.

Each night, I fall asleep thinking about my heavenly Father, who is three people in one, taking care of my soul, which is mine alone and which no one else can touch.

I wonder about my own father, who is two different people. I can tell my two fathers apart by their footsteps. I want the bad part of my father to go away, but I know the good will go away with the bad. The good father can take all my hurt away by putting his arm around my shoulders.

During the secret times, his arm around my shoulders feels like a mountain crushing me.

I fall asleep saying, "Our Father, who art in heaven, hallowed be thy name." I drift away to the floating words "as we forgive those who trespass against us."

My mother has left us alone with him.

There is nowhere to run or hide when he has his plan. My heart pounds, and I can't feel my fingertips or toes, because my mother is putting her coat on and telling us she won't be long.

I can't concentrate on watching television with my brother because I know what is about to happen. My father goes to the window to see if my mother's out of the yard. He locks the front door and makes sure that all the blinds are closed. He tells Raymond to come down to the basement with him. He has crayons and a coloring book, and they go downstairs together. Soon I hear my father's footsteps coming up from the basement, where he's left Raymond alone to color. He closes the basement door, and I hear the bolt lock snap shut. My father comes into the parlor. We are alone, and he takes my hand, saying, "Let's go in the bedroom now."

I ask, "Can I have a glass of water?" to stall what I know is about to happen.

He gets me one. I sip slowly.

"Come on. Hurry up and finish," he says.

I ask, "Can I watch another program first?"

"No. Now, come on into the room," he says impatiently.

I try one more stalling tactic, asking, "Can I go outside until Mom gets home?"

He asks disappointedly, "What's the matter with you, Mary? Come on. I thought you liked the things I have been teaching you."

All I can think to say is "I do, but I don't feel good tonight, Daddy. Do I have to?"

He pulls at my hand, saying, "Stop being a baby, and let's go in the room."

I follow the bad father's dark footsteps as he leads me into the bedroom I share with Ray, with the twin beds. In the distance, I hear my brother banging on the basement door and crying for my father. "Daddy, let me out of the basement!"

Each time, in a translucent dream, a horse takes me away and then leaves me at the edge, and I fall into harsh colors and jagged forms and then back into my body. I see his feet arching and his toenails curling. He is finished and looking at me, but I won't look at him. I am in limbo, and that makes him angry.

He glares at me with ice-blue eyes, saying, "I wish you would show some enthusiasm. Don't you trust that I won't hurt you? There's a lot more to learn, but I don't push you, do I? I know you're young just yet, but see how nicely your body is developing thanks to me?"

He pats my breast with a finger, smiling pure evil like the snake on the tree pictured in my catechism, tempting Adam and Eve to eat the fruit. He whispers, "I can wait to teach you everything. Yes, I can."

My eyes are closed, and I see red, still stung by his touch. I think to myself that I am the key in Sister Pauline's drawer, which he has taken without permission. *Yes, you can, but you may not.* I cry to myself.

I sit before the television again and watch my father unlock the basement door. Raymond is at the top of the stairway, moaning, "Didn't you hear me, Daddy?"

My father picks him up and hugs him, saying kindly, "Why, no, sport. No, I didn't hear you over that darn TV. I forgot that you were coloring in the basement."

He brings Ray into the parlor, and we all watch television until my mother gets home. Dad asks if she had a good time at her sister's house. He says he was a little worried because she was there so long.

"It's only up the hill for me to walk home from," she tells him. "You shouldn't have worried." She looks around, asking, "Why are all the blinds shut?"

My father says, "It's getting dark. I don't want nosy people looking into our house."

She notices that the cellar door is wide open and complains, "The kids could have fallen down the stairs and gotten hurt."

He ignores her, saying, "Come watch some TV with us, Muffy."

We are a family. We watch program after program, laughing and pointing, until Ray and I fall asleep and wake up in our beds in the morning.

The story in our catechism today is about two women fighting over a baby. Each one says she is the mother. The king is called in to settle the dispute, and he tells both women that if neither will tell the truth, he will just rip the baby in half and give half to each. One woman agrees it should be done, but the other cries, "No!" She is willing to give the baby up rather than see it die. As the other woman tries to grab the baby from the king, he wisely hands it to its real mother, the woman who would rather give it up than see it die.

Someone asks Sister Pauline, "If neither woman had said anything, would he have ripped the baby apart?"

Sister Pauline reminds us that the story ends the way it does to make you ask questions and answer these questions for yourself. She explains that there is a moral to the story and that a moral teaches us right from wrong. "Can anyone tell me the moral of this story?" she asks. We are all quiet, scrunching our lips, looking for answers in our empty heads. Sister Pauline decides to give us the answer: "It is the meaning of true love. It was a way for the king to test the truth about who really loved the baby."

We are all amazed and agree that the king was clever in using love to find the baby's true mom.

I ask Sister why all the stories don't have pictures.

She smiles. "So we can use our imaginations. Sometimes all you need are words to put a picture together in your mind. So if a picture isn't there, imagine what the king or the women look like from what you read about them."

The bell rings, and we are released from learning. We form our familiar lines and then march along the gray winter sidewalk. When I blow my warm breath into the frigid air, it makes smoke. I catch up to my brother after the line breaks, saying, "Look, Ray. I'm smoking. Try it."

He blows his breath into the air, pretending to hold a cigarette in his hand as Mom and Dad do. We smoke all the way home, laughing.

My mother and I are different when my father isn't around. It's quiet, and I can ask her to tell me stories about things, such as the blue bowl, snowflakes, or the name of the bee bird, the hummingbird. I'm safe next to her whenever he isn't there.

Sometimes after dinner, when my parents fight, Ray and I want to go to bed, but my father makes us all sit together and discuss their argument. We all learn to tell him he is right about whatever he says. If he says my mother is a rotten bitch, we agree. Even my mother will agree just so we can end the lecture and get to bed. If my father figures out that we are saying yes just so we can get to bed, he goes on and on some more. We all figure out how to say yes in a way he thinks we really mean it and end his lecture. All of us are so tired that we don't know if we mean it or not anymore.

Sometimes he continues lecturing anyway, no matter what we say.

My mother gives up, announcing, "You are angry at the world, Larry. I don't know what the hell I or anyone else ever did to you, but I'm going to bed."

She walks out, leaving Ray and me to listen to my father call her a bitch. We say, "Yes, Daddy. Can we go to bed now?"

We are on our way to bed, and she has to yell out, "You are a no-good, rotten bastard is what you are, Larry!"

Her outburst starts the whole thing all over again. He makes us go back to the table and listen to his problems until Mom remains quiet.

At times, Ray falls asleep with his head on the table, and I cover for him. Other nights, I fall asleep with my head on the table, and Ray covers for me.

When we get home from school, everything is calm because my dad isn't there, and mom is getting ready for her favorite programs. Then the news is on. She is always shushing us to be quiet so that she can hear all the good things about to happen in the future. We will have a new president named Kennedy. He has a daughter about my age, and I wonder if I will be seeing her at my school. The government will be sending men into space. In between commercials, my mother makes dinner, and I help her set the table with TV dinners that have everything from meat and vegetables to dessert, all frozen and prepared in silver trays.

When Daddy comes in the door, he says, "Mother and I have a surprise for you." They hug and kiss each other, and we are confused. At dinner, there are no complaints or accusations, only proud smiles.

Ray says, "I know—we have a new president."

"No, guess again." My father grins.

"We are getting horses!" Ray screams.

"No," my father says, smiling.

"Oh," I say, "I know—they are sending men to the moon in rocket ships."

"No, no." My father shakes his head, still beaming. "Guess again."

"You won a million dollars from those green lottery tickets that you and Mom buy every week," I guess.

"Oh no," my father says. "This is something money can't buy."

We are quiet. This is a true mystery. My mother and father stare into each other's eyes in a way we never have seen before. "What is it? Tell us. Hurry up!" I say.

"It is"—he pauses—"a brand new baby!"

Ray and I exhale in disappointment at the same time. Ray asks, "What fun is a new baby for us?"

My mother says it will be someone new for us to play with, and she makes a game of picking out a new name. We get to use our imaginations to think of a name for someone we don't have a picture of yet. Time passes into the night until we don't even realize it's time for bed. We all agree for tonight that if it's a girl, we'll name her Rebecca Lynn. We hardly get to start thinking about a boy's name, but there will be plenty of time for that.

In bed, I prop up my ears just right on my pillow so that I can listen in the dark to my parents talk about things when we are supposed to be asleep. It's quiet, so instead, I think about things Sister Pauline says I need to improve on, such as my penmanship. I still must try harder to fit everything within lines on the page. Sister Pauline knows a lot about religion, and her answers make sense, except for the part where Protestants go to hell.

The most important thing Sister Pauline has taught me is to pray to my heavenly Mother and Father, who protect my soul, which is mine and which no one can touch—the soul I must not stain with venial or mortal sins.

⁂

On Saturday morning, my father sits at the head of our round colonial table in the captain's chair, smoking a cigarette and sipping coffee. He wears only a long undershirt, which he's pulled down and wrapped around his crossed legs to hide his privates. My brother hides behind a cereal box while he eats Cheerios floating in a bowl of milk. My mother sits opposite my father, sipping her coffee and wearing her sky-blue silk nightgown with a housecoat over it, cinched nice and tight. I sit opposite my brother, dipping a doughnut in milk beside my father's ashtray full of stinky crushed cigarettes.

Dad sits as if he is the captain of a ship, at the ready should a family crisis arrive, except he's got no pants on. Bored by waiting, he starts an important family discussion about water.

He lifts a glass of water up to the light, admiring it with an evil smile that reminds me of the snake in the tree in the Garden of Eden. He sips the water as if each drop is the last on Earth, savoring its clear purity, and then he says, "Ah, in the future, water will be the most expensive thing you can buy. Even then, you won't be able to buy it this pure." He nods, taking another sip and swallowing the water as if he hasn't been on Earth to taste water's purity for an eternity, as if it is something he'll never get to taste again.

"The best things in life are free," he says after the last sip.

We all watch him, afraid to say anything, for fear it will lead to a long conversation that will keep us in the house all afternoon. I know our kitchen is where my father plans to spend the whole day, contemplating the downfall of humanity and waiting to preach to any ear that will stop by and listen.

It's not how I want to spend my Saturday. He stares at me and says, "Water—someday, Sissy, when you grow up and leave your old dad, there will be a knock at your door, and when you see that it is me, you won't let me in. Why, you won't even offer me a glass of water. You will be on your own, and you won't want a thing to do with your old dad."

"Why would you say that, Dad? I will always give you a glass of water," I say in front of our family.

He smiles. "You're my girl, aren't you?"

Thank God a banging on the pipes comes from upstairs to interrupt the discussion. We hear the upstairs door open, and Nonie yells down in Italian, "*Voglio*!" (I want).

My mother runs to the door, yelling up in Italian, "*Di che cosa?*" (Of what thing?). The word *bowl* floats down, and my mother grabs a bowl, telling me to take it upstairs.

My father yells out, "Cripes! Shut the door, Muffy. Can't you see I'm half naked here?"

He stands up, about to speak in anger, pointing a finger at my mother, when his shirt unfolds, causing his privates to hang down. He continues shaking his finger at my mother, and now his privates are jiggling. Ray and I laugh and point it out to each other. My mom gets mad, scolding him that it's not good for the children to see him this way. He tells her that a man has a right to look any way he wants in the privacy of his own home and that there's nothing wrong with children seeing a naked body. "It's nothing to be ashamed of. They aren't going to grow up frigid like the ones up there." He points up at the ceiling, causing the bobbing again.

Mom retaliates by running around the house and opening all the blinds, yelling at him, "Here you go, Larry! It's daylight and time to start the day. The entire neighborhood can see you, so put some goddamn pants on."

My mother hands me the bowl, giving me an escape to run upstairs and deliver it. I leave Mom singing loudly "Someday My Prince Will Come," a song from *Snow White* that aggravates the hell out of my father, but it shuts him up.

Undone

Papa Non and Nonie's door is open, and I walk inside their peaceful, clean home. It smells of coffee brewing, bread baking, and beeswax floor polish. Papa Non sits at the kitchen table, concentrating on swirling a spoon around the inside of a bowl of hot green water, making lime Jell-O. Nonie calls out to me from her open bedroom door, "Bella, my beautiful little bird." Her room is filled with white lace from the curtains, the bedspread, and the doilies plopped on her dresser like giant snowflakes. She brushes her long dark hair, which flows below her waist. She then wraps and pins it neatly into a doughnut-shaped bun at the back of her head.

She comes into the kitchen, putting on her apron and saying to me, "Come look out the window. We tell Papa Non what's ready to pick in the garden." After a quick look, she says, "Yes, the tomatoes are ready. The squash doesn't look ripe. The birds have picked all the seeds from the sunflowers."

Nonie and I sit at the table as the coffeepot percolates.

She begins to tell me about her old country and how she got here on the back of a whale, when Papa Non's shrieking in the bathroom interrupts us. Nonie runs into the bathroom, and then she comes out, telling me not to move or go in there. She grabs a spoon and bangs it on the radiator pipe. My mother rushes upstairs and through the door, and Nonie is running around in circles. I hear something about blood in broken English. My mother runs to Aunt Sophie's house to phone for an ambulance.

They take Papa Non away, and no one tells me what's wrong with him.

Later that night, my mother tells us Papa Non is back from the hospital and has bleeding ulcers because of his nerves. My brother and I promise not to dig up flowers or ambush him, because if he gets agitated, his stomach will bleed.

Our routine is back to normal. Papa Non sits out at the picnic table with a little glass of red wine, even though he is supposed to eat only Jell-O for two weeks. My father never joins in with Mom's family around the picnic table. He says it's because he works late and has no time for it, but I know it's because he is a Protestant, and Mom's parents are Catholic. Everything about him is different from mom's family. They all have olive skin, black hair, and brown eyes. Dad sticks out with blond hair and blue eyes. He doesn't go to church, and his parents didn't come here from an old country. He hates macaroni, which is what goes around the picnic table most every night with a salad. He doesn't drink any kind of alcohol, and wine is all that Papa Non drinks.

I still look forward to sitting at the picnic table by my

mom's side and listening to Papa Non and Nonie's family laughing until it gets dusky and cold. Papa Non lights the burn barrel to keep everyone warm and chase the bugs away. He wears gloves with the fingertips cut off, shaking a wire basket of chestnuts over glowing charcoal. "*Oh sole mio. Oh sole mio*," he sings. Everyone laughs and joins in. Whenever my mom says her hands are getting chilly, he runs to her and puts warm chestnuts in them. We take turns cracking them open. Their charcoal, sugary taste is delicious, dissolving on my tongue.

Summer is almost over, and I haven't spent much time with my father, because he works extra jobs. Besides his day job at the jewelry factory, he is an usher at the drive-in at night, and he does yard work on the weekends for his boss, Mr. Trine.

This work schedule makes the morning pretty miserable because my parents fight. Dad can't wake up early to get to work on time. Mom pleads with him and then threatens to pour water over his head. This goes on until he realizes how late it is and screams, "Muffy, why the hell didn't you get me up?"

She's been screaming and cursing and pulling at him for an hour, yet I hear him blaming her that he will be late for work and get fired. I hear him running out the door with those footsteps we all know to stay away from.

My mother hasn't left us alone with him in the house for a while. I hear her talking to herself, wondering why my father leaves the blinds shut in the middle of the day when she is out.

One day my father tells her he doesn't spend enough time with me, so she lets me keep him company riding in the car to Mr. Trine's house, where he cuts grass. During our drive, my father pulls the car to the side of the road and tells me that we are going for a walk in the woods. When he speaks to me, I look through him and not at him. I know what's about to happen by the sound of his footsteps and the sneaky expression on his face as he looks around.

The leaves pinch my skin when I lie on them. I go away in my mind, numbing my body. My eyes are in limbo, neither here nor there, giving one last wish for my good father, whose touch makes things better, and not the wicked father. I'm the only one he shows his sins to. Who would believe the things I know about him?

The next Saturday, we drive straight to Mr. Trine's house. Dad finishes mowing and raking the lawn, and I wait inside the garage while he puts the mower away. He locks the garage door from the inside and lays a blanket on the floor behind a trash can. I begin to go away, when I'm jolted by the noise of a door being pushed open. So is my father.

"Who's there?" Mr. Trine calls out as he enters his garage from the back door of his house.

My father jumps up, bumping into the trash cans. "It's me—Larry. I'm putting some tools away," my father answers nervously as Mr. Trine's footsteps reach us. "I thought your family was away this weekend and the house was all locked up. My little girl wasn't feeling well, so I brought her in here to lie down while I put tools away."

His boss smiles at me. My father introduces me as his little girl, Mary. Mr. Trine looks at me, knowing that I'm unhappy—as if he feels sorry for me. He tells my father his family isn't leaving until tomorrow.

"Oh," my father says as we begin walking to the car. "Well, I'll be back next week. All the raked grass is in those trash bags by the side of the yard."

Our car pulls out of the driveway, and I see Mr. Trine out the window, pacing as if he's thinking hard about what to do about something.

A couple of days later, I'm perched in the cigar tree's branches, when I see a car pull into our driveway while Dad is at work. A man gets out, and I recognize him as Mr. Trine. He knocks on our door. My mom answers, he returns the blanket that my father forgot, and they talk for a bit before he leaves.

My father drives our car with me in between my mother and him. The sounds of the highway lull me to sleep.

My mother screams, "I want out! There's no other way. I just want out!"

I'm crushed in between them, suffocating and feeling the hot leather seat sticking to my skin. My mother opens the door to be sucked out. I see shiny chrome wheels spinning fast on the black highway at the bottom of the open car door. My father reaches over, smothering me as he grabs her with one hand, pulls her back in, yanks the car door shut, and snaps the lock. I hear cars screeching as they swerve out of our way. My mother sits weeping.

"Dammit, Muffy! What the hell? Things are going to be different. You'll see. I'll change."

I will always be in between them, and to make a move will cause my mother to die.

⟡

My mom's friends and family still gather at the picnic table, but Papa Non doesn't join in. Since his stomach aggravation, he paces around the yard with his slippers on, saying the same thing over and over: "There's water in the basement."

It's getting dark out, and relatives are still talking. I hear someone say they have to get Papa Non help. Nonie wants to hide him in the house so that the men in the white coats won't come take him away.

The next day, amazingly, Papa Non is his old self, raking in the garden and singing out loud. Nonie is there watching over him while she plucks ripe tomatoes from their stalks and places them in a sack she has made for them from her apron.

In the afternoon, Mom and I watch TV, when we hear a loud banging on the pipes from above. We run upstairs to see what's wrong, only to find Papa Non sitting at the table with a nice plate of sliced tomatoes. His face becomes bright red, and his eyes seem to bulge as he screams, "Those goddamn boyz Gary and Raymond ruined my tomatoes! They's shootin BBs into my perfect tomatoes. I'm take a bite, and I almost choke on a BB. I told you BB gunz not for play. Why they cannot kill the pigeons or the crows? No? A shame they have to destroy the food."

"Papa, I'm sorry. It will never happen again," my mother says.

I hold my hands over my mouth not to laugh and make Papa Non more nervous, knowing that every drop of food is precious and that it's a sin to waste it.

He pushes the dish of tomatoes across the table, and it falls to the floor, breaking with tomatoes askew, while Nonie paces back and forth, not knowing what to do. He opens the window and shouts out to everyone, "That's it! I'm selling this goddamn house because there's water in the cellar and BBs in my tomatoes!"

Eventually, we get used to seeing Papa Non pacing about in the garden, checking for BBs in the tomatoes, and then going to the basement to check for water. My mother keeps hoping that the next day will be a good day and that soon he will be his old self.

My father still has two jobs and continues to get home late. I stay by my mother's side while she waits up for him and reads to me from my storybooks. Now her belly looks like a big ball that sticks way out, with her nightgown stretched over it like a balloon. I still manage to rub its silky blue between my two fingers while listening to her read a story about Hansel and Gretel. They are lost in the woods. (*Ah*, I think, *Nonie's worst nightmare.*) An old witch captures them, and she puts Hansel in a cage and feeds him to fatten him up so that she can cook him and eat him. Every day she asks Hansel to stick out his finger so that she can feel how fat he is getting, but instead, he holds out an old chicken bone to stall the hungry witch from putting him in the oven. Gretel is left to do housework, and she hatches a plan to push the witch into the oven and slam the door shut, killing her.

The witch reminds me of my father, who checks my body to see how far along I'm developing, so he can do things to me like to a woman, but I don't know what things, so I'm scared. My breasts aren't flat anymore. They are kind of swelling. This must be developing, so I worry. This story can't help me figure out a happy ending to stop my father. The story only makes me scared because the evil gets deeper. I ask my mom to read another fairy tale and hope it's one where the hero beats evil with a happy ending.

I try to fall asleep, but I worry inside my head. All that's left to do is listen in secret to adult conversations. I still have not found out a word for what my father does to me. I wonder if there are other children like me, ashamed of a secret and afraid to talk about it.

My good father is the only one I can talk to about anything else. He doesn't yell or get mad, and he helps me find my lost kitten and teaches me fun things, such as how to ride a bike or swim in the ocean. The police will take the good father along with the bad one away from my mother, my brother, the brand-new baby, and me. I love my good father. If only they could take just the bad part of him away.

I lie awake worrying by my mother's side as she reads a newspaper, and then I begin to fall asleep while listening to the crinkling sounds of pages turning. She begins tossing and turning over and over, waking me up. "Augh!" she screams, bolting up and out of bed and running into the kitchen. I see her through the doorway, banging on the radiator pipe with a spoon. Her nightgown's caught on the radiator and is ripping as she hangs on to the pipe with one hand and bangs on it with the other. I think she is dying because there is bloody water everywhere.

"Ah, Mafa!" Papa Non and Nonie scream when they get downstairs and see her like this. They start running in circles.

Finally, an ambulance comes and takes my mother away.

Ray and I are upstairs, trying to sleep in Nonie's big bed while she sits in a rocking chair by our side, praying on each bead of a long black rosary.

"Nonie, what's wrong with our mother?" I ask.

"Shhh. Everything's gonna be okay. She come home soon with a new brother or sister for you. Okay?" She rocks back and forth, singing softly.

Our car pulls into the driveway; we run downstairs from Nonie's apartment, excited to meet our new sister and play with her. We are in shock to see my mother holding a tiny thing all wrapped in a blanket. "How do we play with her?" I say.

My mother says, "It will be awhile before she can play with you."

She puts our tiny sister into a new white cradle that my dad made. It has pink rosebuds painted at the crest. He shows us how it rocks back and forth to put the baby to sleep. We finally see her face, and while she looks perfect, all she does is make strange noises like a cat. Ray and I look at each other. That's it. That's all she does; she just lies there and makes noise.

During the day, my mother isn't working at her mirror, sharing beauty secrets; instead, the baby absorbs our attention. I watch Mom bathing the baby, and she teaches me how to hold a new baby by supporting her head. She points to a soft spot, saying, "This is where her skull hasn't closed yet; you should never touch it. It will go away eventually, just like the cord on her belly button." She puts Rebecca on the bed, dries her with special soft towels, and then sprinkles baby powder on her. "Look how perfect she is," my mother says, touching her fingers and toes. Rebecca looks right at us, smiling and cooing. She has the softest little hand holding tightly on to my finger.

"How innocent and helpless they are," my mother says in wonderment. "How could anyone hurt them?"

I think to myself, *I was a baby once. How could my father hurt me?* But I am not a baby now. I'm a big sister. I'm nine.

Papa Non has sold our houses and property. The new buyers sit at the picnic table with our family, chatting like the old times. Papa Non joins in at the table, wearing his slippers, and then he walks away, continuing to pace around the yard. Then he goes to the garden to check the tomatoes for BBs and back to the house to look for water in the basement. I know Papa Non is unhappy, and we will all soon be moving away from each other. Aunt Sophie bought a new home, and so did Papa Non and Nonie. My dad is building us a new home, and until it is finished, my mom rented an apartment right next door to our old house. That way, we won't have to change schools. My mother explains to Ray and me that our expenses will be much higher, so she will be working a night job at General Electric Company for extra money. We will have to help out by being quiet so that she and our new baby can sleep during the day.

Dad is happy these days at the dinner table as we eat from the blue plates that tell the story of lovebirds and the unhappy prince. He and my mom stay up late, going over blueprints of the house being built on the land they bought.

One day my brother, cousins, and I are running through the gate and into the yard, but our street and driveway are filled with cars, even my dad's. Uncle Frankie is at the picnic table with his head down. I run into our first-floor hallway, surprised to see our door open. No one is there, and I hear a crowd of people talking and crying upstairs with Nonie. My two aunts come down from Nonie's apartment, bringing their children and leaving our older cousins in charge of keeping us under control. My aunts go back up the stairs, sobbing.

All of us cousins huddle together. My oldest cousin finally says, "He's dead. Papa Non is dead."

I run out of the house and find my father alone at the front stairs. I look at him and tell him my cousins are starting trouble and saying things that aren't true about Papa Non. My father is quiet and looks sad. He asks what they said.

"They say Papa Non died!" I cry out.

Quietly, my father nods, saying that it is true.

Papa Non is gone!

He pats my back lightly, talking in a low voice. "He had an accident."

Children aren't allowed at funerals, so a neighbor watches all of us at Nonie's house. Huddled together, we share more of what we heard. I tell them what my dad said—that it was some kind of accident.

Someone asks, "What kind of accident?"

"No, it is worse," a cousin says. "It wasn't an accident."

"Well, what then?" Everyone chimes in.

"He killed himself!"

I walk away from all the kids huddled in a circle and look out the window into the garden at the pink plastic flamingos below, and I hear, "He hung himself. Uncle Frankie found him hung in the basement."

Relatives begin to arrive at Nonie's house after the service. No one talks about anything in front of us children as they bring in food, and some people give Nonie cards with money inside. All of a sudden, Aunt Sophie begins weeping and then cries out loud, "Why, God? Why?" She collapses.

The kids are rounded up again and told to stay in the bedroom with the door closed. We are quiet, and I still don't believe it is true.

It's quiet in our house, and I'm alone with my mother. We sit on the edge of my twin bed, and I watch her folding clothes and matching socks.

I ask, "Mama, is it true?" I can't finish my question.

She looks into my eyes, placing her hands on my shoulders and saying, "Go ahead. Finish your question."

"Is it true that Papa Non killed himself?"

My mother looks down, saying softly, "Yes. It's true, Mary Ellen." She breaks down and sobs.

I whisper, "No."

We both cry. I expect her to push me away so that she can be sad alone. Instead, she pulls me onto her lap, and we hug each other, not believing this truth—together.

7
Mr. Zelka's House

My mother leads us next door to a stinky brown house. We will live on the third floor, which my mother calls an attic apartment. Everything in Papa Non's yard was a shade of green and growing into something; the air outside smelled sweet like pistachio ice cream and church on Sunday, filled with sandalwood incense and ladies' perfumes. This new place is shades of brown and smells half dead. The house is falling apart and has a yard of straw grass and weeds. I find an old cement birdbath, empty of birds and water, as a possible hiding spot where I can go to cry if I get too sad, but my mother yells to stay away because it could fall on me. The worst part is that there is no fence to protect us from the lot boys.

My mother holds our hands, walking Ray and me to our new apartment. I step onto the porch, walking between broken floorboards that creak and pass by a bow window with tattered lace curtains and dark green shades half drawn. Inside the window, I see a man with a large, swollen belly sitting on a rocker. One of his hands rests on a cane across his lap. Flies buzz all around him, but he doesn't move.

As we enter the first-floor hallway, I'm knocked back by a stink worse than Papa Non's freshly delivered manure pile. My mother pulls at me, saying, "Let's go. Keep moving." As we climb up the stairs to the third floor, I ask my mother if the man is dead. "No, he is very old and can't move much," she answers. "Don't ever make fun of him. He lives with his grandson, Jackie, whose mother died, and the grandfather is supposed to take care of him, but it looks like no one can much take care of anything."

I feel bad for Jackie because I can barely stand to pass by the smell, but he has to come home and live in it. I can't imagine how he does it.

We reach the third floor and open the door to our new apartment. It looks a little like our old house, as it has the same furniture, including cloth couches, chairs, blond tables shaped like triangles, and our kitchen set. My mother shows us our room with our familiar twin beds, bedspreads, and curtains, which have been cut shorter to fit the small windows. All the ceilings come down on a slant.

When I look out the window, the first thing I see is Papa Non's old yard below, which seems far away because I'm so high above it. I recognize the gardens, the paths, the flowers, and the silver fence surrounding everything, glittering in the sun. However, it doesn't look real anymore. It seems like a small, faraway, make-believe place like the one inside my snow globe.

I ask my mother how long we will live here. She reminds me this is only a temporary place. By next year, we will be in our new house in the country.

By evening, we are settled in, but there are still boxes of unpacked things. Ray and I find a shoebox full of pictures. My mother comes by and begins looking at the pictures with us, and we ask her who different people are. My father yells out from the parlor, "Bring those out, and let's have a look!" Dad pulls out a large picture and says, "Look. This is my mother. Isn't she an attractive woman? You resemble her, Mary. Look at her delicate complexion. Do you know her secret ingredient? Baby pee!"

"What?" I ask, disgusted.

"Oh yeah," my father says, "each time she changed a baby, she would hold the warm pee diaper to her face."

I can't imagine this smiling face with glasses, pearls, lace collar, and flowered dress warming her face in a wet diaper. We pull out another picture, and I ask, "What high school class is this?"

"That's no school; it's my family, all fourteen of us—seven boys and seven girls," my father proudly says.

I see that they are versions of each other, and like my dad, they could be movie stars with delicate complexions, fair hair, blue eyes, high cheekbones, and wispy smiles like Grandma Sinclair's.

"Yep," my father continues, pulling out another picture, "and there I am. I'm nine." He points to a skinny kid with freckles and hair slicked down except for a cowlick. The kid is wearing a white shirt and jeans cinched up nice and tight with a rope for a belt. He points to a picture of his oldest brother, Art, who was like a father to him because their father died just before this family picture was taken. His father fell off a ladder and lived in the house for three days in a coma before he passed away. "My brothers and sisters all vowed to keep the family together, take care of each other, and share whatever we have with each other, even if one of us became rich one day." My father seems to be reminiscing, and then he nods, saying, "We were like the Musketeers—all for one and one for all. The older ones raised the younger ones."

Ray pulls out a picture of a sailor posing on the deck of a ship, surrounded by waves, with the wind blowing through his hair.

"Oh, look at how handsome your father looked in his uniform. I always loved a man in uniform," my mother says dreamily. "That's when we first met. Remember, Larry, at the USO dance?"

"Oh yeah," my father says, "I loved you the minute I saw you and your shiny black hair."

My father looks at my brother and me, telling us about the first time he came into Nonie's yard to get my mother for a date. "Nonie was sweeping a rug atop the outside stairs. I smiled at her and gave her my best 'How do ya do?' She picked up the rug and shook the dirt all over my white sailor suit, shooing me away like a dog."

Ray and I laugh at the thought, but my father's eyes still glare into the picture as he says, "It's a wonder I ever came back after that."

"Did you like being a sailor, Dad?" Ray asks.

"Not really," he says, looking at the picture and holding his stomach. "I didn't know what I was getting myself into. To this day, I can't eat tuna fish; the smell of it turns my stomach. We ran out of food, and all we ate for weeks was tuna. When we reached the shore, we all went out and got drunk, and I got this tattoo." He flexes his muscle on his left arm, showing us his familiar green tattoo of an eagle with its wings spread and a heart with an arrow through it, surrounded by the words "Mother and Muffy, the Only Tow I Love."

I read *tow* instead of *two* and say, "*Two* is spelled wrong."

My father laughs. "Well, I said we were all drunk, didn't I? The guy spelled it wrong, and it's a tattoo, so I'm stuck with it."

"Who is this?" I ask, pointing to another picture.

"Guess!" my father says.

"I don't know."

"Guess!"

Finally, my mother tells us who the mystery person is. It's Papa Non, her dad, as a young man. I say, "You mean, he used to have hair, and his eyebrows weren't always bushy white? And look, Mama—he's smiling!"

We find a picture of an old car with my father waving from behind the steering wheel. "That's the car I drove all the way down here from Ohio after your mother called me and said she would marry me." He points to the tires. "You see those tires? They were so old and worn that I could only drive on the roads at night, when they were cool, or I'd risk getting a flat on the hot roads during the day. I had no money to get here either, so I stopped at restaurants and hid behind tables, stealing the tip money from them."

My mother rolls her eyes, biting her lips.

"Look at this!" He points to his ear, showing us a little scar. "You know how I got this? A big old rat came up and bit me on the ear. Can you imagine waking up to that?"

"Where did it happen, and when?" I ask.

"Well, I didn't have a place to stay until the wedding, so I got a job right across the street from your mother's house, at Brownie's Doughnut Shop, making doughnuts during the day and sleeping on the floor at night. The rats would come out at night, looking for food, and one chewed on my ear."

We gasp. "Mama, why wouldn't Papa Non and Nonie let him stay with them?" I ask.

"Oh, I don't know. Everything was improper until after the wedding," she says, looking at the floor.

Time flies as we pick through pictures from days before we were born. "It's time for bed," my father says finally. "Look how late it is."

I push for just one more before we go to bed, pulling out a picture of a toddler on a couch in a house.

"Oh, that's you at six months old," my mom says, "at your aunt Doris's in Ohio."

"How did I end up there?"

My mother and father look at each other. My mother says, "Well, after we were married and you were born, we decided to move to Ohio, but it didn't work out. I didn't like it there. You are lucky to be alive."

"Why?" I ask.

My mother says, "We took off in our red Chevy. Do you remember, Larry?"

My father nods. "We should have stayed with my family, Muffy. Things would have been a lot easier on us financially."

"Anyway," my mother says, ignoring him and going on with the story, "we left in the winter, and as we drove, it started snowing, turning into a blizzard on the road. You were asleep in a basket in the backseat. Cars were swerving and slipping all around us, and we were sideswiped. I thought our car would never stop spinning, until we finally ended up in a ditch. Neither of us got a scratch. I reached back to get you, but you were gone, basket and all. I was horrified to see a hole through the plastic window of the convertible top that your basket had broken through. We searched the road, looking for your white basket. Your father and I had just about given up, when a little old woman came up to me, holding the basket and you. It had landed in front of her house, in a mound of snow. There wasn't a scratch on you, and you weren't even crying. You slept through the whole thing. You must have a powerful guardian angel looking over you."

My father reminds us that "Just one more" is over and that it's time for bed. I'm under my sheets. My mother always tucks them so tightly that I can just squeeze my feet under. The sheets smell clean like the wind that blows through them on the clothesline. Best of all, I have a new black kitten named Ebony who curls up right on top of my feet and purrs herself and me to sleep. The nicest thing about this apartment is that Mr. Zelka allows pets in the house. Papa Non and Nonie never allowed animals in the house unless they were for dinner.

"They are food, not pets," I remember Nonie scolding us each time we called our Easter rabbits by name.

I drift into sleep, feeling Ebony's purrs vibrating through the blanket onto my feet. My mother and father are giggling in the other room with their door open, and I hear, "Get those feet away from me; they are ice cold!" I start to giggle, and my father yells out, "You kids get to sleep now!" The last words I hear are "Damn, your feet are cold!"

Even though this is a different house, I wake up to the same morning routine. My mother is home from her night job, and I hear her shrieking at my father to get out of bed. I hear my father curse. "Shit, I'm going to get fired. Why the hell can't you get me out of bed, Muffy? Is that so damn hard?"

I wonder if we are the only family who starts their day this way. On TV, the father gets up and comes to the table smiling and wearing a suit, the mother has a fresh stack of pancakes ready for everyone, there's always plenty of time, and they don't worry about money.

After Dad's angry footsteps pound out the door, I know it is safe to get up. My brother's hiding behind a cereal box while eating Cheerios floating in a bowl of milk. My mother tells us she is going to sleep and jumps into the bed, which is still warm from my father. She yells out, "Your clothes are ready in the bedroom! Get dressed, and don't be late for school or forget your lunches that I made for you. They're sitting on the counter." I kiss my mom and Rebecca Lynn, who is tucked by her side, good-bye. Before I leave, I hear my mother say, half asleep, "Don't stay too late at band practice tonight."

We race down three flights of stairs, holding our breath until we pass the pee-stained man I'm sure is dead. I breathe again once we get to the porch, hopscotching over its missing floorboards. Ray and I look toward our old house with the mint-green paint, the shiny silver fence, and the colorful flowers, which are being watered by the new owner instead of Papa Non.

I love school because it's quiet and peaceful. We are studying our catechism to prepare for confirmation. Sister Angelina says that around our age, twelve, we begin the age of reason. We raise our hands wildly, speaking out of turn, wanting to know what the age of reason is before she gets a chance to explain. Sister waves her clicker wildly in the air, making it quack like a duck, calling us out of control. She reminds us to raise our hands and speak when we are called on, as she can only answer one question at a time.

"I will explain now, class, so be quiet and listen," she says. "Up until now, you learn in school, and then your parents teach you the difference between right and wrong. The age of reason is a time in your life when you begin to reason things out for yourselves. Your confirmation means stepping over into adulthood, where each of you figures out the difference between right and wrong for yourselves."

Someone asks, "Once we are confirmed, we can say no to our parents?"

"Well, of course not," says Sister Angelina, "at least not for certain things." She reminds us that it will be a long road to travel until we are eighteen and completely free to make our own decisions, and confirmation is just stepping over onto this road, but it's an important part of life.

"But," a student asks, "what if our parents told us to kill someone? Could we say no?"

Sister Angelina waves her hands in the air, saying, "Yes," as if to keep him from asking any more questions.

We open our books to a glossy color picture of Adam and Eve, who were the first man and woman on Earth.

They are running away from the Garden of Eden. Behind them are trees and flowers just like the ones in Papa Non's yard. Adam has muscles all over his body, as my father does. One hand covers his privates, and the other holds Eve's hand as they run away. Her long auburn hair covers her body. Above them, a snake hangs from a fruit tree with an evil smile like the one my father gives me when he does bad things.

Underneath the picture, the caption says, "And they were naked and ashamed, and the Lord expelled them from the Garden of Eden, condemning them to toil the earth forever. From then on, they covered their bodies, for they were naked and ashamed."

Sister Angelina emphasizes that it was all because they partook of the forbidden fruit.

What? I think to myself. *All they had to do was what God told them—not take a bite of the fruit. Then they could have run around in their birthday suits forever, never having to work and plucking anything they wanted from trees, and everyone after them until forever could have lived happily ever after. If they hadn't listened to the snake and ruined life for everyone, we wouldn't have to worry at all about jobs, money, or buying food and clothes. It would be just like staying in Papa Non's yard forever, and my mother could make pin curls all day under the sun instead of making flashcubes at General Electric at night and falling asleep all day.*

Sister Angelina's ability to read minds seems to happen whenever the whole class is thinking what I am. Her voice breaks into my thoughts. "The fruit God told them to leave alone was not just fruit. It was a symbol for things forbidden, and taking a bite out meant that they gave in to temptation, which is a sin. The snake is a symbol for temptation to do bad things. Regardless, people are all born carrying Adam and Eve's original sin, which is why no one is allowed to live ever again in the Garden of Eden, which is the symbol of a perfect world.

"You see, along the way in your thinking and reasoning, you will give in to temptation and make mistakes like Adam and Eve. That is why we have confession—so you can admit your sins and vow not to make them again. And then you can go to communion, and everything is clean and white, and you can try again."

This is the first time I hear and see something about being naked and ashamed—my secret. It's also the first time an adult says that it's all right to listen to my own thoughts and reason things out on my own. Someday I will figure out how to say no.

Sister Angelina never gets nervous. Sometimes when she looks down and smiles at me, I think about asking her why I'm so mixed up about my father and me and why his sin became mine too. Even though he tells me he is teaching me things, I know they are bad, because no one else can see. No one talks about this; it's not even on television.

How can I say all this to Sister Angelina? I'm scared she will take me away from my family. How do I know I won't get a new father who'll do the same things? If they take my father away from my mother, how will she take care of everyone and work at General Electric? Her papa is gone; there is no one to take care of us now except my father.

I think that saying no is important. It means that I

believe in myself. Even my mom is always telling me to speak up when someone steps on my toe or gets ahead of me in line, saying, "If you don't speak up for yourself, people will walk all over you."

My father is teaching me a bad habit of being quiet—of pretending it never happened.

8
Lot Boys

Ray and I don't go home right after school, because there's no place to play, and no matter how hard we try, we can never be quiet enough for my mother to sleep. We don't invite our friends over because we want them to think we still live in the mint-green house next door. We stay at school to practice for Father Murphy's band, the Shamrocks, in the schoolyard. Ray carries a drum he beats while walking around, and I twirl a baton in the air, trying to catch it every time. We practice for the big day to march on Broadway in New York City for the St. Patrick's Day parade. I get to lead the band with a baton, wearing a big high hat with a white feather on top and boots with fluffy pom-poms that dangle when I march.

Father Murphy calls everyone into the hall, where he is surrounded by expensive chocolate-nut bars wrapped in silver foil. He gives us a speech about having a contest to see who can sell the most candy bars so that the school can make money to buy our new marching uniforms. Ray and I take a box each and begin to walk home. We pass

Shirley Belsy's mother's car in front of the hall, and her trunk is filled with boxes of candy to sell. Ray and I rush to get to every house on the way home so that we can sell our two boxes.

At door after door that we knock on, a nice person always says the same thing: he or she already bought one, or his or her kid is selling them too. We get tired and sit on the curb, looking at the ground and then at each other. Ray says he's getting kind of hungry. I'm the first one to open my box to count and make sure there are twenty-five bars in there. Ray picks up a bar and unpeels the wrapper; he offers me a bite. Before we know it, four giant bars are gone.

It's getting dark as we reach our yard, and Ray tells me he doesn't feel good. My stomach feels as if it's going to explode. When we open the door, my mother is standing there, furious. "Where have you been? I've been worried sick. What happened?" Raymond looks a little green and runs to the bathroom to puke. I put down the boxes, smile as if nothing happened, and tell my mother we were out selling candy bars on the way home. She figures out the whole story right away and yells, "Irresponsibility! These are expensive." She shuffles through the box, counting how many she has to pay for. "Oh my God, you ate four! You're gonna get worms. You're supposed to sell them, not eat them." She puts the boxes on top of the refrigerator, out of our reach, and tells us to bring the unsold ones back on Monday.

We are both sick on the couch, and for now, we don't have to eat dinner. There's no medicine they can give us or anything they can do for us. "We have to wait until it comes out one end or the other," says my father.

It's Saturday, and there is no morning wake-up fight, because both my parents get to sleep in. Ray and I go outside, exploring the lots behind the house. On our way down the stairs, I decide I'm going to stop on the porch and look into the first-floor window at the old man. I stare through lace curtains decaying like melting snow. He sits in his chair, dressed as if he used to have an important job that he wore a nice suit to. He has a starched white shirt, gold cufflinks, a red silk tie, suspenders, and a fancy cane. It's as if he came home one day a long time ago, took his jacket off, sat down, and never moved again, and now the same clothes hang threadbare from his swollen body. I'm sure he is dead because he doesn't move even though a big fly lands on his nose. His face has stubbles of hair, and a fly lands atop a swollen-shut eyelid. *Yeow! He blinked!* The other eye opens wide, and he stares right back at me. *He's alive!* I race to the lots, looking for my brother.

I find Ray picking through broken glass and junk, and I join in on our game of figuring out what each piece of scrap was once a part of. He holds up some rusty mattress springs, and we attach them to our shoes and jump up and down for a while. Tired of that, we climb a mountain of dirt, finding an old bathtub sitting there. It becomes a boat that we get inside, and we roll it down the hill, sailing through an imaginary ocean of waving grass. We leave the ocean to explore an old junk car with broken windows. It's just getting to be fun, when we hear unfamiliar voices and footsteps coming from the woods. We run away, scared. I imagine Nonie's face with scared dark eyes and her finger pointing as she yells, "Stay away from the lot boyz—run!"

We sit on the porch stairs, watching the lot boys take parts from a junk car, and talk about other places to spend the afternoon. I am surprised to see my mom and dad walk through the porch doors all dressed up with Becky in tow. My father wears a suit, and I haven't seen my mother looking so pretty since her papa died. She walks down the wooden steps in high heels, wearing a soft summer dress with a wide skirt that flows, swirling a printed flower pattern around her. Her black hair is curled again, and her blushed-orange lips smile. They announce that this is an important day, and they are driving into the city after they drop us at Aunt Sophie's, where our aunt will watch us for a while. I'm happy to see them like this; I beg to go with them. Ray wants to go to our aunt's house to see his cousin Gary, and Becky, who never sleeps when we want her to, is sound asleep, so they say I can go with them.

My father parks in a lot behind a People's Savings Bank. He tells Mom to wait at the corner with me and promises he will take us for coffee and banana cream pie after his appointment.

My mother holds my hand while we wait. She arches her back against the cement building, posing, pointing one leg out in front of the other so that when my father comes around the corner, he will notice her legs. She licks her lips and squeezes my hand. I hear my father's footsteps making quick, happy clicking sounds. He whistles at my mom as he comes around the corner. I see Mom smile. He looks at her, saying, "I knew those were your legs; I saw them halfway down the street. We got the loan!" He shows her an envelope and some papers. They haven't been this happy since they told us about our new sister.

They make plans for their house over pie and coffee at the bakery down the street. My mother worries about traveling to work, our new schools, and a sitter for Rebecca. My father keeps saying, "Don't worry; everything will work out," and they don't fight. Their footsteps are proud like mine when I'm in the marching band. I watch my father dreaming as he tucks the envelope safely away inside his jacket pocket.

Instead of lessons that go on and on at night, things are better. We sit at the table as Mom and Dad do sketches and talk about the size of rooms and where the sun will face. I remind Dad about the horses he promised us. Mine will be a black-and-white pinto just like the one that my paternal great-grandmother, who was an Indian squaw, had. Ray says he wants a chestnut mare like the cowboys ride. "Of course," my father says proudly, "and don't forget the saddle and bridle."

When we arrive at school on Monday, there's buzzing excitement about the chocolate-bar drive. On the blackboard, a big thermometer is drawn, with everyone's name on it to show how many bars each person sold. I hand in our unsold bars with an envelope of money for our sale of six bars in all—the four we ate, the one my father ate, and one Uncle Frankie bought. It's a good thing other kids' parents sold bars for them at work, because the chalkboard shows we made a profit and have enough to dress up the Shamrocks in marching uniforms for the St. Patrick's Day parade.

Sister Pauline tells us to simmer down and get back to our studies. Today is an important day. She proudly announces to us that we are going to begin practicing for our first confession, and she teaches us what to say in the confession booth: "Bless me, Father, for I have sinned. It has been"—you say how many days—"since my last confession." Then you confess your sins.

Everyone's nervous about this, and the students ask questions that aggravate Sister Pauline.

"Exactly what happens in the booth?"

"What's the longest we can stay in there?"

"Could the hand of God come down and hit us across the head?"

We practice telling our sins to the nuns inside the booth before our first confession with a priest. They remind us that this is only practice; we can make up sins and tell our real sins to the priest.

I stare at a statue of St. Theresa, the saint our school was named after. She floats forever on marble clouds. Painted red blood drips from a slit below her heart. She shows hardly any suffering in her eyes made of glass, which shed a frozen tear on her pink cheek.

I pick my fake sins by the easiest penance. I think the sins of lying three times and swearing twice will probably get me three Hail Marys.

After confession, we are all sweating it out while waiting to hear what the nuns have to say.

Sister Pauline announces, "You have done very well, and confirmation should go just fine. Although you weren't to tell your real sins, some of you did." She blushes and smiles. "They are safe with me. I will keep them secret in my heart."

⁂

The nuns never pick an exciting place for a school trip, such as the zoo or a carnival. "Today we are going to the public library," Sister Rosette announces. It's a huge cement building with lots of glass and never-ending stairs to climb. Before we are allowed to stampede through the revolving glass doors, we promise, in front of God to Sister Rosette, to be on our best behavior, as if we are in church. We are to whisper, not scream, and to say, "Yes, ma'am," to the librarian.

The librarian tells us she will explain how to look things up alphabetically and then use the card catalog to find books. We can look up any subject and then find a book about it through the Dewey decimal number attached to it. "The system is named after the man who invented it, Mr. Dewey," the librarian tells us.

Sister Rosette nods, looking at us as if to say, "Show some enthusiasm."

The librarian asks me to pick any subject. "Apple," I say.

"Apple," she repeats, leading us to a drawer labeled A. She tells us, "In the A drawer, we look for *apple* just like we do in the dictionary, alphabetically. Everyone gather round. See?" She points to words on the card as she pronounces them. "*Ape*, *appetite*, and here is *apple*. Then we have all different apple categories: apple pie recipes, apple perfume, apple seed planting. You can then find a book matching the number to the right, which is the Dewey decimal number."

We go on hunting for books by the number we researched. Once the librarian is sure we all have the idea, we form a line to get our own library cards, which allow us to take two books home.

I start to spend my Saturday mornings taking a bus to the library and searching for answers alphabetically. I can ask questions and look up answers without being afraid of someone finding things out. Books become my mother. Whatever I can't ask another person openly, I can look privately for in a book.

Books don't hold anything back; it's all there in black and white and sometimes even in full color. Some things are hard to understand, but each time, I pick up more and more. I start with words related to the human body—*human*, *body*, *human body*, *female*—and write down the numbers to the right, and then I head for that section of books. Hours pass while I sit on the floor, reading the titles and looking through books. I search the index in the back of a medical book: "body, female—reproductive system, page 252." When I get to the page, there's a diagram that looks like two peach pits at the end of a Y. It is labeled, "Female uterus and ovaries." I can't believe all that is inside me. I know our lungs breathe air and our brains think, but what are a uterus and ovaries?

I read on further about fallopian tubes, ovulation, and a man's sperm, which is ejaculated from a man who has an orgasm into a woman, who usually has an orgasm as well. I look up *orgasm* and finally connect a name to the pins-and-needles feeling I have been having between my legs that makes me feel dirty and good at the same time. It's called an orgasm. I read on. The man's sperm travels through the vagina into the uterus. It fertilizes an egg that's been dropped from the ovaries. In nine months, a baby is born—coming right out of that small space where the whole thing began. I feel dizzy and put all the books away. I don't want to know any more about how the baby gets out of that space or how the penis gets into that space. I remember my mother screaming in pain with her blue gown half ripped off and her body dripping with water and blood on the night Rebecca was born.

On the bus ride home, I look out the window and can't think straight. I will never let my father do what he has threatened to do my whole life—put it inside me. The book says I will have a baby. How will I ever get away from him? I feel my dream of having my own life slipping away. I'm lost in my father's trap without hope that I'll get away.

He tells me to trust him. Why should I? He lies, and books tell the truth. Does he think my mother will simply disappear? Will she throw us both out? Nothing makes sense: fathers, mothers, and daughters. I don't want to get off the bus at my stop; I want to keep riding and riding, but I get off because I have nowhere else to go.

I sit on the porch, trying to figure out what to do, afraid and alone, wanting so much to have someone to talk to.

I must believe in myself because there is no one else. I have to take a chance and say no. My father has made it so that my whole life with him is never a good choice, only the lesser of two evils.

It's later in the afternoon now and still sunny. I hear

my father's voice call to me from the third-floor window. The sound of his voice makes my heart pound. I won't go in until I know my mother is home. All I know is to head straight for a tree to cry under alone. Holding in tears, I run down the porch stairs, heading toward a lonely tree.

I hear unfamiliar voices calling from behind me, "Hey, where you going? Hey! Wait up."

Footsteps follow me; they're coming closer. I don't even think of running back to the safety of my house. I continue defiantly walking forward toward my crying spot. The footsteps are gaining on me, but I march on deeper into the lots through the high grass. I don't care what happens to me. I don't make it to the tree. I just drop, sitting, hugging myself with my head down, and letting the tears gush out.

The footsteps have caught up to me, and a voice says, "Hey, baby." I look up, full of hate, into the dirty face of a boy much younger than I who tries to push at my shoulder.

I spit out in anger, "Get away from me, you little shit."

By now, the second boy has caught up to join in. He's bigger and older than I am, and he reaches out to touch me.

An inner strength pumps so hard through me that I feel no fear. Through tears gushing, my eyes stare defiantly into his eyes as I say, "Isn't there anyplace left in the world to cry anymore?"

Our eyes lock. Instead of looking mean, his eyes are kind, as if to say, "I understand." He blinks, bows his head, and walks away.

I am sitting on broken glass, hugging myself, making gulping sounds into the wind blowing toward the faraway tree. In the distance, I hear the younger boy's voice whining, "Why'd ya stop me? Let's go back. We can get her."

Their footsteps move farther away. I hear the older voice say, "Let's go. Come on. Leave her alone."

No

My mother, her sisters, and their girlfriends go to our school plays, and everyone is excited to watch our marching band practice for the St. Patty's Day parade. My father hardly goes anywhere or makes friends of his own. He works during the day and takes piecework home from the jewelry factory he works in. He has turned our basement into a workshop and spends hours heating colored glass sticks with a torch and turning them into glass ball earrings.

This Saturday, there's great excitement as my brother and I try on our new uniforms that the chocolate-bar sales paid for. My mother helps us button buttons; she fluffs the feather on my hat and admires how perfectly our uniforms fit us. We all try to talk my father into going to watch the rehearsal.

My mother gives it one last try. "Larry, please come with us."

He blows smoke into the air, saying, "No, you go. I've got too much work to do here with the piecework. I've got a lot of pieces to get in by Monday. I'm gonna have a cup of coffee and a cigarette and get to work." He winks and points at me, wishing me luck. "Don't drop the baton" are the last words I hear as I head out the door.

After rehearsal, we visit Nonie, who lives in a small new house with Uncle Frankie. He went to school and got a better job. He drives a tractor-trailer truck, which is parked in the driveway. There is a little yard with shrubs and no garden, but I can see plants and flowers inside her front bow window. She waits for us at the front door with her arms held out and her voice calling out to me, "Bella, my little birdie."

Once we're inside, she shows me all the plants growing in her sunny window, which is like a miniature greenhouse. She is most proud of her orange tree that grew little oranges. "Look at my baby oranges!" She throws bread crumbs out the back door, saying, "Looka the birds," as they flutter toward the crumbs.

We follow her to the kitchen and sit at the table. "Have some meat-ah-balls *mangare*," Nonie says. The meatballs are in a pan in the center of the table, in warm tomato sauce. They aren't in the shape of balls but are egg shaped. Her hands are so crippled from arthritis that she can only roll oval shapes of meat. They taste as delicious as ever, though. My mother and I devour her spaghetti and meatballs flavored with garlic, basil, and salami. Then we dip warm bread in olive oil while conversing.

Nonie asks my mother to bring some things up from the basement because she has a hard time going up and down the stairs. A necklace of garlic hangs on the basement door to keep evil away. I ask her if she is afraid Papa's ghost might be there. She shakes her head, saying tearfully, "Once someone diez, he goes forever, never coming back to this world. Not even as the ghost."

My mother asks about Uncle Frankie's condition, as he is in the hospital for clogged arteries and heart disease.

"How is Frankie doing? Will Leah take you to see him in the hospital?"

"Ah, yes." Nonie gets angry and speaks slowly. "They starve my poor Frankie at that hospital with bad food. I bring him that basket of good food."

My mother pulls salami out of the basket and holds it up, scolding Nonie. "This is full of salt and could kill him! The nurses told you to stop this."

Nonie's eyes flash. "I'm no gonna kill my boy with this good food. They kill him with nothing to eat, ah! Mafa, I will nevah go to the hospital. Don't ever take me there. They starve people to death." Her eyes are watery.

"Bella, good-bye, my little birdie," she calls as we say good-bye, leaving her at the kitchen table.

The lot boys aren't scary, evil warlocks. My father has made friends with them. At night, when my mother and father talk, he says all those boys need is some guidance and to be kept busy by channeling their energy into work. He pays them to help clear out our land in the country. He also hires Jackie, who lives on the first floor, and his friend Mousy to help build the foundation. They are sixteen. He gives them a little money, and my mother feeds them at night. Mousy is strange. He can't help yelling out of the blue, "Mahampt, mah how yeah!" We never know when one of his fits is coming. At first, it's scary, like someone coming up behind you and saying, "Boo!" But then we all get used to him and hardly notice it. I think Mousy would work for free just to be around people who don't think him different because of his fits.

When Ray and I visit the land my father bought, we expect the Ponderosa Ranch. It is only woods with poison ivy and a brook trickling in the rain. We both look blankly into our father's face. I wonder what he's seeing that we don't see. He holds our hands and says, "Use your imagination." He points. "The house is going to go right there, and we will make a small pond from the brook with a crossing bridge and a wishing well. The horses will live there with paths for you two to ride through."

Next, we visit an old hermit named Silas, who lives across the street from our land. His yard is filled with carved wooden windmills that spin as we walk with my father and knock on the door of his log cabin. Silas opens the door, and a musty smell comes from inside, where I can see a fire glowing. My father says someone recommended Silas to help figure out where the best water source is to dig a well on our land. The man invites us in and shows us all his hand-carved Indian tepee toys and peace pipes decorated with feathers and beads. They hang on the walls, which are logs on the inside, the same as on the outside. Old Silas tells my father he'd be happy to help, and he hands me a little tepee made of birch bark as a present.

Silas walks to our land and picks a Y-shaped branch from a particular tree. He holds the Y-shaped twig with the end of the V in each hand, pointing the end of the

845-255-5030

6/27/18 1:06 PM
Items checked out to null

TITLE: A girl's courage / Mary Ellen
BARCODE: 32913000859229
DUE DATE: 07-18-18

TITLE: Mating in captivity :
BARCODE: 38051000158765
DUE DATE: 07-18-18

Total items checked out:2

You just saved $34 by using the Elting Memorial Library today.

stick straight out. We follow him as he walks holding the twig straight out while nothing happens. "No, not here," he says. He walks and walks, and we follow. Finally, the long, straight end of the twig shakes, pointing downward. "You see," Silas says, "it's drawing down toward water. Dig a well here, and it will never go dry."

We tell my father Silas moved the stick, but my father says he didn't. It's an old Indian method that works, and only certain old-timers who pass it down from generation to generation can do it. Even after the method is shown to a person, he still has to have a gift, a feel for it.

On days when it's soggy and wet, my father drives up to the land with Ray, Mousy, Jackie, and me, and we all sit in the car and talk, waiting for the rain to stop. Until then, they make plans to dig a foundation. Dad brought an old junk car that had been sitting in the lots under the rain and left it in the middle of the land. He points and explains why one tire is off the drive wheel with a long chain around it. We are going to use it to haul rocks. It's not a car anymore but a gas-powered rock-moving machine.

On sunny days, Ray and I watch the machine haul one rock after another. My father and Jackie wrap a rock in a chain while Mousy hits the gas at just the right time, crying out, "Mahampt, mah how yeah!" amid the sounds of rocks dragging in the dirt. Soon the area becomes a big, square-shaped hole—a foundation of rocks.

At home, my mother worries about running out of money. Dad sits down and figures out a way to build things himself with the lot boys, Jackie, and Mousy. He orders wood and has it delivered. Ray and I watch each weekend, until one day they have created the frame of a house. We finally get to help, along with my mother, by picking out rocks that we think are perfect for the inside fireplace. My mother stands inside the open frame, trying to figure out the kitchen.

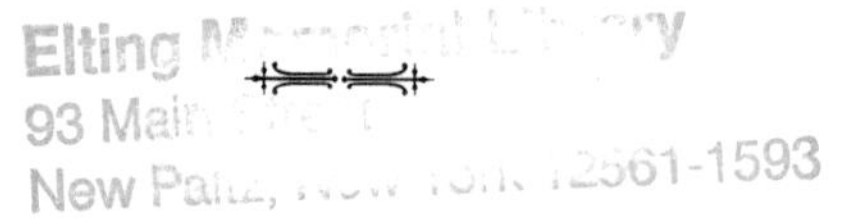

Just when I think my life will remain normal with a happy mom and dad, I'm caught off guard. I am alone with him in the house, and from my bedroom, I sense all the sounds and smells of his evil routine beginning. I hear his footsteps shuffling as he locks the door and then pulls down the shades and goes into the bathroom to wash and shave. I smell the sickly sweet scent of his Old Spice aftershave, which I know is the final step, as if he's getting ready to go out on a date. Instead, he enters my room.

He puts pressure on me to be a woman and get excited about the things he's trying to teach me. He says I don't show any enthusiasm or act as if I care. "Why can't you smile once in a while?" he says. "None of the boys are going to like you with a pout like that. If you don't start cooperating soon, you won't develop properly."

He takes out a film projector from the closet and starts winding film around it, saying, "Now I'm going to show you how a real woman acts with a man."

I don't want to see it, but I want to see it, and I feel ashamed and curious at the same time. However, it doesn't matter what I want anyway. My father starts the projector.

In gray and black silhouettes, a man is doing to a woman what my father says he will do to me. Instead of stiffening up and closing her eyes, the woman in the film makes moaning sounds, and she is asking for it. "You see how she likes it?" my father asks.

I look at my father, and I feel dirty. When I freeze up and try to go away, I am pulled down into my body by my own sensations. I'm drawn inside myself, never letting on about feelings inside me. My mind is desperately trying to figure out how to escape his plan.

My father says he has something to help loosen me up. He hands me a glass of liquid, saying, "Drink this. Gobble it down, and you won't be so frigid."

I fake a slow sip, stalling for time. The liquid burns my lips like fire. I have never seen alcohol in my house, nor have I seen my father drink. I am afraid of this stranger before me. Sister Pauline's words come into my head: "You're at an age now when you can start to reason things out for yourself."

He interrupts my thinking. "Come on, and finish up that glass. Watch me, and don't be such a damn baby," he says. He takes a big swig and releases a stinking breath on my face, sending goose bumps of hate down my spine.

"Why do I have to do this?" I ask nonchalantly, as if he is making me do more homework or eat a vegetable.

"Come on," he says. "I'm not making you do anything. I'm teaching you. Don't you want to learn? Don't you trust your old dad? Take another sip, and before you know it, you will be asking me for it. Go on," he commands. "I will not do it unless you ask for it like the woman in the film. Ask me to fuck you."

I find the courage to say no. "I love you, Daddy. No." I

sob, looking into his eyes, and I feel more courage. "I love you so much, Daddy. Why do you hurt me?"

He breaks down crying. My father sobs uncontrollably with his head down, unable to look at me.

It's the first time I've ever seen him cry. We both sob with our heads down, not looking at each other and not touching each other.

I am naked and ashamed, and I walk away. He doesn't stop me. I am thirteen years old.

I said no.

I'm free.

10
Confessing Sins

It's still dark out, and my mother's alarm rings. It's St. Patrick's Day. She gets Ray and me ready and drives us to the school bus that will take us all the way to New York City for the parade. My mother brings us to the bus and makes sure that the chaperones have our sandwiches and that boxes with our hats are aboard. She waves good-bye as the bus leaves.

Ray and I fall asleep the minute the bus gets moving on the highway, and we wake up to find our bus in the middle of a street that has been closed off for the parade. The sign on the telephone pole says Broadway. When I step off the bus onto the street, I see skyscrapers towering above. Endless rows of friendly people are waving from behind blue wooden barriers. Police officers ride around on proud horses that prance and snort in the brisk air.

I practice throwing my baton into the air and catching it. My brother is drumming away with the other drummers. Father Murphy beams proudly at me, swishing his hand to the side and bowing, as he says to me, "It's time to lead the band."

The band plays, and we march proudly. My feet barely touch the ground. The pom-poms on my boots fly from side to side; confetti mixes with all the colors of the people; and I twirl the baton, watching it swirl in circles high above me and rejoicing in my new freedom. The higher I throw it, the more I feel free—and the easier it becomes to catch it.

On the bus ride home from New York, we get hot chocolate and sandwiches. I'm covered in green, from my uniform to my emerald-green birthstone ring. I begin to nod off with sweet memories, smelling Papa Non's freshly cut grass and feeling as proud as a princess once again. I dream of Ikit and wait for him to appear through translucent serenity, but he is not here for me. Instead, I float in a universe of stars, cradled by a soft female voice: "He is not here because you no longer need him. You are free. Just let go."

I fall through space in starlight without the familiar feel of Ikit's soft hairs. I wish to ride him one last time, not for him to take me away but for us to gallop with my new feeling of freedom.

I awaken, along with all my classmates, at the bus stop in Providence. Mom and Aunt Sophie are waiting for us, excited, saying they saw us on television. The Shamrocks are TV stars—celebrities!

I sit in a church pew in front of the same statue of St. Theresa. She stands on a marble cloud. Her glass eyes look upward and her heart bleeds as I wait for my first real confession in front of a priest.

Since today is a true confession, not practice, I feel this is a private place in the dark with just the priest and me, and I will confess and be forgiven for the secret sin of my father and me and will leave with a clean slate.

I worry that the priest might come running out of the booth and take me to a home or call the police to take my father away. However, Sister Pauline has promised that confession will be between God and me; sins are reported and forgiven with no strings attached. I decide today is the day.

Inside the confession booth, it is hot and uncomfortable, and the wool from the footrest scratches my knees. I say, "Bless me, Father, for I have sinned." I'm quiet, and the priest remains silent for what seems like an eternity. My eyes adjust to the darkness, and I can see the shadow of a priest through the screen. I stutter, trying to continue, but no sins leave my lips. I wait for the priest to say something—perhaps "Yes, my child" in a kindly way—to jump-start my confession of my father and me, but he says nothing.

Through the still silence, he finally responds—with earth-shattering snores. I see from his shadow that his body is slouched over in sleep. I figure that the church probably put the sleeping priest on duty for children's confessions, thinking nothing important was going to come through. I sneak out quietly so as not to wake him.

Ray and I get ready for Mass on Sunday while my

parents stay home in bed. My father says he doesn't have to go because he's Protestant, and my mother says it's the only time she can get some damn sleep. My parents get to break all the rules and do things they tell us not to do, such as smoking, swearing, and skipping Mass on Sunday.

I'm sure my soul is now clean enough to receive the body of Christ, and I line up with all the kids for the wafer that represents the body of Christ. The priest sings the Latin words *Dominos Nabiscos*, making my stomach growl for chocolate Nabisco cookies with cream filling and a glass of milk. Father Gibbons doles out the wafers seemingly in slow motion, as if he is about to fall asleep again.

Thank God the church is so dazzling that it distracts me from having the body of Christ stuck to the roof of my mouth. I sit through Father's sermon, trying to pry the wafer lose with my tongue and admiring the golden ceilings with painted angels hovering above. The stained-glass windows reflect rainbows of colorful light that bounce off crystal lamps and gilded fixtures.

Father Gibbons, still talking in Latin, gets tired and sits down, so another priest takes over. In the background, Father Gibbons is hunched forward, asleep again. People fidget when his snores echo through the church as loudly as the roars of a lion in the jungle.

Glowing votive candles flicker inside the glass eyes on the statues, making them look real. It's as if they are reporting what they see to God. It's not a place where Father Gibbons should be snoring.

11

Foster, Rhode Island; Tiki; and Zombie

It is summer, and soon I will start the ninth grade in a public high school. Although our house in the country isn't quite ready, my mother and father say they can make do, because they don't want us to spend another summer in Mr. Zelka's house with the smell and the lots in the back. They can't afford both a mortgage and rent anyway. Things will be tight, but my father promises my mother, "We're gonna make it."

Ray and I walk around, listening to our footsteps echo off the plasterboard walls. My mother and father are in the kitchen, looking through boxes and pulling out all the things we need to use.

"Only the bare necessities," my mother says to him. "We don't want to ruin everything with paint, plaster, and dust. Let's not unpack until the house is finished. Why didn't you hook up the hot water before we moved in?"

My father is so happy that he doesn't get angry at

anything. "Don't worry," he says to her. "By next week, the hot water will be in, and then the heat will be working before the summer is over, and—"

"But, Larry," she interrupts, "we don't even have a stove."

He has answers to all her complaints. "We're going to cook out, barbecue, and pick up ready-made foods at a diner so you won't have to cook. We can use this little hot plate here to boil water for our cups of java." He grins and continues. "Before you know it, we will have enough saved up for the stove, washer, and dryer." He picks her up and twirls her in the air, saying, "Soon you will be cooking with gas, baby."

The living room is large and empty. It has wooden-plank floors and a bow window looking out into trees with rain dropping on them. "The fieldstone fireplace is solid as a rock and drawing perfectly," my father says proudly from his perch on a kitchen chair in front of the fire. Just as they planned, wagon wheels separate the entrance way between the living and dining rooms, and my father has made one wheel into a chandelier. It hangs from a black chain, marking the spot where our new dining room table and chairs will go.

"After we get a hot-water tank, stove, washer, and dryer," my mother says.

The summer is passing, and each day grows warmer than the next. There isn't much to explore outside except for trees, leaves, and a brook. We know we are safe because my father tells us that it is our land and no one can trespass. We don't need a fence. It's not the same as the lots; there is never anyone around to scare us away. Ray and I find a fort, which is an old abandoned shack in the woods, complete with bottles and dishes. We hide inside, watching deer, squirrels, and rabbits run by.

There isn't a yard yet, just a clearing around the house and a big hole to the right of the driveway, not far from the front door. When my father was clearing the land, he discovered a bump in the path of the driveway. He tried to dig up the bump, but it was part of a gigantic underlying rock. The deeper my father dug, the bigger the rock got, but he was determined to get rid of the bump. He didn't have the manpower or equipment to move it, so he hired a man with a bulldozer to dig up the whole thing. I think the battle between my father and the rock got expensive, and he ran out of money to buy fill, so now we have an uncovered hole that a car would fit in taking up most of the front yard. I think he should have left the bump alone. My mother constantly worries one of us will fall into the hole. She reminds us to stay away from it and nags at my father to get some fill to cover it because it is dangerous. At least we have something to do while sitting on the cement stairs in front of the house: we throw rocks into the hole.

I expect that this is how we will be spending our summer, and I can't wait until September to get back to school.

My dad's car drives up with another car pulling a trailer behind him. He gets out of the car and walks to us. "I have a surprise for you," he says, beaming.

Ray and I look at each other, and I whisper, "I hope it's not a new brother or sister." Dad takes us by the hand and brings us over to the trailer. He opens the back doors, and Ray and I are speechless. I can't believe it. No, I'm dreaming. Inside are two horses bobbing their heads. Our jaws drop in awe as we watch Dad lead a black-and-white pinto with a long black mane and tail down the ramp. I want to touch it, but I'm afraid I'll wake up, and everything will disappear. It's wearing a halter, and my father ties it to a tree with a rope. Next, Dad walks out a chestnut horse with a fiery red mane as it swishes its tail in the air and snorts.

The man in the other car seems to be happy that the horses have a new home, and he drives away with the empty trailer, smiling.

My mother looks out the window and yells, "Larry, what the hell is this? What did you do?"

"Ah, Muff," he says, "I'll be in to explain in a minute."

My brother and I stand together, looking up at the two horses as they look down on us. My father goes to his car, opens the trunk, pulls out two saddles, and carries them one on top of the other. He tells me the black one is for my pinto. I study the saddle, which is made of black leather with designs carved into it, and imagine myself sitting in it and holding on to the silver horn with my feet in the stirrups. He shows Ray a tan leather saddle and orange woolen blanket for his horse. My father's riding lesson begins with my pinto as he picks up a red blanket and shows us how to first put the blanket on and then put the saddle over it.

"Watch how I buckle and pull the straps secure around his belly. Feel this tension, how it is tight enough to keep the saddle on but not too tight to hurt the horse. For now, I'll put the bridle on."

Before I'm finished asking, "How am I going to get

up on top?" my father picks me up, and I'm in the saddle, which fits me like a glove. *Wow, the whole world looks different from up here.*

Next, he saddles up the chestnut horse and puts Ray on top.

My brother and I look at each other and smile, knowing this is not a dream.

Dad returns to my horse to check the saddle straps one last time, saying, "Just as I suspected, they are loose. This horse is smart. He held his breath and puffed out his belly till I was finished cinching the straps, then he let his breath out, and now the straps are loose. Watch this guy whenever you put the saddle on by yourself."

He checks Ray's saddle once more and then steps back, smiling slowly, enjoying the moment. Then he says, "That's it! You see the bridle? It has a metal bar called a bit with long leather reins attached on each side." He puts the straps into my hands, explaining, "To go left, gently pull the left rein; to go right, pull the right rein. To stop, pull back evenly on both reins. Never yank on anything because the horse's mouth is very sensitive. Oh, and be very careful about digging your feet into the horse's belly; that's their signal to gallop as fast as they can, and you have to prepare to hang on tight."

We practice using a delicate touch on the reins, turning, and stopping in circles, waiting for my father to say we are ready to ride.

My mother comes out with a horrified look. We want her to be as happy as we are. We call to her from atop our horses, "Look! Look at us!" but she is busy talking to my father. We hear her ask, "How are we going to afford this?"

My father answers in a low voice, "Wait. Shhh."

He comes back into our riding circle and says we can go exploring because we are doing so well. As I go down the hill, he reminds us how to prepare for a gallop by pushing our heels into each side of his belly and making a *chit-chit* sound. I imitate my father by squeezing my teeth on the side of my mouth and sucking in and out to make the *chit-chit* sound. He says that's good enough. The horse will understand.

As we ride slowly down the country road, my father calls out, "Don't gallop until you feel comfortable! Don't get hurt now. Go. Have fun."

I am in heaven, pretending to be my great-grandmother, the Indian squaw from my father's side. After a while of riding along tree-lined dirt roads, I see an open field and call out to Ray, "Let's gallop!" Ray's a little scared. I yell out, "Watch me!" I feel my bare heels bouncing off the soft hairs on the horse's belly as I loosen the reins while making the *chit-chit* sound. His ears perk up. I was not prepared for his immediate takeoff, which is as fast as a bullet in the wind. I jerk backward, dropping the reins, and grab on to the saddle horn in just enough time to stop falling to the ground. Dust and wind surround me as trees along the road pass by me in streaks of brown and green. The reins flap in the air all around the horse's neck, tangled in his black mane. His upper leg muscles cause creaking sounds against the leather saddle. I'm scared he's never going to stop as his galloping hooves kick up dirt below me. I can't catch the reins to pull back on them to stop him. Then he begins puffing, out of breath, and stops on his own. He stands there, breathing in and out, snorting and then relaxing.

He looks back up at me as if to say, "Have you had enough?" I rub my hand along the side of his neck and say, "Good boy. Good boy." I love him. I name him Tiki.

I let him rest until his breathing is calm. I see my brother down at the other end of the road. "Come on, Tiki." I suck the *chit-chit* sound between my tongue and right cheek and gallop again, loving the feel of his warm belly against my bare heels again. We reach my brother, who says he's ready to gallop too. He clicks his heels, and they gallop off. It's as beautiful to watch as it is to feel it. Tiki and I stay back and watch my brother, and then we catch up with him, continuing to ride around paths and roads.

My brother names his horse Zombie. We agree it is a cool, tough name.

We can't wait to get back to tell Mom and Dad how we feel and what we've seen. I want my mother to gallop and feel the wind. Instead, when we get back, we hear my parents arguing in the house. We tie our new horses to a tree in the driveway. We then sit on the front steps and listen to my mother's and father's words blowing out the kitchen window.

"Do you know how much it costs to feed two horses?" my mother yells.

My father answers, "All they eat is hay and a little grain. Hay is the cheapest stuff on Earth. They can graze all summer behind the house."

"And where will we put them?" my mother asks, still using an angry tone but softening a little.

My father jumps in, detecting that she's softening a bit. "Horses don't need a barn. They are perfectly happy, like wild horses, right in the backyard. I'll build a fence, and they can stay under the trees until I build a shelter."

My mother says, "It is irresponsible, Larry—irresponsible on your part. Doesn't it make sense to make a shelter and then get the horses? We can't even afford the mortgage payments. What about a stove, a washer, a dryer, and a dining room table?"

"Ah, Muffy, it wouldn't have been a surprise for the kids, now, would it, if they had seen the shelter?" My father's voice gives one last pathetic pitch.

They are quiet. My father opens the front door and sits down on the steps with Ray and me. I'm hoping he doesn't say that Tiki and Zombie have to go back. He asks us how we did. We tell him how excited we are. He shows us, for tonight, how to tie the horses up in the back and how to give them grain and some hay and water that he has already set up behind the house. We spend a long time brushing them and admiring them before finally strapping blankets over them and saying, "Good night." We promise to help my father build a wire fence tomorrow and, later, a shelter. I wish my mother would just jump on and gallop once. If she did, she wouldn't worry about a stove or a hot-water heater anymore.

My mother won't even look at them, but all Ray and I do is watch over Tiki and Zombie from our bedroom window. Sometimes Mom softens up and asks us if they have eaten enough, because if we don't feed them, she certainly won't. Every morning we get up looking forward to riding and exploring. We take turns putting Rebecca on the front of the saddles on our horses. We then get two puppies—more surprises—that follow us on our horses.

We own the Ponderosa, just as my father said we would.

What a different place this is from the city, with its fresh air outside. I love taking in deep breaths and smelling the clay dirt, horsehair, and wild roses. I hear wind rustling through leaves in the trees and water gurgling through brooks in the woods.

Each day, Ray, Becky, and I explore from the backs of our horses with the dogs trailing behind. We move like ducks in a row, as we did when we used to meet Nonie at the wool mills. There aren't any people around to bother us, and each path we take leads into a vast field or apple orchard. No one seems to be around to chase us away.

We follow an old wooden sign in the shape of an arrow that says Willoughby's Road. It's a narrow dirt path, long and winding, with thick trees along the sides. It seems to go nowhere and gets deeper downhill. We are about to turn back, when the road ends at a row of tall, pointed pine trees and a second sign pointing to Willoughby's Lake. It is the most incredible lake I've ever seen. I am stunned by how small I feel beside its vastness. My horse and I are like a bee on a flower. Tiki walks into the water up to his knees and starts drinking slowly, making ripples in the still lake water and nosing aside the floating water lilies.

This can't be real. I close my eyes and open them again. In front of me is the exact place I carried in my mind for so many years to protect me. It is real, and I'm riding a real horse into it. I see the exact oak tree I imagined right across the lake. It can't be that such a place exists, yet I am here. My horse bows his head to take another drink and then stands silently, observing as if this is a place he has been many times before.

I jump off Tiki into the clear water up to my knees in my cutoff jeans and run deeper until I'm submerged up to my neck. My body is soft all over, from the ends of my hair to my heels dug into the soft sand. Ray and Becky follow behind me, splashing away the silence and sending ripples to the edges, where the dogs are the only ones afraid to go in. They stand there barking as if to say, "Don't go in too far."

We explore no more. We don't need to. We have found heaven, and we go there every day and have the whole place to ourselves. I see another sign pointing to Willoughby's House. There's a house in the distance, but no one seems to be home. I wonder what Mr. Willoughby looks like and if he is a nice person. I wonder if Mr. Willoughby might be like old Mr. Zelka, stuck in the house and unable to come out.

For the remaining days of summer, I sit under the oak tree by the lake and watch my horse drink water. It's like having Papa Non's yard back but even better because no one ever chases us away. There are no adults working the land, raking, or singing Italian songs. The magic just happens every day in natural features, such as the sun, rain, rainbows, water bugs, birds, soothing sounds, and reflections. I can cry here, laugh here, or simply lie in the grass, imagining animals floating by in cloud shapes above. The endless water lilies that float by keep Becky curious, hypnotizing her as she laughs into the water at squiggling creatures. Raymond swings from a rope tied to a tree branch, and then he lets go of it, flying into the lake water. He screams, getting out all his energy, and no one cares. There is so much space around us that all our noise fades into the sky.

At dusk, crickets and fireflies whisper, "It's time to go home."

12
September

It is September, and preparing for public school is different because there is no uniform to wear. My mother takes me shopping for school clothes. I pick one dress. It is a moss-green wool jumper with a mock olive-green vest that has two brass buttons and chains that look as if they clasp it together in the front. I get to pick out any shoes I want. I pick pointy-toed Hush Puppies of light green suede that match my mock vest. My mother and I figure this is my new uniform, because I can wear it all year paired with different-colored knee socks, blouses, and sweaters worn on different days to change the way it looks.

Since I'm now in high school, Ray and I go our separate ways. We don't walk to school together, and we take different buses.

My bus picks me up at the bottom of the road. All-new faces look at me as I grab a seat and try to blend in. The girl next to me is wearing a metal brace to hold her head up. It connects all the way down to her spine. She smiles at me, and I say, "I'm Mary Ellen." Her name is Anna.

Everyone giggles, turning and pointing to the back of the bus. "Oh," Anna says, "that's Cheryl and Al. They are the school lovers; they're seniors who don't have a car. They take the bus every day and sit in the back, kissing and smooching." I turn around to see them with their faces stuck together. I watch the whole ride. They never stop, smooching as the bus goes *rickety-rack* down the road with the trees disappearing behind them in the distance.

The teachers in public school are men and women like my parents. It's not religious, so there are no nuns. There are no familiar faces, and I'm introduced as the new girl. Everyone's nice and smiling.

One thing I missed during the summer in the country was having a library to go to, but I discover there is a whole library right in the school where we can study and do research for our homework. There's a gym, where we get to practice gymnastics, and I watch boys play basketball. Everything is bigger and better than it was at the Catholic schoolhouse. There are no religion classes. There are signs for dances, and art is a regular class in its own room, where I get to paint with watercolor once a day. Again, my favorite teacher is the art teacher. His name is Mr. Aiello. He has curly dark hair and wears black-framed glasses. He smiles and signs his name on the blackboard as just a circle. "That's something Michelangelo could do that no one else could do—draw a perfect circle," he says, laughing. "Michelangelo didn't have to sign his name because he was known by the mark of a perfect circle."

Regular teachers are cool. I don't miss the Catholic nuns at all.

The bus takes us home again. I sit next to Anna

because no one seems to want to. I always get on or off before her, so I don't know how she walks or if she can. But she is always smiling, and so am I when we sit together. Kids are giggling at Cheryl and Al smooching and sticking to each other's faces as our bus *clickity-clacks* down the road. I look at Anna, and she looks at me as if to say, "How do they breathe?"

It's now Thanksgiving, and we still don't have a stove or hot-water heater. My mother complains that it's going to get cold and insists we should get these appliances soon. She tells my father she never wanted the horses, and she asks when he is going to make some kind of shelter. He tells her that horses roam in the wild, living in the woods and fields, all the time. "And the kids are taking good care of them by feeding, brushing, and blanketing them at night," he says.

"What about the rain and snow?" my mother asks. "It's going to start getting colder and wet out."

"The temporary shelter with the tarp over it is good-enough protection from the weather for now. Don't worry; soon enough, I'll have everything done like magic," my father says. "And now, for our Thanksgiving treat, how about we all go out to eat?" my father asks, smiling.

"Yeah!" Ray and I holler.

My mother grits her teeth, saying quietly to my father, "No money, Larry. No money. Why do you always try to do things with no money?"

Nothing gets my father upset anymore. He's still smiling as he says, "Come on, Muff. You worry too much about money."

We get in the car. We drive around and stop at

different restaurants. "Too expensive," my mother says, "and you have to call to reserve a table in advance. It's Thanksgiving." We find a diner, and I go in to order our food.

The waitress behind the counter looks just as miserable working on Thanksgiving as we are driving around looking for a turkey dinner. I ask her for four turkey dinners to go. She smiles and says, "Will that be with gravy and all the trimmings?"

"Yes." I smile. She's making me hungry now. She hands me a big bag with four aluminum dishes clamped shut with white cardboard on top. "Happy Thanksgiving," we say to each other.

At home, we eat by the stone fireplace with a fire going. The chandelier glows brightly, still marking the spot where our dining room set is going to be. My father says we can sit in a circle with our legs crossed like Indians. My mother brings out her good tablecloth and says it will be like a picnic. We open our turkey specials; my mother goes through the package for forks and napkins and says, "Oh, look, and what's in these four extra packages? The waitress gave us four pieces of apple pie for free!"

Everyone's happy. Our house is warm; the dinner is delicious, with cranberry sauce, stuffing, and dessert; and my mother smiles.

We talk about school and about Raymond's project for the science fair. He wants to build a model of the planets, and he has a book about them from the library, so we go over pictures of the universe and how the planets orbit the sun.

My father sets up a workbench under the chandelier,

made of sawhorses and a sheet of plywood. He brings out boxes packed from his workshop and finds a little motor, some paints, glue, wire, and different-sized balls and beads of glass from the jewelry factory. He and my brother work from the pictures in the book. We read out loud late into the night and debate about whether or not someone could live on another planet.

We enjoy staying up late and working until the project is finished. We hold our breath, waiting for the moment my father will hit the switch and the motor will turn, moving all the wires attached to the painted planets floating in the universe. He hits the switch. *ZZZzzzt. ZZZzzzt.* The motor makes a sound as if it wants to turn, but it doesn't. Nothing happens. The planets don't move. My brother is about to cry because of all the long hours we put in, and without the movement, the model looks kind of dumb.

My father says to have patience. Raymond and I watch. "One more adjustment," my father says. "System's on." *ZZZzzzt. ZZZzzzt.* The motor winds away.

The planets revolve on their wobbling wires, which soon become invisible; before our eyes is a miniature universe. My father turns all the lights out with the chandelier dimly lit, and we leave all the planets and the universe atop the dining table and head to bed.

Going to school all day and then coming home and doing homework is all Ray and I can keep up with. We didn't realize how much work it is to take care of Tiki and Zombie. By the time we are done feeding them, shoveling manure, moving hay, brushing, and blanketing them, there is no time to ride, because it gets dark early. We manage to get it all done, finishing with a "Good night" to them and a special treat of a little grain. As we feed Zombie, Ray notices his belly seems swollen. We tell my father about this, and he thinks we should cut back on the grain for a while.

One Saturday, we are looking forward to riding to Willoughby's Lake. We bring our blankets and saddles around the back, only to find Zombie on the ground, stiff. My brother just looks at the ground, not knowing what's wrong, but I know he is dead. I run into the house to get my father.

My father tells us to go inside the house once he sees Zombie.

The next morning, Ray is standing at the edge of the hole in the front yard, staring down at Zombie at the bottom. My father somehow managed to get Zombie's body into the hole during the night. I think he used the rock-towing car machine, but I don't tell Ray, who doesn't talk or ask questions or cry in front of me; he just looks at the ground.

My father moves us away from the hole, telling us to get back in the house. We watch from the window as a truck drives up, and a man with a badge introduces himself. We read the initials SPCA on the side of the truck and ask my mother what the acronym stands for. "That's Society for the Prevention of Cruelty to Animals," my mother says. "I hope they don't arrest your father and take him to jail for killing the horse. I told him not to leave these animals out in the cold and wet like that. Irresponsible—that's your father."

My father talks to the man, who then drives away in his truck. My father comes into the house and gets on the phone to order a truck full of dirt and a couple of bags of lime. My mother asks him what the man from the SPCA said. He tells her that a woman across the street called to report the horse's death. I know their daughter, and sometimes I watch her from my window as she jumps English-style on her thoroughbreds. She practices for competitions.

My father tells my mother that the man from the SPCA said the horse was probably sick when he bought it, but my father had no way of knowing. He took down the name of the man Dad bought the horses from so that he could check on other horses he might have. He looked at Tiki and said he is fine, but to be safe, he said we should put Tiki in a barn. My mother says old Silas called and offered us a little shed on his land that Tiki will just fit in.

I watch in the window alone. I see my father throw lime down the hole, and the dump truck fills the hole up to the top with red dirt that matches Zombie's coloring. Ray is nowhere to be found.

Each night, after school, I visit Tiki in his shed, feed him, and clean out the manure. He whinnies and neighs in hunger every night when I get to him. He waits impatiently for me, bobbing his head and mane up and down. I can't ride him much, because Ray and I were a team. It isn't the same without the whole caravan. I feel selfish still having a horse without Ray having one. It gets cold and dark early these days; Christmas and snow are just around the corner. I know that Tiki is suffering from lack of exercise and from being cooped up in Silas's little shed. Taking care of a horse is a lot of work.

When my father says they've decided that the horse should go and that they are going to sell him, I understand. I want the horse, and I don't want him. Tiki was part of the whole package with my brother, the caravan, and the lake, so how can I ride around galloping and being happy in front of him? I know my brother too well to think he would want to share Tiki with me. It would never be the same for him. My parents can't afford another horse, and I don't think he wants another one.

I hear my father's sad, understanding footsteps come into my room. He sits at the edge of the bed, puts his arm around me, and says, "Tiki is gone. I sold him to a very nice man who will keep him on a farm with big fields and a barn and other horses."

He is not gone. He is in my mind. I will always remember him under the tree with his reins falling, his head bobbing up and down, and his thick black mane glistening. I was just getting to understand his personality. Whenever I clicked my bare heels into his soft belly toward a place he was afraid to go, he would neigh, lifting his head up and down with his big black eyes bulging, reminding me of Nonie when she said, "Stay away from the lotz." Sometimes after a long walk, when I wanted him to gallop, he'd let out a snort as if to complain. Then he'd start to gallop when he felt like it.

Tiki took me into such a wonderful, safe place all summer. As always, I know it is not a place I can stay in forever.

I did not watch him go away. I did not say good-bye.

My fourteenth summer will always be a memory of Tiki.

Circle

Ponaganset High School was named after an Indian, Chief Ponaganset, who was not a God or a saint. This big public school is very different from the little schoolhouse of St. Theresa. I think about Christmas coming while waiting in the cold for the school bus.

Anna and I sit together on the bus, preparing to giggle at the smoochers, but Cheryl sits alone in the back without Al, or Kissy Face. That is our nickname for him. It's gloomy because there's no one to laugh and point at. No one talks to Cheryl. She sits there smiling. It's the first time I've seen her lipstick not smudged from all the kissing. She stares into space with her head bobbing along with the bus on the bumpy road. Then I see the girl from across the street, whose mother called the SPCA. She looks at me and smiles. I feel self-conscious because of what happened with Zombie, but she is always nice at school and waves to me in the corridors.

By now, it's getting harder for me to keep my hair, which is still down to my back, clean. The lake water is too cold to wash with, and I'm too lazy to boil water every night. I'm getting embarrassed about the dress uniform that my mother and I thought up. All the other kids wear different outfits, except one or two who are in the same boat I am. I'm about out of combinations, wearing orange socks one day and an olive sweater the next.

I leave the door of our house feeling self-conscious, trying not to walk over the spot I know Zombie is buried under and yelling at our dogs to go back into the yard. They are out of control, untied, and still barking. I still have the secret scar that no one can see, the one from my father and me. If anyone ever knew what happened, I might never leave the house again.

What happened to me in the past makes me feel like a leper. I pretend it never happened, but the memories haunt me. I try to push them away, but they never disappear. They simply become smaller and further away.

On Christmas Day, there is gloom in the house. My father sits at the table, as always, with a cup of coffee and a cigarette, wearing a T-shirt without underwear. He has no plans for moving the entire day; he blows his problems into the air through cigarette smoke, up to God. I think it must be his way of praying. When he gets no answer, he gulps down his cup of java. No one wants to sit at the table next to him. It's a trap, where we have to listen to him go on and on about the world and the state it's in. We learn to let him sit there, and we try to escape by the television in front of the stone fireplace.

There is no Christmas tree with toys under it. Secretly, Ray and I think there is going to be some big surprise on Christmas Eve; later, we might drive somewhere and look for a diner where we can order Christmas dinners to take home and eat in front of the fire. Maybe we will just talk and look in the cardboard box at photographs.

At least we have some peace and quiet, I think, until my mother suddenly runs out of the bedroom, saying, "There's absolutely no money, Larry. No money. We are three months behind on the mortgage, and the bank is going to take the house. What are you going to do about this? What are we going to do? You and your promises and your big ideas." She sobs.

My father sits with no response, staring into the air as if she isn't there, puffing smoke, crossing his legs, and grasping his coffee cup.

Getting no response from him, she runs back into their room and then comes out again, slamming the door behind her. She holds a small white box. "Here," she says with an angry voice. "It's a Christmas present." She hands it to me as if it is a bomb, angry because this is the only present there is.

Inside the box is a white slip in between tissue paper. "Thank you," I say, looking down at the floor.

"Thank God I bought something before all this mess happened," she says out loud to everyone. "Larry," she says, trying to get some response from my father. "Larry, it's Christmas, and we have nothing. We are going to lose the house, and we can't even drive out and get some food. Larry, you promised." She breaks down crying. She moans. We all want my father to comfort her and us and say everything is going to be okay.

"Larry?" she cries. We watch him stare at the wall while avoiding her eyes. "That's it!" she calls out. "I swear

I'll kill myself. I'm going to do it this time because I have nothing to live for."

I'm thinking he has no heart. Why doesn't he go to her and hold her? Instead, he gets up and walks calmly and slowly past her to their bedroom. There's an angry, bitter, hateful look in his eyes, and his privates dangle below his T-shirt. He appears in front of her, carrying a gun. Ray, Becky, and I stare at both of them, too stunned and scared to move. He's loading the gun surely, calmly, and with great force. "Go ahead," he says. "It's ready and loaded. Kill yourself." I can't breathe. The air is still. How could he? I will never forgive him.

My mother stops crying.

Still looking hateful, he puts the gun into her hands. She holds it, aiming it at him, and then she turns it around awkwardly toward herself. She looks into our eyes, which stare back, begging her not to.

She drops the gun onto the floor and runs into the bedroom, crying out, "Damn you, Larry! Damn you."

We listen to her sobbing alone on the bed.

My father goes back to his ritual at the table, staring straight ahead at the wall, inhaling smoke from a cigarette, gulping coffee, and pulling his T-shirt down over crossed legs. On his arm, I read the tattoo that says, "Mother and Muffy, the Only Tow I Love," written in a green heart, with an American eagle proudly spreading its wings across my father's muscle.

He turns his face toward us and says calmly and softly, "She wasn't going to kill herself."

It's dead quiet. Then the sounds of him sucking coffee, puffing a cigarette, and tapping his fingernails on the table echo through the house. He continues talking to the wall. "I had to call her bluff. I'm tired of her years of threatening. I'm tired of stopping her from doing it."

We hear his toenails tapping on the wood floor as he walks away from all of us down to the basement.

I vow never to forgive him for taking such a chance. Why couldn't he pick her up and twirl her in the air, saying, "Don't worry, baby; soon enough, you'll be cookin' with gas"? Maybe she would have laughed instead. It would have been better to try to make her laugh than to hand her a loaded gun.

I confirm my promise to myself that I will have my own apartment someday. It will be quiet, and I'm going to live alone without children, because my mother and father always say that if they hadn't had us, they could've had a lot of things and done something with their lives. They wouldn't have such money problems if it weren't for us.

Maybe I'll have a husband in my apartment, but we will never argue, and we will say, "How was your day?" to each other. He will be my best friend, and we will read books or talk and laugh in the dark like all the other families on television.

14 Serendipity: The Faculty of Making Fortunate Discoveries by Accident

When I'm at school, kids seem to like me for who I am. They don't see my parents arguing, Papa Non's ghost in Nonie's basement, the dead horse buried in the front yard, our empty house with no stove or hot water, or the barking dogs out of control. Kids seem to see me as me.

Maybe it's because I'm new. They give me a nickname, Dino, like the mascot dinosaur on Sinclair gas stations. Sinclair is a rich name that doesn't match my family. I end up on student council. We work on posters and plan dances and activities. I think I'm popular and can't figure out why.

Although the teachers are not nuns, they are serious about what we have to learn. Not everyone is Catholic. It's the first place I've been where kids are all different religions. We don't study any religion, and there are fun classes, such as art and gym, which I look forward to. Most of all, I enjoy the library in the building. I don't have to travel to get to it, and we get study period for an hour a day at the library to look things up to our hearts' content.

The librarian sits at her desk, reading while we study. Whenever I ask her to help me find something, she says, "Look it up." It seems a librarian's job is saying, "Shhh," or "Look it up," whenever we ask her a question.

In the middle of the room is a monstrous Webster's dictionary that sits on a pedestal, inviting me to turn its pages. I'm drawn to it, and I look up words I already know just for fun to check if they are in the dictionary.

I become a detective, searching for a word to lead me to other words to explain the secret of my father. So far, I've hit a dead end with words that don't lead to answers, but I continue to search, asking questions and looking up answers.

I ask myself, *What was I when this happened to me? Answer: a child.*

I look down the page of definitions:

> *child*: Function: noun
> a young person <a movie for both children and adults>
> Synonyms: bud, chick, chickabiddy, chit, juvenile, kid, moppet, nipper, puss, youngling, young one, youngster, youth
> plural: *children*
> Synonyms: offspring, begats, brood, descendants, issue, posterity, progeny, scions, seed—children, the care of: see *pediatrics*

I look up *pediatrics.*

> *pediatrics*: Pronunciation: pE-dE-'a-triks
> Function: noun plural but singular or plural in construction
> Date: 1884
> a branch of medicine dealing with the development, care, and diseases of children

In alphabetical order directly below, I spot an unusual word:

> *pedophile*: Pronunciation: pE-dA-fIl
> Function: noun
> Date: 1951
> one affected with pe·do·phil·ia

I look up *pedophilia* and find the following:

> Pronunciation: pE-dA-fi-lE-A
> Function: noun
> Etymology: New Latin
> Date: 1906
> sexual perversion in which children are the preferred sexual object

I've found the answer I've been looking for my whole life. I read the words again with my heart pounding, my finger outlining the definition: "Sexual perversion in which children are the preferred sexual object." He's afflicted with a sickness worse than a disease like cancer.

The dictionary has given me all it can: the definition for his affliction. I still have no answer for what, if anything, to do about it.

It's January and a new year. On student council, I help organize dances, make banners, and decorate the gym, which is a big space with high ceilings and hardwood floors where all the dances are held. The dances are called sock hops because we dance in our socks.

I'm self-conscious about dancing, but then a boy taps me on the shoulder and asks me to dance. *Eyeyeeyee!* He's one of the cute basketball players. We begin flailing arms and feet along with everyone else to the music, having fun.

The school hired a real band, the Cowsils, who sing away and change into different outfits. The chaperones are yawning at the doorways, and the band plays on until the time to go home comes too fast. We all dig for our shoes in a big pile. I head home like Cinderella racing everyone to the bus home.

As I begin to fall asleep, thinking about dancing with boys and watching seniors kiss atop the bleachers, feelings come over me like when my father used to do things to me. I hated him doing those things to me, but my body wants these feelings for myself, as if I'm craving a drug he gave me. Now I am free of him, but I still want the drug and don't know how to get it.

I try to give myself pleasure by touching myself all over, but nothing happens. I fall asleep feeling confused, with my blood rushing and my heart pounding to nowhere.

Back in school, studying in the library, I watch the librarian immersed in her book. In the hall, I see the basketball player who danced with me that night, and my mind wanders to those feelings again. I should be doing a lot of things, such as research or homework, but I daydream. Maybe I can find a book about pleasuring myself like the ones my father showed me. Then I could relieve my cravings and fall sleep at night.

I know my father hides magazines in my parents' bedroom, in the top drawer of the bureau. I would not take a chance to go in there or be near his things. I'd be asking for trouble if he ever caught me or even felt his magazines were amiss. I will never go near him or his bedroom. I know he has a sickness now, but what I feel is not a sickness. It's between me and my thoughts and my body, and the throbbing isn't going to stop unless I do something about it.

It is all I search for when I'm at the library. It's getting to be all I think about. I grasp for words to lead me to a book, a dirty book with no words, just pictures, but I'm back to a dead end. I do research like a blind person trying to cross the street in the rain, taking a chance on all the dirty words I know. As usual, really dirty words aren't defined at all. According to Mr. Webster, they do not exist, just as the word *aint* doesn't. So I start with medical words—*penis*, *vagina*, *uterus*—which lead me to gory scientific pictures.

I start to wander around the room to peek at the books behind the librarian's desk. Every time I try to get to the books behind her, she slams the book she's reading shut, annoyed, as if she doesn't want me to see what she's reading. "These stacks of literature aren't for you; they're novels for an older age level. You should be researching for geography class. Now, get back to work," she says, pointing to the geography section.

Bingo! Novels for a much older level. Aha! I'm onto something here; her description sounds like a cover-up for a dirty book if I've ever heard one. I'm sure all the books behind her are nasty ones. Of course they would be hidden away somewhere where everyone knows where they are but nobody says anything, like at my house. That's why the librarian guards them.

I pretend to read Webster's dictionary until I see her leaving her post. She puts her book down and goes to the door for a moment to chat with a teacher. I run to the stacks, grab a book, and walk away as unsuspiciously as possible.

My cheeks are flushed red. I also have a couple of science books to check out, so I slip the dirty book, with its pink cover, amid the others, disguising it at the checkout desk, worried that the clerk won't let me check it out. She stamps it along with the others, anxious to get back to reading her own book. I'm feeling cocky. I say to myself what my mother says to me: *Mary Ellen, sometimes you're too smart for your own good.*

I hide the book in my knapsack, vowing never to let anyone find it. I will keep it for a private moment all to myself.

It is Saturday, and my mother and I are the only ones home this afternoon. Alone in my room, I pull my hidden book from my knapsack. Finally, the moment I have been waiting for arrives. I nestle naked in my bed with the thick, heavy book in my left hand, my right hand at the ready. I rip open page after page, expecting exciting pictures to help me pleasure myself. *What? What's this?* The text is all words without one lousy picture. Could I have been wrong?

I close the book and read the title: *For Whom the Bell Tolls* by Ernest Hemingway.

Hmmm. I open the book, unable to admit defeat, reading on, hoping to find sensual writing. I continue as the book gets heavier in my left hand, with the right hand still hopeful.

It begins, "He lay flat on the pine needle forest." I read on and on, determined to find a seductive scene. Roberto, the hero of the story, is in the midst of trying to blow up a bridge in the middle of a war going on, when he comes upon a band of gypsies in the desert who have taken in a girl named Maria. They found her after men did terrible things to her, such as cutting off her hair and other things she can't talk about.

I think, *So Roberto will do the same, right? She's already ruined. Will he pull her clothes off? This will be described.* I read further. *No! Their eyes meet, and the earth turns?*

I begin to read on with both hands gripping the book, forgetting what I got it for in the first place, slowly savoring the gentle words describing how she slept in his tent on a cold, snowy night. He felt her short hair, soft between his fingers, and she wanted to give herself to him, but he was afraid to hurt her.

He loved her. I cry to myself. I can't stop reading. Roberto fell in love with her, and it didn't matter what had happened to her before. What those men did to her didn't make her ugly. He loved her, and he never even touched her.

At the end, I close the book slowly, dreaming about that inner feeling that words can't describe that Roberto and Maria had and the things money can't buy and remembering my soul.

I think about the characters, especially the old gypsy woman who took Maria in and what she said to her—that she was a little rabbit who did not know how it felt to be ugly on the outside and feel beautiful on the inside, as the old woman did. No, Maria was the opposite of her; she was beautiful on the outside and felt ugly on the inside.

There's banging on my door. My mother yells, "Mary Ellen, what in the world have you been doing in your room all day? It's not healthy, locking yourself up in there." She pushes the door open, saying, "Look at you with the covers pulled up to your chin. Get dressed, and go outside. The sun is shining."

I leave my book under my bed and read it every night. The due date comes and goes, and I can't return the book.

All my life, my hair has been long, down to my waist. My father never allowed me to cut it. He would stroke it, saying, "Never cut that beautiful hair."

I decide to cut my own hair short like Maria's. I don't ask anyone's permission. I get scissors and cut away.

In the morning, at the table, my mother's and father's mouths hang open when they see me. My mother gasps. "What happened to your hair?"

"I cut it. I wanted to try it shorter," I say, shrugging.

My father looks disappointed but says, "If that's the way you want it, Mary."

In school, I am the buzz of the corridor. I didn't think people noticed me—or my hair, for that matter. Kids who didn't talk to me before call out, "What happened to your hair?"

Then it happens: I feel the earth move under my feet. As if in slow motion, my eyes and a pair of blue eyes lock. Maybe I'm a little dizzy. We stop walking. Maybe the feeling is more like butterflies in my stomach. He looks right into my soul, trying to say, "Didn't you have long hair yesterday?"

He stutters, trying to get the words out, and I feel kind of dopey answering, "I wanted to try a different look."

He smiles. "Hello. My name is Steve," he finally says, stumbling again over his words and breaking our silence.

I understand how it feels to be self-conscious about something I have no control over. I tell him my name is Mary Ellen.

Some boys walk past us, breaking our spell. Someone yells out, "You'd better watch it! She's jailbait." I know he's a senior about to graduate. Steve asks how old I am.

"Fourteen and a half," I say, emphasizing the *half* so that he'll think I'm practically fifteen. He doesn't seem to mind. I make a mental note of the word *jailbait* to see what *Webster's* has to say.

I spend all my time on school activities and come home late to avoid being home. My father asks me questions: "Who is this boy you have been spending so much time with? He's not a boyfriend, is he? He's driving you home later and later after school. You're not going on dates, are you? You're too young to date, young lady."

I'm embarrassed and say, "He's just a friend."

My mother defends me. "She needs a good friend right now. There's nothing wrong with her getting out of the house, especially with all the hollering and fighting going on in here."

I come home with his sweater, which is big enough to be a dress, and his class ring with tape rolled around the bottom to make it fit my finger. I don't wear it in the house; I keep it under my bed with my book so that my father won't know we are going steady.

Steve and I are both on student council, so whenever we work late at school to decorate the gym for events, he drives me home afterward. Even though I think about smooching on our walk to the door, I run inside, leaving him standing there.

It's springtime. I have made many new friends, and I'm looking forward to next year, especially more sock hops and art classes. I spend holidays and weekends at Steve's house; his parents have practically adopted me. His mother is a hairdresser and has white-blonde hair styled like Marilyn Monroe's. His father builds houses. They have three boys, and I think his mother always wanted a girl. They live in a neat house with a lake in the back.

Steve and I read gushy love poems and tell stories. Mostly, we laugh a lot in the dark. We share secrets—not my scar, though. I don't think I'll ever be able to talk to another person about the secret that hangs over my head. It has taken the form of the ugly me inside my head, and I feel that anyone who sees it will not like me.

On the last day of school, when I get home, my mother and father give me bad news: we are moving back to the city. They don't give a reason; they just say we are moving because things didn't work out here with the house. From listening to their arguments at night, I know they can't keep up the mortgage payments. It's too far for my father to drive back and forth every day to the city with no time to work on the house. My mother says she can work again in the city and help out financially. They will get a sitter for Rebecca. "No more night shifts, though," my mother says. "That was killing me."

I gush out all the bad news to Steve. I think that he will be gone too, just like the country and Tiki. He's not worried at all and says, "I can drive my mother's car, so I can see you anywhere you live—and I will."

What a big difference a car makes! I thought he would be gone forever.

15
Looneyville

A Simon and Garfunkel song plays on the radio: "Lad dada dada—feelin' groovy. Life, I love ya. Lad dada dada."

We are back in our old neighborhood in Providence, near Olneyville, nicknamed Looneyville. Our apartment is on the first floor of an old Victorian house on the corner of two streets. At least it is in the school district of St. Theresa's, so I can return to a familiar school in September. Inside, the house is aged but neat and clean. Half a wooden fence that barely stands partially protects the yard. My mother and father turn the den into their bedroom so that Ray can have his own room, and I share a bedroom with Rebecca. We have the same old twin beds.

I unpack a box of my possessions: Steve's sweater with the fuzzy letter *P* on it, a photograph of me and Tiki at the lake, trinkets, and ticket stubs from school events. I close the drawer on mementos of the past. *For Whom the Bell Tolls* is now my book because I could not bear to return it to the library. I hide it under my bed, fearing that the library police will come to arrest me and confiscate it.

My mother got her night job back at General Electric. It looks like a long, hot summer ahead for me, with nothing to do but watch my sister, Rebecca, listen to the radio and wait for the weekends with Steve by the lake. I don't have to hide his ring anymore. My parents figured out we are going steady.

My brother seems to come in and out of the house, and when I ask where he is going, he says he's going out. I ask, "Where?"

He always says, "Just out." Ever since I started high school, we aren't as close.

On the radio, I hear a jingle: "For fifteen cents, a nickel and a dime, at Burger Chef, we will make your money rhyme." An announcer says, "That's right, folks; fifteen cents will get you a delicious, juicy broiled hamburger or fresh, crispy french fries. There's no point in staying at home and cooking anymore. At these prices, the whole family can afford to go out to eat every night. And by the way, the folks at Burger Chef are looking for help, so stop by and fill out an application."

Wow, I think, *if I had a job, I could start saving money to get my own apartment.*

The minute my mother gets in the door, I ambush her, asking, "Mom, can you take me to Burger Chef? I want to apply for a job there."

"Wait," she says. "Let me sit down and take my shoes

off. I just got out of work." She bends down to untie her shoes.

"Mom, if I don't get down there and fill out an application, someone else is going to get the job."

She looks at me and says, "It's not that simple. You need a Social Security card because you are only fifteen."

"Fifteen and a half," I remind her.

"You need to file for working papers."

"Can't I at least go fill out the application? Then you can help me get all the other papers later. Please?" I beg.

"All right," she moans. "Hey, maybe then we can buy some hamburgers and french fries so I won't have to cook supper. I'm tired."

I get the job.

My mother hands me some papers, looking serious and saying, "This is your Social Security card. Put it in a safe place. Never lose it. This card will be with you the rest of your life. It's your number. No one else in the United States will ever have the same number."

I read the numbers as if they are snowflakes captured for me and given to me by the government as proof that no other is like me. This is a serious part of life, like confession or communion, a stepping-stone to another level. I memorize my number in case I lose the card.

"There are two papers you will need the rest of your life," my mother continues, breaking into my trance, "this Social Security card and your birth certificate. You will need these two things for everything you apply for."

I hold the two pieces of paper—my keys to freedom and opportunity, the reasons Nonie came here all the way from Italy on the back of a whale. I place them safely in my drawer, and I fall asleep remembering my soul.

I get to work behind the counter at Burger Chef, where I smile and take people's nickels and dimes for burgers and fries. I'm allowed to eat all I want. The people ordering are happy because they don't have to cook after a hard day's work, and I bring dinner home, so my mother doesn't have to cook.

I pass by Old Stone Bank on my walk to work, reading a sign in the window: "Come in and open a savings account." A lightbulb goes off in my mind. *I need a safe place for all my hard-earned money.*

I return to the bank and bravely present my birth certificate and Social Security card to the manager, who smiles and hands me papers to fill out. He says he is impressed with all my proof of identification, but until I'm the magical age of eighteen, a parent must cosign for me.

Mom helps me sign papers, proud of me for saving money. She reminds me to keep my bankbook in a safe place.

By the end of summer, I have saved $300. While Miss Karmodey scared the living daylights out of me by screeching the times tables, multiplication comes in handy in double-checking the bank's math on my deposits and interest. My mind goes blank when it comes to seven times seven, though; I freeze, remembering a vase flying past my head and shattering glass bits on the floor.

It's Saturday afternoon, and I decide to take the bus into the city to go shopping. For the first time, I don't have to ask anyone if I can buy something. Looking through the window of my favorite boutique, I see a shirt I love on display. Inside the store, I examine the white shirt's soft, crinkly fabric, and then I try it on, admiring its unusual buttons, which look like big nickels. I buy it.

I walk on air all the way home, singing to myself, "For fifteen cents, a nickel and a dime, at Burger Chef, we will make your money rhyme."

The summer is over, and so is my job. I'm back at St. Theresa's, catching up on Latin and religion lessons that I missed while at my public school. I miss gym and art classes. I still have Steve, and as promised, he is there for me every Friday. I look forward to seeing his maroon Pontiac and spending weekends at his house with his family. We sit by the lake or go to the park or the movies.

My mother likes him and says Steve is the only good thing to come out of our move to the country.

My morning ritual is getting dressed in my uniform and then opening my drawer to look at Tiki's picture and my savings book, which looks as if it has been moved. I check the balance, which has not changed. Seeing my money grow gives me hope for having my own apartment and a new life once I'm eighteen.

Hearing my girlfriend's car horn beeping, I rush to get ready, dropping my head down and giving my hair a quick brush. I stand up quickly, feeling dizzy. Rushing out the door, I ask my mother, who is sitting at the kitchen table, "Mom, how do I look? What can I do about my hair flying all around my face like a weed?"

It's not her words but the way she says them while

admiring me that strikes me: "You look fine, Mary Ellen—so fine. You've got nothing to worry about. You'll have the world on a string."

I think about her on my ride to school—sitting tiredly at the kitchen table and having coffee and a cigarette before she tries to get some sleep. She budgets money so tightly, and we are so wasteful. She works hard for her money and then comes home to cooking and cleaning. I feel guilty that I am fine and that everything is going to be okay for me. Someday I will walk out the door for good, leaving her there to fight with my father, work the night shift, and try to get some peace and quiet to fall asleep by.

I feel ashamed for saving my money so that I can leave home.

16

Sublime

Another school year comes to a close, and I begin my search for a summer job. The not-having-to-cook-dinner idea for mothers is a big hit, and burger places are popping up everywhere. "Job security," my mother says. "Don't worry. With your experience, you'll get something."

I've applied to two new places: Burger King and McDonald's.

It's May 15, my sixteenth birthday. My mother is so excited that she spills a big secret the minute I get home. "You know I can't keep a secret. Your father's got a present for you. Now that you have your learner's permit and will soon drive, well, he bought you a car. It needs some work, but soon enough, you will have your very own car. When you blow out the candles tonight and he tells you about the car, act surprised."

Just as Mom said, the moment I blow out the candles and make a wish, I see a car being towed in front of our house. Everyone gathers on the sidewalk, and my father says, "Happy birthday!" I act surprised and am in shock because it's barely recognizable as a car. I was hoping for a neat, dependable car that might need a little polishing and cleaning. All the paint has been removed down to the metal. The front fenders are off and piled on the sidewalk with some other chrome pieces stacked beside them.

Acting happy and excited, I ask, "What kind of car is it once it's all put together?"

My father proudly smiles that old use-your-imagination smile, answering, "It's a very rare 1957 bubble-top MGA. You will be the only one with a car like this. Of course, you will have to help me work on it. The engine needs a couple of parts, but I'll have it purring like a kitten in no time at all, provided the English haven't gotten too many things backward. It's an English design, and those damn English are notorious for doing things backward. They drive on the wrong side of the road, you know. The interior headliner and seats need to be redone, but with how well you sew, that should be easy. We don't have a garage, but we can work on it in a parking space I paid for in the lot across the street."

"Can I do the interior and paint it any color I want?" I ask.

"Of course, it's your car," he says, smiling.

I pick out a color swatch—number 525, sublime—for the outside paint. It is a bright Day-Glo green that hits me right away. When I tell the man at the body shop the color I've picked, he is practically in tears as he says, "You're not going to put that color on this classic, are you?"

I shrug, answering, "Why not? Why offer this color if you cringe when someone picks it out?"

He just shakes his head and looks at the ground.

Next, I go to the fabric shop, because I want to have material ready for the interior as soon as it gets painted. Bolts of materials bombard me, but nothing strikes me, until my eye is drawn to an olive-green color at the end of the aisle. Upon closer inspection, I find that it is stretch vinyl snakeskin. *Wow! What a find.* I imagine a snakeskin interior with a sublime-green exterior, and I buy the bolt of imitation snakeskin, hoping there will be enough to cover the seats too.

My father works on the car every night after work in the lot, under a streetlamp and using a flashlight. I do my work in the house, sewing a new headliner and seat covers, and I have enough extra vinyl for door panels and armrests.

There are only a couple of adjustments left now, and I help my father by holding the flashlight and handing him tools. We are as serious as doctors operating on a patient.

"Flashlight," he says.

I repeat, "Flashlight," shining a light on the spot that he's wiggling.

"Phillips-head," he says.

"Phillips-head," I repeat, handing him one.

Occasionally, he calls out, "Damn, those English do everything in reverse! I'd be done by now if it weren't for the way they do things."

"I thought it would never be done," I tell my father as we admire our handiwork. My MGA's green paint sparkles in the sun. We both agree that the snakeskin interior looks original.

Dad says, "I told you to be patient and that it would be worth waiting for." He opens a small box and unwraps something from tissue paper. It's a miniature golden eagle like one that goes on top of a flagpole. "I couldn't find a hood ornament to replace the original one that's missing, but won't this look great?" he asks as he hands it to me as if giving me a trophy.

It's the finishing touch, a shiny gold eagle as a hood ornament, with its wings spread, glistening in the sun. We sit inside the car, and I try to start it up to take it for a spin. When I turn the key, nothing happens. "Two reasons," my father says. "First, the damn English have an extra button, so you have to turn the key and then hit this round button to start it. I put in a kill switch too. You don't want anyone stealing this baby after all our hard work." He points to a hidden switch that turns the gas pump on.

"Look at that! Under the lighter, it says *cigar* instead of *cigarette*," I say.

"It is so English." My father laughs.

I start the engine, and it purrs like a kitten. It drives like a regular car, but I have to get the hang of shifting gears. I'm ready to give up going up and down hills, until I learn to balance the clutch with the brake. If I don't shift just right when I stop uphill, the car rolls backward; then, when I stop downhill, it rolls forward. I sweat every time I see a hill. My father says I've got it, but I need to keep doing it over and over. Then I'll stop sweating.

I'm feeling cool as the chrome wire wheels shimmer, spinning us toward the highway, where we can test the car at faster speeds. Everyone stares at me and points. I finally realize that a person is pointing to a wheel spinning along ahead of me.

"Dad, isn't that our wheel?" I scream out as the car buzzes along on three wheels.

"Remain calm, and pull over slowly," my father says.

With the car stopped on the roadside, my father gets out and chases the wheel down an embankment. He brings it back and stands before me, wheezing from the run. He says, "I'll hook it up temporarily. You'd better let me drive home." He winks and says halfheartedly, "Back to the drawing board."

I'm back on the road in a week. My father figured out the threads were stripped on the hubs, so he came up with the ingenious idea of drilling holes through the wheels and shafts and inserting a bolt through them with a nut screwed tightly on each end so that the wheels can't come loose again. The only problem is that the bolts are longer than the wheel shaft, so when the wheels turn, they make a clanging sound. I drive down the streets to the clanging of all four wheels.

"Don't worry; that sound will stop at higher speeds on the highway. It's better to be safe than sorry. You can drive it on your own now. Have a good time, and don't get hurt." He waves good-bye to me.

I clang down the street, feeling proud in my sublime-green MGA with the dazzling golden eagle hood ornament leading the way. I drive it everywhere, including work and school. It gets a lot of attention from onlookers, and I feel as if I'm driving the yellow submarine in the psychedelic Beatles song.

Since I had the courage to say no to my dad, he's stopped doing bad things to me, but he's also no longer been good to me. It is a peculiar relief. I am neither here nor there to him, as if I don't exist. Now, with my birthday, the car, and us working together, I want to believe that the past is behind us and that a genuinely good part of my dad still exists, yet my doubting Thomas thoughts nag: *This is all part of a plan or trap, and now he wants something in return from me.*

⟿

At school, talk is wild in the cafeteria. Everyone is clamoring about what we will choose to prepare for: college or business classes. I meet in a little room with a nun, almost as if I'm making a confession. Sister Katrina looks at me while shuffling folders on her desk until she pulls out mine. She compliments my grades, saying, "Very good indeed."

"Then I'll go to college," I say, smiling.

She seems sad as she tells me that it's not that simple. "After going over your family's financials, I don't think they can afford to send you to college. Take a business course. Learn to file and type, and take shorthand. Choose a profession to earn money for yourself."

"Okay." My voice squeaks.

I leave feeling disappointed and embarrassed about what she said about my parents' financials. My mother said we are middle class, but I have figured out that we are poor. The high school divides into two groups—the business group, whose families can't afford college, and the group whose parents can afford to send them to college.

In the cafeteria, I listen to seniors' conversations about which colleges to apply to. Others are talking about planning their weddings, excited about picking out the gown and shoes, renting a hall filled with flowers, selecting a cake, and dancing. One girl says her parents are even giving the couple money to buy their first house.

Amid our chatter, sandwiches, and milk, someone yells out, "Kathy, sing!" She interrupts us with her rendition of the song "House of the Rising Sun." She belts out the lyrics in a deep, emotional voice just like a man. She modestly brings the whole cafeteria to silence as she finishes her rendition, belting out the closing verse: "Oh, Mother, tell your children not to do what I have done, spend your lives in sin and misery in the house of the rising sun."

Everyone claps wildly. We all sigh and get back to chattering, clinking cups, and finishing our sandwiches.

My next class is typing. Sister Marie says, "Fast, accurate typing is the key to a good job." She makes typing fun, creating contests to see who can type the most words in a minute. She calls out a sentence for us to type that has every letter of the alphabet in it: "The quick brown fox jumps over the lazy dog."

She straightens her shoulders, swipes her habit behind her head, and then waves her clicker wildly in the air, commanding us to begin, as if she is a maestro and we are the orchestra in rows of typewriters beating in unison: *Clickity-clack, clickity-clack. Slam. Bang.* The cartridge springs back. *Clickity-clack.*

"Don't look back. Type faster!" she says. "'The quick brown fox jumps over the lazy dog.' Type faster—the more words per minute, the more you get paid."

The school year whizzes by with more words-per-minute typing. We memorize shorthand squiggles and learn formats for business letters.

Things are no better between my mother and father. He works during the day, comes home, lies on the bed, and falls asleep with his work clothes and shoes on. My mother yells from the kitchen, "Larry, get up and eat! Come on! We have some nice hot burgers and fries here. Come spend some time with me before I go to work."

My father yells out, "In a minute, Muff! I'm not sleeping; I'm just resting my eyes."

He doesn't come out, and my mother goes to work. When she is back in the morning, he's leaving for work. At least they don't argue, because they aren't around each other during the week, and they seem to enjoy sleeping in on the weekends together.

I am seventeen, and another school year ends with a summer job at Burger King. The owner is sleazy; both his wife and girlfriend are pregnant at the same, and neither one knows about the other. I work the front and chomp on fries, watching for his wife to come. She barely misses his girlfriend, who just left. His sister, who is a bit older than I am, is beautiful and wins all kinds of beauty pageants. Joey, the owner, puts her on a pedestal. He always brags about her, and she works whenever she wants. Still, I'm happy to have this job, because it allows me to keep saving up money. It's only a year until I graduate high school. I will start a secretarial career and have money, a car, and my own apartment.

Getting dressed in the morning I go through my ritual of checking my savings book. Again, I notice that it looks as if someone's moved it, but the amount is the same. My hard-earned balance of $700 hasn't changed.

Saturday afternoon, I sit outside on the cement stairs with a kite while waiting for Steve to pick me up. I hear my father's footsteps behind me, and he sits by my side and puts his hand on my shoulder, saying, "How's my girl? Where are you off to today?"

"Oh, I'm just going to the park with Steve and my friends Paula and Tony to fly kites. Look how windy it is." I show him my ball of rolled string on a wooden handle and the paper bird kite I've made with a long tail of rags tied in bows.

"Well, that's great. Go out and have some fun," he says. He then gets serious. He looks around to see if anyone's listening before he whispers, "Now, Sissy, I noticed you have some money saved up in that book you and your mother have been hiding from me."

"I wasn't hiding it, Daddy, just saving up," I say guiltily.

"Well, it doesn't matter to your old dad. But I need to borrow that money from you. I'm in a little scrape, and I don't want you to tell your mother. I'll put the money back as soon as I can."

My feet and hands go numb, as they did in the old days. I feel everything draining from me, and the pressure of his arm draped over my shoulders feels like a ton of bricks. That savings book holds the key to my freedom, and he's asking me to turn it over to him.

My words come while I gulp. "Yeah, sure, Dad."

He says, "You know, your mother and I never asked you

for rent money or anything all the time that you have been working, even though it's been hard for us to send you to school, and you bought that expensive blouse hanging in your closet."

"Oh." I swallow. "Do you need all of it?"

"Yes," he says, "but don't worry. Your old dad won't let you down. I'll pay you back before you know it. And not a word of this to your mother; it's our little secret."

He takes my hope away and turns this loan into our little secret. What's next? I wonder if he is going to try to start doing the things he did in the old days. He had better not. I have a boyfriend now. I will give him my money but not me anymore.

How I hate those words: *our little secret*. I don't like keeping things from my mother, but I would not have told her anyway, because it would be another problem for her, another thing to fight over. I protect her by keeping the peace. She can't take any more bad news.

The wind blows wildly as Steve's convertible pulls up across the street. He beeps and waves, and I run toward him, leaving my father sitting on the stairs. I turn back to wave good-bye. I hardly seeing him through my hair blowing around my face, but I catch a glimpse of him winking his secret wink, and I race away with the kite tail dragging behind me, hearing my father yell, "Have a good time, you kids, and don't get hurt!"

To make things worse, on our drive home, Steve gives me some bad news. He will probably get drafted to fight in Vietnam, because all his friends are, and they are the same age and status as he is. To avoid the draft, he enlists in the reserves so that he will only serve six months at a military base in Texas and then come home, where he'll go to monthly meetings as a reserve.

It's been a month since I withdrew the money and gave it to Dad. I've saved up a small amount again. Saving money and watching the balance grow keeps me going. I will leave home one way or another.

I should have realized Dad would interrupt my plans by not making things easy for me. Yes, he gave me the car, but as always, he wants something in return. Having Steve away makes me more vulnerable. I worry that my father might try something again. He winks at me lately, and that's the first sign. I can't stand the thought of it. I know now how right it feels to be in love with someone and how wrong his sickness that no one talks about is.

I lie awake in bed at night, trying to get the guts to stand up for myself and tell him the way things are going to be. One night, I jump from the bed and open the basement doorway. From the top of the stairway, I feel like a giant looking down upon a small man working in a musty cellar at the bottom of the stairs. He works under a lamp, melting and twirling glass rods over a torch flame and then dropping sparkling balls into a bucket of sand. I feel a surge of power and courageously roar down to him, "Dad?"

He doesn't even look up as he answers, "Yeah, Sissy?"

I spit out my words. "You know those things you used to make me do? I will never do them again."

He stops everything, turning around to look back up

at me, saying calmly, "Well, if that's the way you want it, Sissy." He shrugs as if to say it doesn't matter.

I turn away and quickly slam the door shut before he has a chance to say another word.

17
Debutante

deb·u·tante: noun: a young woman who is being introduced formally into society by appearing at a public event such as a dance or party.

We are in study hall, and Sister Superior interrupts our silence to make an announcement. She reads a letter from a prestigious department store while speaking into a silver microphone. The management of Cherry and Webb is inviting our school to participate in its search for Miss Cherry Deb. The *Deb* in the name Miss Cherry Deb is short for *debutante*. The letter says, "She will represent your school in our store as a fashion liaison for all the girls, reporting back fashion trends during the school season. Each high school in Rhode Island will submit one candidate, and then, from all the candidates, Cherry and Webb's board will select five special Cherry Debs. Our Cherry Debs get paid to work in the store and participate in fashion shows, and they will receive a complete Cherry

Deb outfit to keep and wear in the young girls' department. Each Cherry Deb will have her own storefront window with her picture and the outfits she will wear in upcoming fashion shows."

Everyone's jaw drops. We are surprised that nuns would approve of such a thing. The cafeteria becomes so quiet that you could hear a pin drop. Every girl's eyes stare at the paper that holds the news. Sister Superior, whom we've nicknamed Soup, has a thin body wrapped in flowing black cloth, with large wooden rosary beads hanging from her waist. She smiles while looking out at us through her pointed horn-rimmed glasses, saying, "I know a girl from our school will win. First, everyone has to vote for one girl." We buzz like bees swarming while Sister hands out slips of paper and asks us to write down one girl's name.

I sit looking at the paper, wondering what's to stop me from putting down my own name. As always, nuns, being married to God, can read minds. Sister yells out, "Of course, if everyone voted for themselves, we wouldn't have a winner, now, would we?"

For a second, I imagine it being me, but I've come to believe I don't deserve such things. I write down Peggy Short's name. She is the most beautiful girl in the whole school. She is perfect, with a little nose that wiggles like a bunny rabbit's, long blonde hair like a Barbie doll's, and big blue eyes. Her lips always smile. Everyone stares at her.

I wonder how other girls see me. People tell me I'm beautiful on the outside. When I look in the mirror, I see a pretty face, a perfect combination of my mother and father. No one sees the ugliness of the secret I hold inside, which stops me from believing I deserve good things. The French nun calls me petite, and I think all models are tall.

Sister Superior breaks into my thoughts, announcing that she has finished tallying the votes. She lifts her glasses up and down, staring at her results, and then calls over other nuns to verify her findings. She speaks into the microphone: "Girls, it's a tie between Peggy Short and Mary Ellen Sinclair!"

Everyone sighs disappointedly in perfect unison. I am shocked. It's impossible. Things like this don't happen to me. Soup decides that Peggy and I should go home and prepare speeches to give to the class the next day about what being Miss Cherry Deb would mean for us.

I spend the night writing my speech while my mom paces back and forth, hopeful for me.

Giving speeches and dancing make my knees shake. I sit, waiting to go onstage after Peggy to speak.

Soup calls me up to the stage. To my amazement, my voice doesn't shake. It comes through the microphone loud and clear as I speak confidently. "I would be honored to represent all the girls at St. Theresa's. If elected as Miss Cherry Deb, I will dedicate myself to sharing the latest fashion trends between Cherry and Webb and the girls at St. Theresa's." Walking away from the stage, I can hear my footsteps echo.

We vote again. Peggy and I sit across from each other, and our eyes meet. I vote for Peggy. I know this can't happen for me anyway. I don't want to get my hopes up.

"And the winner is"—Soup holds the paper in the air, spitting excitedly through buckteeth—"Mary Ellen Sinclair!"

Everyone jumps up, screaming and applauding. I look into Peggy's face and cry, which makes everyone sigh in unison.

The next day, hardly able to believe what's happened, I report to my boss at Burger King that there is a slight chance I might be leaving my job.

"Oh yeah, why?" he asks.

"Well," I answer, "I was nominated for Miss Cherry Deb."

He says, "Oh yeah, I've heard of that. My sister was picked from her school last year just like you, but they only pick five girls, and with over a hundred girls, you'll never make it. If my sister didn't make it, you won't, but good luck."

I read the paper that Soup gave me about how to prepare for the interview and what questions the board at Cherry and Webb might ask. The letter ends, "Wear a special outfit to the interview that depicts fashion of today." I look in my closet at that one special blouse I bought long ago. I washed it, ignoring the label that said, "100 Percent Silk, Dry-Clean Only," and it shrunk. It wouldn't fit a doll now, but I couldn't throw it away, so it hangs in the closet with its oversized nickel-colored buttons.

I sit outside on the cement steps, miserable because there isn't enough money in my savings account to buy a new outfit. *What's the use anyway? I'm not going to win.* I hear my father's footsteps coming from behind me. He sits beside me, wanting to know what's got me down. In tears, I blurt out the whole problem.

"Is that all? Don't worry a second longer. I've got the money to pay you back. You can buy a dress, and you'll be picked for sure," he says, patting my shoulder, making me feel better.

The next day, he tells me he's got the money if I need it, but he is wondering if I will try something else first. "What?" I ask.

"You are so good at sewing, and Mrs. Cabana, the lady I do yard work for, gave me a sewing machine and a lot of material and patterns. I bet you could make something better than anything you could buy at a store."

"You think I could, Dad?"

"I'm sure," he says with confidence and pride. "Come on in the house, and look at what I've got."

He leaves me alone with a big cardboard box of stuff and a shiny white sewing machine. I find Simplicity patterns complete with instructions and pictures. I pick out an outfit with a skirt, vest, and blouse. Rummaging through the box of materials, I find a yellow crepe for the skirt and vest and a sheer flowered silk for the blouse.

I want to give up right away because I can't figure out how to thread the machine, and I feel lost in the map of instructions. My father helps me solve the threading problem, and I begin to enjoy playing around with pinning tissue pattern pieces onto fabrics. Memories of sewing in home economics class at public school come back to me as I work every night for a week until my outfit is finished.

Dad was right. It looks like an expensive outfit that you couldn't buy anywhere, and no other girl will have one like it.

I wait for the interview in an office of Cherry and Webb, wearing my creation. A tall, thin man opens the door, introducing himself as Mr. Casey, and then he escorts me into a room full of smiling adults sitting around a table. Mr. Casey mentions that my last name is Sinclair and asks me if am related to Dodi Sinclair, who owns Cherry and Webb. If so, I will be disqualified. I tell him I'm not related in any way. I pose, fluffing my flowery sleeve so that they will notice it. He asks me about drugs, and all the other board members' eyebrows rise as they look at me. I tell them about the lectures at school and about how dangerous and harmful drugs are. I say I would never take drugs. Everyone's eyebrows relax, and they smile.

Before I know it, the interview is over. Mr. Casey smiles cordially, showing me the door and thanking me for coming. He tells me that I will be notified by mail one way or the other.

I walk out, leaving the room full of pretty girls sweating and wondering how they will answer Mr. Casey's questions.

I come home from school one night to find my mom deliriously excited. "You got it! You're a Cherry Deb! The letter is on the table. Read it. Want me to read it to you? I had to open and read it. I'm so happy for you."

We jump up and down. I don't believe it. She phones all her girlfriends and tells them her daughter is a Cherry Deb.

A whole new world opens. I can't believe I'm getting paid to dress up and be in fashion shows on the weekends and then work after school in the teen department while wearing my special outfit. I talk to girls my age and show them the latest styles in clothing. I take being a fashion liaison seriously, feeling that this is my future. I never want it to end. I won't have to type and take shorthand notes. Maybe I can work as a salesgirl full-time after I graduate.

What a grand day it is when I tell my boss at Burger

King that I'm leaving. I'm a Cherry Deb, and his sister can have my hours at the counter.

All the girls at school who voted me in and sighed when I cried now walk around school with their noses in the air, pretending I don't exist. They never come into the store for my fashion advice. It doesn't matter, because I still have Steve and four new girlfriends—the other Cherry Debs. We are an inseparable fashion clique, singing and dancing. We have sleepovers while we compare fashion notebooks of what's in and what's not.

We spend a lot of time at the house of Terry, a Cherry Deb who's an only child. She seems rich, and the beautiful, neat home she lives in has a swimming pool. I ask her if it's lonely having no other kids around. She says she wished for a brother or sister and was angry with her parents because they only had her. Her parents told her they didn't want to share their love with anyone else but her.

Steve and I walk by the window of Cherry and Webb with my picture in it, and I feel lucky. He says he would like to get engaged when he gets back from the reserves in six months. We vow eternal love and promise to write each other every day.

Each day I drive to school in my lime-green MGA and work at Cherry and Webb afterward. I spend my weekends practicing for fashion shows. After one rehearsal, I hear a commotion coming from one of the dressing rooms. I look down the hall to see Terry summoning me into the dressing room. She sits in her bra and panties, smoking a cigarette and flicking the ashes into the top of a lipstick tube. Two other Cherry Debs, Beth and Donna, are getting dressed as Terry tells me she is collecting money from everyone to buy a birthday present for Jane, the fifth Cherry Deb. She says that everyone is pitching in a quarter.

I happily give my quarter, thinking nothing of it.

The next week, as I work at the store, Mr. Casey's secretary comes onto the floor and asks me to stop by his office. I think that since we will soon give up our titles to next year's candidates and I already have a year's experience on the selling floor, this is a good time to ask for a full-time job once I graduate. I'm surprised to find Mr. Casey with a sourpuss look upon his face as he sits behind his desk. He tells me in a matter-of-fact tone that I will no longer be working at Cherry and Webb. He holds up a little statue I have never seen before and hands it to me. It is a plastic joke gift with a plaque on it that says, "Jerk of the Year Award." He says Jane came into his office crying because she found it in her locker. "Terry told me that all of you girls pitched in to give this to Jane. This is not the behavior we expect from our team here, and we have decided to release everyone except Jane."

Mr. Casey has a sad look on his face, as if he is disappointed in himself for not detecting our character flaws at the original interviews.

I want to say I had no part in this and tell him what I now realize: Terry tricked everyone into attacking Jane because of her own personal jealousy toward her and maybe even us. Instead of defending myself or explaining my side to Mr. Casey, I resort to my ingrained means of defense by freezing, going away, and accepting a wrong done to me.

It all ends just like that. I am ashamed that I leave Mr. Casey with such a bad impression of me. Each one of us is released privately, and we never say good-bye or talk among ourselves about what happened. My illusion of us as a family of inseparable friends vanishes.

After months pass, I go back into Cherry and Webb and look into my old department. I pretend to be looking at some coats just outside the elevator to see Jane working in her Cherry Deb outfit. She sees me from a distance. I want to go to her to apologize and explain how I was tricked. I freeze when she gives me a dirty look with a strange smile on her face that seems to say, "Stay away. I won. The job is mine."

My whole life is changing. Steve has returned from the reserves, and his hair has grown back to normal. Having long hair is important. It's a way to identify that one is for peace and love. Those branded with short military haircuts are labeled as war mongers fighting the Vietnam War.

People tell me I'm beginning to look like Janis Joplin. While I don't drink, I let my long hair frizz, and I wear flowers in it. I decide that I don't want to be engaged and then married, because it scares me to think of ending up like my parents, hollering and screaming, with no money and too many children.

As hard as I try to bring back my feelings of love for Steve and my desire to get married, I can't. My feelings are gone.

The strange thing about love is that one has no control over falling in or out of it. I'm also losing my best friend.

I imagine it must be a rotten feeling for him, still feeling love for someone who can no longer return it.

At nineteen, I have a full-time job. I work in a room full of desks with other typists wearing earphones and transcribing legal documents. The boss sits in a small office with his feet on his desk, watching everyone through a glass door that has the company logo in gold letters across it. I hear him tell my supervisor, "That kid works right up until five o'clock!" He doesn't know that in my mind, I'm racing, reliving my typing contest with Sister Marie. I envision her raising her arms like a maestro and saying that the faster we type, the more we get paid. She was correct.

When I get home at night, I look at my mother sleeping on the bed and snoring loudly. Her stomach is starting to look round, and she is gaining more and more weight. I wonder if she could be pregnant.

Tonight my mother makes pork chops and mashed potatoes for dinner, and she says, "Mmm, delicious," while spooning out my favorite, mashed potatoes. My brother sits across from Rebecca, who is almost ten now and has long blonde hair and Mom's signature bangs, trimmed short. My parents fill the table with a happy mood, smiling together. My father announces that they have a surprise for us.

Rebecca can hardly sit still, asking, "What is it?"

I remember noticing my mother's stomach, but I keep my idea to myself. He asks Rebecca to guess, as she's the most excited of all. He tells her, "It is something very special that money can't buy." When the words "A new baby" come from my father's lips, she is as dumbfounded as Ray and I once were about her.

"What kind of surprise is that?" she asks, disappointed.

They explain the joy of a brother or sister to play with and how a new life is something money can't buy.

What they say is true yet confusing, because my parents always complain that life would be a lot easier if it weren't for us kids. Why would they have another kid? I don't get it. Ray and I will be out of the house soon, and Becky is in school during the day. My mother can work during the day and have some peace and quiet.

Ray and I sit with our mouths open. I'm still lost in thought. I see how genuinely happy this new baby makes them. What does it matter to me anyway? I'll be out of the house.

At the end of dinner, we all throw names into the air until we hear my mother's voice say from the kitchen, "Melissa is the name I picked."

My mother gets the final word, and Dad says over and over, "Melissa is a beautiful girl's name."

Expecting a baby makes them happier, and they don't argue. My father tells my mother he wants to start a new business because he's never going to get ahead by working in factories. He wants to rent a storefront and make his own jewelry. He'll supply each one of his brothers and sisters in Ohio, who will sell the jewelry in their own stores. They will sell it and send him money, keeping the promise his brothers and sisters made to each other when their father died: that someday they would all take care of each other and become rich doing it.

Because everyone is family, it will be a big success, he says. My mother thinks he's taking a chance with a new baby on the way, but she still believes in him, saying this could be the idea that makes us rich.

Ray and I help screw hooks into the mouths of plastic fishing lures, letting Mom sleep. We are about to give up because screwing the hooks with pliers goes slowly. My father invents a machine to clamp the fish tails into a revolving motor at one end, and we hold pliers with the hooks at the fish's mouths, letting the machine do all the work. Production picks up as fish fly, filling box after box. My father happily works alongside us, saying, "Faster. I'll put some water on for a cup of java. It's going to be a long night for me. You kids get to bed." We desert him before he finishes his sentence.

It's Saturday, and my aunt Sophie has invited us to a backyard picnic at her house. She lives in a beautiful new Cape-style house, and the interior has modern light switches. She shows us how the lights can be dimmed by moving a circular knob. My mother says under her breath that Aunt Sophie pilfered the switches from her night job at General Electric. "She could never afford to buy them. They are compliments of GE," she says behind Aunt Sophie's back while she's at the grill cooking.

My father doesn't go to Mom's family gatherings. He still feels that his family is in Ohio and that none of my mother's family ever accepted him. My mother, my aunts, and their girlfriends gather at the picnic table, eating, talking, and laughing. When they find out my mother's pregnant, everyone congratulates her, but when she leaves the table, her girlfriends whisper about her right in front of me, as if I can't hear. One says, "Can you believe it at her age? Well, if it was up to me, I just wouldn't have it. She's taking a big chance. It could be a mongoloid."

Another woman giggles and says, "Well, better her than me." A chain of laughter goes around the table.

After all the company goes home, Aunt Sophie asks my mother and me to stay to help her get ready for a big night out. She shows us her new blue silk dress. My mother says, "Whew, that is gorgeous, Sophie. Let's put your hair up in French curls. Have you got bobby pins and hairspray?" We pile her hair up into a bouffant of puffy curls and spray them stiff.

We watch her put makeup on in front of the mirror. She looks at a picture in a magazine of Elizabeth Taylor's face for inspiration. She puts white powder on her eyelids and then paints black eyeliner above her lashes, ending each line in a painted curl. The last step is to apply false eyelashes. They sit on the bureau like centipedes. I volunteer to do this finishing touch and ask Aunt Sophie to sit with her head back in the chair, as if I am a beautician. I hold the tube of glue while my mother reads me the instructions: "Put a little line of glue along the edge of each lash, and then place it on the eyelid from left to right." *Done!*

The directions say to wait a minute before opening each eye, so I fan her closed eyes while we wait. My mother inspects my aunt's face, admiring the great job I've done. "Time's up," I proudly say, holding a mirror in front of her eyes. She's still sitting with her head back in the chair. The eyelashes look perfect, but she can't open her eyes. I've glued them shut!

Sophie starts to laugh with her eyes still closed, and black tears fall in watery lines down her face, making a mess and ruining her makeup job. I rip off the lashes, and Aunt Sophie escorts us to the door, saying she will finish her makeup.

Before we leave, we admire how beautiful she looks and tell her to have a good time.

On our walk home, without thinking, I repeat to my mother what her girlfriend said: "Well, if it was up to me, I just wouldn't have it" and "Better her than me."

My mother stops walking, looking hurt by the words I repeated. She says, "Well, maybe it is better me than her, because I'm going to have my baby, and I'm going to love it no matter what God sends me. A baby is a gift from God."

I feel like a stupid kid next to my mother, realizing she has thought long and hard about her predicament, and despite being worried about her age, she has decided to have the baby. My mother knows the chance she is taking, and she doesn't need people making fun of her.

I remember the deformed baby I saw long ago cooing in her carriage, dressed in pink, with her mother rocking her, in a trance.

I love my mother. We hold hands while walking home across a bridge. It's dusk, and she is afraid someone is hiding underneath, about to jump out and get us. "Don't worry, Mom. We are safe together," I tell her as we squeeze hands.

She thinks out loud in front of me: "I'm getting my tubes tied after this. There'll be no more surprises. No more children once I get through this."

Ray and I still help my father with piecework he brings home from the shop, working into the night, screwing hooks into the mouths of the orange plastic fishing lures using the machine Dad rigged up. We fill boxes by throwing the finished lures into them while talking and singing songs. My brother starts singing along to a song on the radio: "We gotta get out of this place if it's the last thing we ever do. Girl, there's a better life for me and you." He sings the lyrics over and over to the beat of the machine winding hooks into the lures.

My mother passes by, hears this, and tells him to stop singing, because the words aren't nice.

"What, Ma? It's a song I'm singing along to on the radio."

"Oh!" She laughs. "I didn't know it was a song. I thought you meant it, that you had to get out of here."

We all laugh at the fact that she doesn't know the lyrics of this song or the band the Animals.

18 Composition

I hear my mother screaming at my father that he is going to be late for work and threatening to pour a glass of water on his head. I wake from dreaming to utter peace and solitude realizing that this is my first morning in my own apartment.

I am almost twenty, and I begin my first day of a new job, making more money typing at a legal firm. I can pay my rent, buy groceries and gas, and put some away for a rainy day.

My roommate, Nancy, rents one bedroom in this two-bedroom apartment on Grape Street. I'm the new roommate, so she has made me a cup of tea, and we go over the rules of respecting each other's privacy and other basics, such as keeping the kitchen, bathroom, and living room clean. We get along right away like sisters sitting around the kitchen table.

I wonder how my father got himself into financial situations over his head all the time. He blamed it on having children to take care of, which I think is unfair.

Yet I now understand how important it is to be able to come and go, work, and do fun things without having a child yet. I vow not to have children until I'm sure I can provide for myself first.

My sublime MGA sits in a parking lot behind my apartment building because it stopped running. My father gave me another car that barely runs as his way of repaying the money he borrowed. While it is efficient on gas, it has a strange habit that no one can fix: under speeds of thirty miles per hour, it hiccups, stopping, starting, and skipping down the street. Everyone laughs as I drive by. Even the gas station attendant seems to wait for me each morning with a grin as my car hiccups up to the pump. He chuckles when I ask for fifty cents' worth of gas. I don't know what strikes him as so funny. It's an economical car that drives smoothly once on the highway. I can see him cheering me on from my rearview mirror.

An even better secretarial job comes my way, and I now work in a building on a college campus. The Department of Labor has offices in the basement, and there are college classes on the upper floors. I take dictation, type, and answer the phone, so I make even more money.

I arrive each day a little early and sit in my car that's hiccupped its way into a parking spot. I meditate in a cross-legged yoga position, chanting, "Ohm. Ohm." I've become enlightened and think of God now as a higher power but not one in the image of a man.

I work for Mr. O'Farrell, who is nothing like Joey at

Burger King. He is, by nature, a positive person, and it is nice working with him on his plight to help people. His eyes always sparkle, and he has pictures of his wife, children, and dog everywhere. I have my own desk; everything is neat and orderly. One advantage to working hard is that it makes lunchtime arrive quickly.

There's a nice cafeteria upstairs, where mostly art students have lunch. On my way back, I go down stairs and then through a long corridor, passing open doorways with art classes in session. I stop to watch a teacher giving a lecture. He seems to be in great agony while critiquing two drawings. He commands everyone's undivided attention, including mine. He points to two drawings done in black lines on newsprint taped to the blackboard. Jiggling the left one, he says, "This student has done a wonderful facsimile of a bell, but it is nothing more than a reproduction." He jiggles the right one and asks, "Can you see the difference between these two drawings? This one has composition!" I study the drawing with composition from the doorway, seeing nothing but swirling black lines, until I see that the whole page is really full of bells drawn. They are disguised and locked together, large ones and small ones, filling the page.

He says, "The bells are drawn well but are also composed in such a way that they reveal themselves to the eye through designs and shapes."

I understand his point: art isn't only about drawing a perfect reproduction but drawing images creatively. He continues struggling to get everyone to see the difference between the two drawings and then finishes his lecture by staring seriously into the student audience and practically fainting as he whispers the word *composition*.

I want to yell out, "I get it!"

A plaque beside the door reads Mr. Ballou. I can't figure out his first name because someone has scratched the word *Cat* over it. They call him Cat Ballou in the corridors after class is dismissed.

In the afternoons at work, I think about what is going on above me: the classes, the cafeteria talk about professors and classes, Cat Ballou's compositional frustration, the smell of oil paints and chalk, and rows of easels in classrooms. While I'm typing and taking dictation, my shorthand notes aren't symbols for words anymore but compositions on a page.

Whenever I pass by the art room, I want to be there.

I think about my father soldering the same posts to earrings day in and day out at the jewelry factory and my mother inspecting rows of flashcubes all night on an assembly line at General Electric. I've been doing the same thing over and over, working different clerical jobs in offices—taking notes, transcribing them, and typing to make a living. I want more out of life.

Until I can figure out how to make this dream come true, I spend lunches in the cafeteria, sitting among the students and listening to their conversations. Someone taps me on the shoulder. It's my cousin Charlene. We've lost touch over the years.

"Oh, Mary Ellen, are you going to school here?" she asks.

"No, I work downstairs and eat my lunch up here," I say.

She tells me how much she loves going to school here and says it's her last semester before graduation. We sit and have lunch like the old days back in the yard by the pool. I can always ask Charlene anything, and I respect her opinion because she always tells the truth.

"How did you get to go here?" I ask, knowing that my aunt was in the same boat as my mother—unable to afford to send her children to college.

Magic words come from her mouth. "Oh, it's easy—financial aid and student loans." She turns around and points to an office down at the end of a long corridor. "Stop in there, and get an application," she says, smiling, as if it is that simple.

Eventually, I stop by the financial aid office. A woman behind a desk asks, "Are you a student here?"

"No, but I was thinking of it for next semester," I say hopefully.

"Why don't you make an appointment with a counselor and talk about which courses you should take and how much money you will need?" she says.

We set a time and date, and as I leave, she hands me several pamphlets. "Read these," she says, "especially the applications for admission, student loans, and financial aid."

I start to feel depressed, thinking I can never give up my full-time job to go to classes. But then I picture my cousin Charlene at the pool with me as a little girl with braids and bangs. If she can go to college, I can too.

It must be fate that my new job is located on a college campus and that all the offices and registration appointments for art school are right above me, making it easy to spend lunch hours and breaks at the financial aid office with a counselor. After a few appointments, the counselor hands me a package for review.

I qualify for some grant money and a portion of student loans that I don't have to pay back until after I graduate, and they will be low payments spaced out over ten years after. If I join the Peace Corps or remain a full-time student, my payments will be frozen. I am still short on living expenses, but he tells me about work-study jobs, meaning I can study and work at the college part-time.

"What skills do you have for part-time work?" he asks.

I say confidently, "I can type and take shorthand."

"That's perfect." He gives me a list of clerical jobs to apply for. Some are right here in the college art department.

Next, I talk with an adviser about how to apply to the art department without a portfolio, because I came from a Catholic school without art classes and took business courses. He says not to worry, because that's why most people go to a junior college—to take courses they didn't have in high school. After two years of art classes, I will have a portfolio to apply to a four-year art college. Many of the junior college classes are transferable, so most people start out as sophomores.

My dream is coming true. I walk past the art classes back to my job downstairs, picturing myself inside the classrooms this September. The nuns were right and wrong at the same time. Rather than getting me through life, the skills I learned will get me through college for a better life.

My boss, Mr. O'Farrell, pretends not to notice that I'm late returning from lunch. It's as if he knows what's going on and is happy for me. Finally, I get the courage to talk to him and give my two weeks' notice, which was a requirement when he hired me. When I tell him I am leaving to go to college, he looks at me proudly, as if he is my own father. "Very good, and I appreciate the notice," he says, and he wishes me luck. As I turn to leave, he says, "Mary Ellen, there is a matter of one week's paid vacation that you are entitled to. Technically, you have not been here a whole year, but I will push it through for you because you gave notice. You crossed all your t's and dotted all your i's."

I think he probably went to Catholic school.

I've never been paid for not working before, and the week off is a gift that allows me to get ready for classes.

There it is—Creative Art 101—the sign on the door that I know so well. I enter my first class and sit right in front of Cat Ballou. He is thin, wears black horn-rimmed glasses, and has a goatee and an earring in one ear. He begins his dramatic speech about drawing and composition. He strains to get his point across, putting all his guts, heart, and soul into his lecture. I feel exhausted for him as I watch the word *composition* shoot from his mouth. His body clenches inward, causing his hands to flail in the air. He bows and raises himself up slowly. Breathing in and out deeply, he musters enough energy to hold up a twenty-four-by-thirty-six-inch pad of newsprint and a black Conté crayon. He asks us to buy these items at the bookstore for our next class.

I listen to students talk about what they've heard about our cool teacher. He came from a place called Greenwich

Village in New York City, where beatniks spend their days writing poetry and their nights in dimly lit, smoke-filled coffeehouses, listening to bongo drums and poetry readings. Someone says he's tough because New York City is dangerous. People get shot there just walking down the street at night. Someone else says that weirdos walk around in the streets in broad daylight and that no one even notices.

Wow! What a place. I dream about living there, a place with many different people mixing their ideas. I imagine both danger and excitement, and I picture factory buildings at night, with lights in the windows, shining on artists creating and poets contemplating.

The only New York I know is from the St. Patrick's Day parade and from the words my mother used to cry out when we ran around tracking dirt all over her clean floor: "This place is like Grand Central Station!"

We would ask as we trampled, "What's Grand Central Station?"

"Augh," she would moan. "It's a place in New York City with a floor that no one ever stops walking on twenty-four hours a day."

I'm half asleep when my father calls and excitedly tells me, "It's a girl! She's a normal, healthy seven-pound-two-ounce beautiful girl, twenty-one inches long. Your mother is doing just fine, but she had to have a cesarean section because of her age. She's still groggy and can't talk to me."

"It's three o'clock in the morning, Dad. I'll get to the

hospital before school to see our new Melissa and Mom. Love ya."

Why are babies always born hours before the crack of dawn, waking everyone from a deep sleep and getting people out of bed and running around in circles? Why can't they come into the world at a convenient time, such as a quarter after ten, when everyone's on coffee break?

The hospital is quiet as I go up to the nursery window and search for the baby with the wristband that spells out the name Sinclair in pink and white beads. There she is—a tiny, doll-like angel fast asleep and perfect in every way.

I sit by my sleeping mother in her room, and her eyes open halfway. She turns to look at me, and I hold her hand. "You know it's a girl, Mom?"

She nods. "Yes." Then she asks, "Is she beautiful, Mary Ellen?"

"Yes," I tell her, "so beautiful, Mom. I just saw her."

"And smart, Mary Ellen?" she asks, holding back tears.

I say, "I can tell. She's going to be as smart as a whip."

My mother cries and holds on to my hand. She falls in and out of sleep, waking up occasionally to ask questions that make no sense, such as, "Where's my son's motorcycle?"

I realize Mom's been worrying alone all this time about Melissa being normal because of her age. I remember our walk on the bridge, when she told me that she was going to have this baby and love it no matter what God sent her and that a baby is a gift from God. I never have forgotten the baby I saw under the tree long ago, and I burst into tears, holding my mother's hand while she sleeps. I respect and love her—and our sweet Melissa.

We are all in the room, and I hear a nurse whisper—so Nonie won't hear—that Mom had her tubes tied. Then Aunt Sophie says, "I'll go count the baby's fingers and toes." It's a family tradition to count them right away because Nonie was born with an extra finger and toe on each hand and foot. They removed the extra fingers in Italy when she was born, but they did not remove the extra toes, because they would be hidden by her shoes.

"Yes, she has only ten fingers and toes," Aunt Sophie announces. All the relatives smile and agree that Melissa got most of her beauty from their side of the family, except for the blonde hair, which comes from Dad's side of the family.

19

If I Only Had a Million Dollars

I feel safe and happy living on my own. Sometimes the familiar black dots of abuse keep me awake, lingering in my memory like floaters in my eyes. Until I figure out what to do about these remembrances, I put them in an imaginary glass jar like jam preserved, close the lid tightly, and put the jar on a shelf until I'm ready to open it.

In the morning, I drive to my parents' house when I know Dad won't be around. Entering the back door, I find my mom watching TV and holding Melissa. Ray is never home. He rides his motorcycle to his girlfriend's house and spends all his time there. My sister Rebecca is almost ten years old and has bright blue eyes and long blonde hair. She enjoys being a big sister to Melissa, as I was to her. Mom finally puts baby Melissa on my lap, and we all enjoy sitting close to each other on the couch.

"Oh, Mary Ellen," my mom says, grasping my arm excitedly, "I have some unbelievable news. We are going to be millionaires!"

"What?" I laugh. "Did you finally win the lottery?"

"No." Her voice quivers with excitement bordering on disbelief. "Your dad's brother Don in Ohio has been working on an invention that is going to revolutionize electricity."

"So what has that got to do with us?" I ask.

"Well," she says, "your father and his family have been talking with Don on the phone for over a month about an electrical device that Don invented. He has a patent on it, and he is in the process of signing papers with General Electric to purchase it. As soon as all the legal work is done, GE wants to put this invention in every home in America. Don will also get royalties, making him richer than his wildest dreams. He is giving each of his brothers and sisters a million dollars and then some!"

The back door opens, and I hear my father's proud footsteps. From the parlor, I see his face grinning from ear to ear. He sits down right away in his captain's chair at the kitchen table, and my mother eagerly joins him, leaving Rebecca, Melissa, and me in the parlor.

"Sissy, come in the kitchen and talk with me and your mom while we smoke a cigarette," he says. From the corner of my eye, I see his hand motioning for me to hurry, and he rolls a cigarette down the table to my mom. "Put some water on for coffee." He cleverly times his request as I'm walking past the kitchen stove.

I sit at the table, wondering how many cups of coffee I have made for my father, as his words penetrate my thoughts. "I have unbelievable news," he says. "We are millionaires!"

"What?" I act excited, pretending not to know.

"We are rich," he says, sipping slowly, looking up over his cup.

My mother chimes in. "I always knew we would be rich one day."

My father announces that he has closed his shop and needs to get to Ohio right away to sign legal papers. He will drive there with Rebecca and live with Aunt Rosie, and later, Mom and Melissa will fly commercially. All his family members are excited about the profits and royalties, and Aunt Rosie has already put a deposit on a new yacht.

It is all happening too fast. Within a week, everyone will relocate to Ohio. Even Raymond and his girlfriend have decided to move to Ohio after they are married.

"We are starting over," my mother says. "We will build a new house."

"Of course." My father agrees with anything she says.

I'm glad that good fortune finally has come their way, but Ohio seems so far away, as if it is another country. Even though I couldn't wait to grow up and be on my own, I can't imagine life without visiting my sisters and going to cookouts with my mother and her family. I see a whole chunk of my life moving away—as always, taking the good along with the bad.

"Don't you worry, Sissy; we will be able to help you out," my father says proudly. "You can go to school and not have to work, and you can buy anything you want. Of course, there are still things money can't buy, but it will be nice not worrying about bills. If you started buying things today, you couldn't finish spending a million dollars in your lifetime!" My father beams proudly, as if he has caught the biggest fish in the largest ocean and is holding it up for everyone to see.

We sit quietly, watching my father at the head of our round colonial table. "I'll be starting my life over again—picking up the pieces and beginning a whole new life in Ohio with my side of the family, where I always wanted to be," he says, as if he has been waiting patiently for this moment for a long time.

My parents are on air. I listen to their new hopes and dreams and more about the miraculous invention over and over again. Time passes while they pour more hot water into their mugs, sprinkle in coffee crystals, and stir everything up with a spoon. In between talking, they sip coffee and puff cigarettes.

"Oh, look there," Mom says, amazed. "Dad blew a perfect smoke ring!"

It hovers in the middle of the table, floating above everyone like a big halo.

"You couldn't do that again if you tried," she says. We all laugh.

Months pass, and Mom calls to update me on the status of Don's invention, telling me of lavish family get-togethers with fancy dinners and board meetings afterward. Each one of his brothers and sisters, waiting on his or her fortune, takes turns picking up the tab for Uncle Don.

With each conversation, their luck seems to become less and less exciting. Mom confides that everyone is beginning to lose faith in Uncle Don, as they have not received any dividends. Of course, Uncle Don is still the family celebrity.

Although I have not met him, I'm beginning to mistrust him.

My suspicions are confirmed when my mom confides in her latest phone call to me that negative comments about Don and his invention have been floating around private family discussions. They are all tapped out, having given all their savings to Don. Now, until the money comes through, my parents have to get jobs. They can't keep living with Aunt Rosie forever. My father is working at a gas station, pumping gas, and Mom put in an application to work as a corrections officer at a women's prison. She is not giving up hope, though, as Uncle Don continues to ask everyone to be patient. At the latest dinner board meeting, he gave a speech ending with a motto for the family to help them keep faith in the invention: "Don't say *if* the money comes through, my family. Say *when* the money comes in."

After months of being patient and hopeful, my mom calls me, frustrated, with unbelievable news. Uncle Don is still talking about his invention that will make everyone rich, but no one has any more money to give to Don. They are tired of his slogan.

They hired a private investigator to follow Uncle Don, suspicious about his life and whereabouts. The detective report came in with shocking news: Don has been spending his time at the horse races, gambling the family's money away. It turns out that he has an electrical patent, but there are no records of GE buying it. The paperwork everyone signed for dividends is bogus. The detective also discovered that Uncle Don carried out this same scam on a woman named Ruby, and he bilked her entire family out of all their savings too.

"Ruby." I gasp, interrupting my mother over the phone. "Isn't she his girlfriend?"

"Yeah," my mom says. "Unbelievable. After he left her drained of money, Ruby joined in with Don to carry on the same charade with his own family. The detective had pictures of them living it up at the race track. Who would expect a brother to take advantage of his family like that?"

My father's voice erupts from the background, saying, "Just forget the whole thing. Our family isn't going to put their own brother in jail. Would all that money really have made us any happier anyway? I'm here with my family, where I always wanted to be. We have each other and our health. I'm going to get ahead."

I hear the familiar sounds of the teapot whistling, my dad's footsteps, water being poured, and the tinkling of a spoon swirling coffee crystals around hot water.

I remember the excitement in Rebecca's blue eyes as she waved good-bye to me from my dad's car on their drive to Ohio. I recall watching Melissa as a toddler, running down the airport corridor and vanishing into splashes of swirling colors and lace. Then and now, my heartstrings break.

I cry alone, not about a million dollars but for the happiness it cannot buy—and for myself too, at being nothing more than one of my father's past hurts he left behind to start a new life.

I rip open the envelope and read a letter from Rhode Island College: "The admissions office is proud to inform you of your acceptance in the master of fine arts program."

I did it! I've been accepted into an official four-year master of fine arts program. There's more. Grant money has been allotted to me, and the work-study job I applied for has been approved.

I think it odd that my family picked up and moved away, but I have made a new family of other artists and creative thinkers. We go to peace rallies protesting the Vietnam War dressed in brightly colored clothes, tattered bell-bottom jeans, and love beads. We stand for peace, armed only with flower power, pot, and love.

Time flies when I'm doing what I love: creating art. I'm glad to have part-time secretarial work in the art office, so I can pay my bills. At night, I fall asleep the minute my head hits the pillow.

On Friday nights, my girlfriends and I pile into one car and head to the college coffeehouse, where we sit at tables around a dimly lit stage, listening to a folk singer strumming a guitar.

When we get to the parking lot one night, everything is different. Our coffeehouse has changed. There's a new sign in the window: The Frat House. Loud music is blaring from the open doors. I'm disappointed because I can't dance, and I have trouble mingling and chatting with strangers. It's understood that whoever drives makes the rules on what time we get home. I want to go somewhere else or home, but our driver says, "I'm not driving anywhere else. I have to be in my parents' house by midnight and drop all you girls off beforehand, so let's go in and see how we like it. Let's spread out inside and all meet in front of the ladies' room in one hour to decide if we'll leave early."

Once inside, our group scatters to mingle. Carla and

I stick together, standing at the edge of the dance floor, talking above the noise. We point out cute guys and girls in cool dresses. Couples dance by us like fish swimming through water. They smile under black lights, which make teeth and white shirts glow in the dark. Strobe lights streak around the room, bouncing off a crystal ball chandelier hanging from the middle of the ceiling.

Across the dance floor, we see our group gathering in a circle outside the ladies' room.

"Probably a new plan to head home early," Carla says. "I'll head over and motion you by the exit door if we are heading to the car."

I've still got another twenty minutes to kill according to the clock, which seems to be moving in slow motion. I stroll unhurriedly past the bar, hoping for a miracle to find an empty seat. Out of the darkness and loud music, a figure dances toward me with one hand holding a luminous cigarette and the other pointing toward me, beckoning me to dance. Behind him, I see Carla wildly waving to me under the red-lit Exit sign, which is our signal that we are heading out. My dancer approaches me, wearing cool, nice bell-bottom jeans and sandals. However, he has a military haircut, of all things. "Wanna dance?" he asks, spinning around me. I wave my arms, feeling awkward and self-conscious, trying to dance while watching my last friend leave. The door closes behind her. My dancer makes a turn-around disco move, and while his back is to me, I bolt for the door.

Inside the car, everyone agrees that the club was a bust.

20 Weaver

For the first time, art school becomes discouraging. There are required courses I have to take, and none of them appeal to me. After I struggle through them, I have to decide on one area to major in. Ceramics involves complicated mathematical equations for glazes. I hate getting my hands dirty, and I don't like the feel of rough mud as I try to form a clay pot that eventually spins off my disk onto the floor. Painting a nude model makes me feel sorry for the model sitting naked while everyone stares at her body, painting it onto a canvas, even though she has a flawless figure, is not posed obscenely in any way, and seems completely relaxed. There's no joy for me in swishing paint around with a brush and waiting for it to dry. It smells nasty, and so does the turpentine. It's what made Van Gogh crazy—he drank his turpentine at the end of a long, hard day of painting under the sun. That's about the only interesting thing I learned in art history class, which is in a dark room with a projector humming and an art history professor who has such a melodious voice that I fall asleep at my desk, along with half the class.

It seems fate always shows me my future as I walk down a hall on my way to a cafeteria. I pass a room with a sign over the door: Fiber Arts. It smells fresh like cotton and wool. I'm drawn into the room by weavings of students' work hanging on the walls, made of brightly colored woven and knotted yarns and threads. Sewing machines and draped fabrics cover the workroom tables, making me feel as if I've found a new home.

I sign up for as many fiber arts classes as I can. I learn how to loop strands of yarn to weave scarves and then blankets and wall hangings. I spend hours working, until everyone's gone home. Above me outside a window, a big black spider diligently weaves its web, keeping me company. Through the window and this spider's magnificent net, I see a student setting up a sculpture in the grass. It's impressively gargantuan, and although it is made of polished aluminum, its airfoil shapes float delicately, dancing in the wind. He looks vaguely familiar shadowed in silhouette by the sun, with long, curly dark hair and a body like Michelangelo's *David*, but I can't place him. A crowd gathers round him and his sculpture, and there's great excitement. I think I've seen him talking to my roommate, Nancy, in the cafeteria.

Steve is still my good friend, and he lives in the neighborhood with a roommate. We decide to celebrate his acceptance into MIT at Ronnie's Rascal House with burgers and fries. He picks me up after school, and we stop by his apartment so that he can change clothes. After we walk up the stairs to his third-floor attic apartment, the first thing I see when he opens the door is a sink full of dirty dishes. Otherwise, the place is neat and clean. While waiting for Steve, I sit at the kitchen table and notice a watch on top of a paperback novel, *Steppenwolf.* There's a typed term paper, and I read the title page: "The Social Life of Eskimos." I yell out to Steve, "Whose stuff is this on the table?"

He replies, "My roommate's. He works a lot and is hardly here—doesn't do dishes either."

These simple remains of the day, belonging to someone I've never met, intrigue me. I see a Post-it note and pen and sketch a still life of dishes piled in the sink. Then I get up and wash them out of boredom from waiting.

Steve is finally ready, and as we prepare to leave, he laughs, noticing that I did the dishes. "Why?" he asks.

"I have no idea," I say, sticking the note above the clean sink on my way out.

It's a small world and neighborhood. One day Steve knocks on my door, and when I open it, his roommate, Michael, is with him.

"Hello," I say, feeling a mixture of confusion and panic as the mysterious roommate stands before me. We scrutinize each other carefully and recognize each other from that night at the Frat House.

"Hey, you are the girl who ran away from me in the middle of a dance at the club."

My face turns red from embarrassment about the incident, and I joke, "Yup, that was me. So how have you been?"

We both burst into laughter. My roommate, Nancy, appears and says hi to Michael as if she were expecting him. She explains to me that they have lunch together most every day at the college cafeteria. Steve butts in and says he and Michael decided to stop over for a visit with us.

I think about how different Michael looks with long, curly dark hair and ask, "Didn't you have really short hair that night at the club?"

"Yeah, I was on leave from the military. It's the official buzz cut. Since I've been at college, it's grown back." I recognize him also as the familiar-looking student who was installing the sculpture I saw outside my window from the weaving studio.

I introduce myself. "I'm Mary Ellen."

To my surprise, he says, "Oh, I know who you are."

We all have a good time playing cards at the kitchen table into the night.

My roommate, Nancy, is an excellent baker, and she usually leaves her pies out for me to taste-test whenever I want. Lately, though, she puts a pie on the counter and says she's saving it. This has come to be a signal that Steve's roommate, Michael, is visiting her alone. I study in my room with the door shut while they sit at the kitchen table, chatting over coffee and pie.

Thanksgiving is around the corner, and Nancy tells me she is going away to her parents' for the holiday. I look forward to enjoying the apartment to myself, but the holiday turns out to be miserable for me. During the night, I wake up with a pounding headache and an unbearable toothache. I end up in emergency surgery, having four impacted wisdom teeth removed.

Thanksgiving morning, I wake to someone knocking at the door. I'm still sedated from the drugs. My face is swollen, and my jaws are stuffed with cotton. I can't yell out or get up, so I wait for the banging to stop. The knocking continues, so I hobble to the door.

Not able to talk, I write a note and slip it under the door. "Who is it?"

I hear, "Michael."

I open the door a crack and slip out another note: "Nancy's at her parents' for the holiday."

He says he didn't realize she had already left and then looks at my face. Taken aback, he asks if I'm okay. I nod, tired of writing notes.

The next morning, I find a note under my door, asking how I am. We communicate this way, and by the end of the week, we are spending time together, first having coffee and then going for drives in the evenings and stopping to sit by the ocean, eating clam cakes and talking for hours, aware that Nancy will be back soon.

We begin spending nights together, and we are watching television in my bedroom, when the inevitable happens. We hear the front door open, and Nancy calls out, "Hi! I'm home early." She passes my open bedroom door, holding a pumpkin pie in one hand. She figures out what is going on and then throws the pie directly at us.

Michael and I decide to find our own apartment and live together. We fix it up with bright painted walls and unusual furniture that we refinish or buy from artists. We even have fish together in a big tropical tank. Everything falls into place, and we work as a team, using our creativity and survival skills. After paying for rent, books, art supplies, and tuition, we don't have extra money, but we aren't starving artists. We cook for each other combining recipes from our heritages making Italian, English, Jewish, and Greek dishes. Life together is the happiest ever.

It's a good thing I love my new roommate, as he has a strange addiction to engines and the mechanics of how they work. I think he sees them as sculptures, or his art revolves around their principles. At first, I am surprised to see him carrying a heavy, beat-up engine up a flight of stairs and into our spare bedroom, thereby claiming it as his shop. But in time, I see a polished, new-looking engine going out the door, down the stairs, and into a motorcycle. When I hear the engine roar, it's more exciting than the earth turning beneath my feet.

He sells the motorcycle and makes a nice chunk of extra money. I hope he will put it away for a rainy day, and I'm a little worried that he won't tell me what he is spending it on.

He surprises me one night, saying we are going to a

restaurant for dinner. I have become my mother, reading the menu and thinking it's too expensive. When I look across the table, he is holding an open box with a ring in it. At that moment, a waitress appears to take our order, and she stares at me and says, "Aww," alerting the whole restaurant. The other diners quietly look on with her and Michael, waiting for my answer.

This doesn't faze Michael; he enjoys the attention of the moment. All my life, I've imagined a wedding proposal as a private, intimate moment between two lovers vowing to spend the rest of their lives together. Now everyone is gawking at me. I look at the ring and say, "This isn't real." The waitress scats. Silence is broken, and everyone goes back to eating and chatting again.

"Why did you say this isn't real?" he asks. "Of course it is real."

"You don't understand the importance of privacy to me. I thought if I pretended it wasn't a diamond and you weren't proposing, it would get rid of the waitress and people staring, and we could be alone and start over."

Holding the box under the table, I put the ring on. I then place my hand on the tabletop, wearing the diamond. We look into each other's eyes, and we are engaged.

I got our private moment in spite of my nearly turning the evening into a worse fiasco than when we first met.

The waitress takes our order, noticing the ring on my finger. Michael and I begin planning our wedding, and I think we should elope because we don't have money for a reception. Michael, being a positive thinker, tells me not to worry and says that everything will work out.

I've never told anyone my secret. The scar my father

gave me surfaces whenever something important to me is about to happen, causing me to sabotage myself. I get nervous at the thought of my father walking me down the aisle and at the hypocrisy of the symbolic giving me away. The thought of a church full of people staring at me is a living nightmare. I keep this all to myself, as always.

It's been three years since our wedding and our reception, which was a New England clambake. After adding up the money in the envelopes, we paid for the food, cut the cake, changed clothes, and played baseball for the rest of the afternoon. We had enough cash left for our honeymoon to camp out at Daytona Beach in Florida.

Today we throw our graduation caps to the wind. Tomorrow we move to Pratt Institute in Brooklyn to become masters of fine art. We've paid our first semester's tuition with money from the sale of a car Michael bought and restored. We both got work-study jobs too.

Lost in Brooklyn, we drive around in circles, looking for Pratt. I walk into a grocery store and see a cashier protected behind thick Plexiglas walls, as if the store were a bank. Before I have a chance to ask, the cashier speaks. "Looking for the college?"

I nod.

He points, saying, "It is across the street, surrounded by the wrought-iron fence." As I leave, he says, "Hold your handbag with the zipper front by your side."

At the medieval-looking gate, we push away the ivy from two granite pillars engraved with the words *Pratt*

Institute. Michael looks at me, saying, "Some people work their lives to get out of this neighborhood, and here we are, moving in!" We open the gate and enter a little utopia in the middle of a ghetto. Surrounded by a metal fence are the buildings, library, and student housing.

We make a vow to each other to leave the moment we get our teaching degrees in art and to travel wherever our first teaching jobs take us.

21

1981

Twenty-Second Street, New York City

Instead of running for the hills after graduating from Pratt, we live in New York City in the Flatiron District, which is named after a building that looks like an old-fashioned flatiron standing on the corner of Fifth Avenue and Broadway. Our loft is a big, open space on the second floor of a six-story building with old-style schoolhouse windows that run from the tin ceilings to the wooden floors. It has redbrick walls on one side and a hand-operated elevator that opens into the loft. It was once Miss Weber's millinery shop in the 1930s.

For a while, Michael worked part-time at one of his art professor's special effects shops. Now he runs his own similar shop here in the loft. His studio workshop is in the front, our kitchen is in the middle, and we sleep in the back. Machines have been going in and out of our home since the day we met, so I'm used to this. The difference is that Michael now gets paid well as the work goes out.

Time ticks by lightning fast with endless hectic deadlines and frantic art directors to deal with.

I have an art studio around the corner, and I am represented by a gallery that sells my fiber art.

My parents remain in Ohio in a new home in the suburbs. Melissa is now nine years old. She rides a bicycle around the cul-de-sac and goes to a nice school. Rebecca is now twenty and married with a child, living in my parents' neighborhood. Raymond and his wife moved to Colorado. In his last letter, he wrote about working construction in the mountains with a crew of guys and watching wild stallions run every day.

My father and I have an unspoken understanding that nothing happened. Keeping the secret is our only bond now. It maintains family peace and the illusion of a normal childhood. I run to the store at the last minute to buy a card for Father's Day or his birthday. Those days are nothing more than a noose of duty and obligation around my neck. I rarely visit Ohio, see him, or speak to him. I talk to my mom and keep track of my sisters growing up from photos she sends me.

Michael and I are cooking together, preparing dinner for my mom and Melissa, who will soon be staying here. It is important to me that Mom is making a special trip to see an exhibit of my artwork and bringing Melissa, whom I miss terribly.

After the exhibition, she takes a picture of Melissa and me in front of the big black doors of OK Harris gallery in SoHo, enjoying this proud moment. She calls out from behind her camera, "Smile," and then snaps a picture. "Your first one-woman show, Mary Ellen! You got your start, and you're on your way." She is here for me, while my father stays home.

On Saturday morning, my mother and I sip coffee while everyone else sleeps. I open her gift, which is a lovely white satin slip with lace and pearls stitched on the neckline. She tells me she got Michael boxer shorts. We laugh, but she says that tight underwear lowers sperm count, and between these two gifts, she's bound to get a grandchild from us soon. She reminds me that my biological clock is ticking.

"Mom, you know we have done everything possible to get pregnant, and now the doctors say the only thing left to do is relax, and maybe it will happen. Life is strange, isn't it? Not every woman makes babies."

She looks into my eyes, saying in desperation, "Adopt!"

Everyone is up now, and after we eat french toast, my mother says her spending money is burning a hole in her pocket, so we head out for a shopping spree on Canal Street. We throw our money around, buying Gucci pocketbooks, Fendi perfume, and Rolex watches as if we are millionaires. The highest price for any item is ten dollars. My mother wonders why the police don't confiscate the imitation brand-name items. "Oh, Ma," I say. "In the city, police have bigger fish to fry than this!"

We walk to Chinatown for all the food we can eat. My mother gives up on the use of chopsticks, but Melissa and I press on, rice grain after rice grain.

We buy paper umbrellas to walk under the sun with, silk pillows, and Chinese teapots. We then pick through bins of new clothes and shoes displayed on tables along the streets. My mother buys two pairs of children's shoes, saying, "I'll find some little kid who needs these in Ohio. They're such a bargain."

Our last stop is Little Italy for dessert and cappuccino. We eat cannoli and watch the sunset while sitting outside the café at wooden tables, as if we are back at the picnic table in Papa Non's yard in Rhode Island. My mother comments on how delicious real Italian pastry is.

"Don't they have Italian pastry in Ohio, Mom?" I ask.

"Ah." She waves her hand in the air. "They have all kinds of stuff they call Italian, but it's not the real thing. It's the Ohio version. I had to fight with the manager at the supermarket in Marysville just to get him to put real olive oil on the shelves."

Before I know it, we are saying good-bye at the airport. "Don't forget to call to let me know you got home safely," I say, waving.

They return home with suitcases full of treasures. Mom promises to mail me copies of the photos she took as soon as they are developed.

I picture my father at home, waiting for my mother to report all the excitement as he sits at the round oak table, puffing cigarette smoke into the air, pouring hot water into his coffee crystals, and thinking out loud, saying, "One more cup of java, and I'll start my day."

My mother calls to let me know she got home safely and had so much fun that she's exhausted. I hear my father in the background, calling out items and souvenirs from her opened suitcase. "What is this paper umbrella and brass teapot? Gucci watches? And who's the perfume for?"

She reports how happy my father is for me for having a one-woman art exhibit and such an interesting loft home.

He picks up the phone and says, "So you're all right up there? You're doing just great, I hear! Maybe next time, I'll come with your mother. Say, when are you coming to Ohio?"

I tell him I'll visit soon and end with "Love ya, Dad."

My mother takes the phone from him to say good-bye, and as I hang up the phone, I overhear her say, "She's doing just fine, Larry."

It's a hot summer's day as I walk to my studio on Twenty-Third Street. Aromas of bacon and fried eggs blow out the restaurant vents, and ambulance sirens blare. I arrive at the building my studio is in and I see my landlady, Mrs. Babel who is eighty- five years old. She is wearing a blue hat with a feather and manages to walk here every day using a cane. She greets me with a shocked look in her eyes and says she just caught a man urinating on the front door in the alcove. "Lucky I had my cane," she says, holding it up and pointing it at an imaginary groin. "I hit him right there with it before he got a chance to zipper it up. Ah, it was horrible." She holds her heart, shaking her head from left to right.

Edna's deceased husband, Irving, made her promise on his death bed that she would never sell the building. It was once an elaborate building. The first floor was a showroom for baby grand pianos. Now used office furniture is sold there, and the building is crooked and run down. Her handyman is the same age she is and does all the repairs in the building with one solution: slapping coats of paint over any problem. Occasionally, he will hammer a big nail into something if the paint doesn't do the trick. He lives illegally in his studio at Edna's building and has worked on the same painting for the last twenty years. Rumor around the building is that he was once Edna's lover.

I climb the stairs, unlock my studio door, turn on the lights, and set the fan to spin on high. It's going to be a long, hot day. I organize my fabrics and prepare for a second show, entitled "Illusions with Thread." Instead of weaving thread, I now create miniature embroideries that appear to be normal everyday objects, such as matchbooks, cigar boxes, or playing cards.

I am finishing a fabric-and-thread version of a bag of potato chips complete with silk chips on my work table, when Mrs. Babel knocks on the door. She is concerned that the peeing perpetrator she whacked with her cane might be lurking in the corridors. She sees my work on the table and says, "I'll let you get back to your lunch!" I tune in to the radio and settle into work.

Before I know it, it's afternoon, and the phone rings. I expect it to be Michael and am surprised to hear my mother's voice. She says, "Honey, I've got some bad news for you; it's about Ray."

I ask, "What, Ma? Has there been a car accident?"

"No." Her voice shakes. "He had a nervous breakdown. We got a call from his wife. They were having marital problems. She said he was acting strangely, and then he checked himself into a psychiatric hospital. She's left him and called to tell us the name of the hospital he is in."

"What? Where's Dad?" I ask.

My mother says, "He's driving to Colorado to get him.

According to Roberta, Ray's in a bad state and doesn't even know who he is. When I have any more news, I'll let you know."

"Okay, Ma," I say, pretending to be calm. I hang up the phone in a trance, sweating profusely. I'm angry and yell at God, "Why is there always bad news from my family?"

I kick a soda can, and it spills all over a work I've labored over for weeks. "Good! I'll destroy the rest of my work in here. Better still, I'll throw it all out the window." Rage gives me strength like Sampson, and the window flies open. A force of frozen air blasts me right in the face, stopping my rage immediately, as if someone has slapped me in the face. My window is opposite a church's stained-glass window. It is so close I can reach out and touch it. It has an open section, making a chute directly from my windowsill down into the church, giving me a bird's-eye view of the choir chanting chamber music, and free air-conditioning swirls into my studio, cooling the place.

I laugh hysterically, remembering Sister Pauline with her pitch pipe in one hand and her clicker in the other, saying, "God sees and hears everything."

I start working frantically, losing myself in my work. There's something about the creative flow that gives me positive energy. I explore my feelings and release them, good or bad, into my artwork. Whatever I can't say in words comes out through creating.

While working, I listen to talk radio. People call in with personal problems, and a radio psychologist asks them questions. It's interesting to hear him chip away at their phony answers as they tiptoe around the truth about who they really are or acknowledge their wrongdoings.

Analysis could help me sort out the effects of what my father did to me as a girl. I believe it is all behind me, and I have a happy life full of love and contentment. Am I dancing around the truth like the anonymous callers I listen to?

22

Open

I can see by the many degrees on Dr. Hansk's wall that he is an accomplished psychologist. He greets me with a friendly gaze and a genuine smile. An aura of kindness surrounds him. He offers me a seat opposite his chair. Now his tall, lanky body sits in his chair. He looks the image of a classic dad portrayed on television.

I'm nervous and afraid I might cry in front of a complete stranger, even though he is a doctor. He begins with simple questions about who I am and my family. I tell him that I'm an artist. I've been married for seven years, am the oldest of four children, and am thirty-one. My brother is twenty-nine, one sister is twenty-one, and the youngest sister is eleven.

"All from the same mother and father?" he asks.

"Yes."

He takes notes, commenting about the unusual age gaps between my siblings. Before I know it, forty-five minutes have passed, and I'm only up to Papa Non and Nonie and growing up in Rhode Island. I wonder how long it will take until we discuss the secret, if ever. We decide to meet every Monday evening for a session.

I trust him more and more. He extracts pain with as few tears as possible until I can talk of my father's abuse.

He asks, "From what age did the abuse begin and end?"

I tell him it was from as far back as I can remember until I was twelve or thirteen, but I'm not sure of exact dates or ages because it happened so long ago. I explain how memories keep resurfacing, but I push them back. "I fear if I push them into the background any longer, I will forget, and I promised myself to remember what my father did to me. I started getting dark feelings that if I let myself forget, something bad would happen. A little voice inside me nagged, 'Don't let it slip away. Don't forget. Tell someone.' So here I am, lost about what to do about my father and my memories."

He asks me if I ever told anyone else. I tell him the first and only person I felt comfortable telling was Michael, and even then, I wasn't sure what he would think of me. It took me a year or two after we got married to tell him.

"And what did he say? What did he think?" Dr. Hansk asks.

I tell him how relieved I was when Michael just hugged me in the dark as I wept and said, "I'm so sorry that happened to you. I love you."

It was the first time someone said, "I'm sorry. It's got nothing to do with you. It doesn't make you a bad person." His words gave me courage and a good feeling about myself. I felt more positive in looking at the world after that. I could hold my head up. The secret was out, and I was still a good person, with someone who loved me, and it didn't make a difference to him.

"Very good. You have a highly supportive husband, and it's important at a time like this," Dr. Hansk says, rocking back in his chair and putting his pen to his lips.

In each session, we go over my memories more and more, from being small and escaping into my mind to the time I tried to tell the sleeping priest in confession to Mr. Trine's garage, with my father standing over me naked. Whatever I say doesn't shock him, which makes me feel more normal.

Most importantly, he says what Michael said: "It's not your fault." It was never my fault. I was never guilty; all the guilt belongs to my father. As an adult, I might think I know this—I might think I have come to terms with this—but inwardly, I still hold the weight of his crime and carry his burden for him on my shoulders.

Dr. Hansk explains what a powerful force denial is. It allows a person to believe something never happened, because he or she cannot deal with it. It's a way to avoid reality when it's too painful. He explains that my father brainwashed me from an early age, as if he hypnotized me into believing we were in this together. But it didn't work, because I'm normal, and he is abnormal—wired wrong. The more I talk and go over memories, the more I see the ugly reality of his actions as a conscious decision to hurt his own daughter simply for a sexual addiction.

Before I went into therapy, I lived with two parallel childhoods in my mind, one with a good father and one with a bad father, and I kept the bad father in the background, believing in the good one and portraying that existence to myself and others. Now I see that he is one and the same; his evil side conquered the good. The acts of kindness I remember are too few and far between compared to his selfish acts of cruelty.

Dr. Hansk has helped me untangle memories of deceit for a long time now, and today I'm finally beginning to understand where he has been leading me, which is to take my power now as a woman and heal my inner child from incest by confronting my father about his abuse. I stop protecting him.

I'm strong enough to open the lid on the imaginary jar of memories and release them to the rightful owner, my father. By standing up to him, I no longer protect him.

Dr. Hansk shocks me with a bombshell: "There's another important aspect about confronting him. You are not only protecting your inner child; you're protecting other children from him as well."

"What do you mean by that?" I ask.

"Pedophiles don't stop at one child. Most often, it's a lifetime addiction leaving many victims behind."

A ton of emotional bricks hit me. I always thought that his actions were a freak of nature and that when the abuse stopped between us, it stopped altogether. Now I have survivor's guilt over saving myself but leaving my sisters behind to burn. It didn't dawn on me that he would move on to other victims, such as my sisters, neighbors, nieces, or friends' children.

I tell Michael of my decision to confront my father, and he says he is here for me however I decide to do this.

It's three in the afternoon, and I'm alone at my studio, preparing to call my father. He works the night shift, so this is the time when he will be sitting at the table, having his coffee. I have no plan regarding what to say; all I want is the courage to stand up for the little girl inside me. As I dial his number, adrenaline pumps through my body to the beat of my pounding heart.

"Hellew?" his melodic voice answers.

"Hi, Dad. It's me."

"Hello there, Sissy. What ya doin' calling your old dad in the middle of the day? Is everything all right?"

I sternly tell him there is something important I want to talk to him about, and the strength of my voice surprises me.

He says in a calm but suspicious voice, "Hold on; give me a minute to make my cup of java."

I hear the microwave beep three times, signaling that his mug of hot water is ready. I hear the spoon clinking as he stirs the coffee crystals into the cup. Then there is silence.

"Dad, are you there?" I ask into the phone.

"I'm here," he says through a puff of breath. He has his props ready: coffee and a smoke.

I blurt out, "Dad, I want to talk to you about the things that you did to me while I was growing up."

I hear puffing, gulping, clinking, and then silence. He says, "Why, what things?"

My voice is unyielding. "You know what stuff."

"I don't know what you're talking about." His voice reeks of guilt.

I say, "You abused me when I was a girl."

"What! That wasn't what you think it was," he says. I hear puffing, tapping, and then silence.

"What was it then? I want to know."

Clink. Slurp. Clink.

"I'm waiting for an answer, Dad. What was it then?"

"Nothing," he says. "I dunno."

"Nothing?" I yell angrily into the phone as my body shakes. "How dare you say it was nothing!"

I hear the doorbell ringing and his footsteps walking to answer the door.

"I gotta go," he says. "There are some people here to look at the house. Your mom and I have it up for sale, you know. Listen, I'll call you back."

"You'd better call me back tonight, because I'm not gonna let this go."

Hanging up the phone, I'm amazed at how free I feel. When I get home, I tell Michael that I confronted my father on the phone. "Some people came over, so he couldn't talk anymore, but he is calling me back tonight."

Michael and I watch television as if waiting for a bomb to drop. The phone rings, and I go upstairs to answer it in private. I'm glad that I am home and that Michael is here.

"Hello?"

"It's me—your father," he whispers. "You don't know how long I have wanted to talk about this."

There is silence.

I ask, "Why—"

He interrupts, whispering to me as if I'm a child once

more. "Oh yes, for so long, I've had no one to talk to about this. You're my girl, aren't you? I never let you down, did I?"

I say angrily, "What's wrong with you? All the hours you spent convincing me to trust you. And the hurt, shame, and fear you gave me that I carried inside my whole life. That's not letting someone down?"

He continues whispering as if he hasn't heard my response at all. "You know that scarf you made me for Christmas? I've been looking at it hanging in the closet, and well, I've been thinking of—"

I interrupt him. "Don't change the subject. Do you even realize what you did was wrong?"

"Of course I knew it was wrong." He giggles like a guilty child caught with his hand in the cookie jar.

I hear puffing, gulping, more puffing, tapping, and then dead, heavy silence.

I savor the feeling of turning the tables on him for the first time in my life, making him feel trapped like a bug in a jar with no way out and no air to breathe. The tide has turned.

He doesn't answer for a moment and then continues his childlike whispering. "Oh, Sissy, for so long, I've had no one to talk to about this."

He's trying to turn my confrontation into me being there for him!

"Dad, I'm not calling to help you feel better. I'm calling to make me feel better by standing up to you for all the hurt you caused. You are sick, and you need help. It's not my duty to help you this time."

"I'll call you back" is all he has to say. "I'll call you back."

I'm trembling. I did it! I'm free, just as I was the first time I looked down at him in the basement from atop the stairs and said no.

I no longer tremble.

I go downstairs, and Michael has red roses and champagne on the table. We don't talk about my conversation; we simply enjoy having each other.

In the morning, I awaken as a whole person for the first time. It's as if I have finally found something I lost long ago—as if I have dreamed of climbing Mt. Everest and am now at the top. I went back to fight for myself as a little girl, for all those times she had no power. I am finally free of the mountain of shame I carried all these years. I've put it on my father's shoulders, where it belongs.

When I get dressed, I put on a red blouse with matching red lipstick. I have a desire to be noticed and not blend into the woodwork. I am free of my father's hold on me.

At the studio, I have so much energy that work flows through me. At three o'clock, the phone rings. It's my father, wanting to talk some more. "Sure, Dad," I say, feeling amazingly calm and rational.

He announces, "Well, I decided I'm going to get help."

"That's good, Dad, but—"

He interrupts. "I was wondering if you wouldn't mention this to your mother until then. I made an appointment with a psychiatrist for this Monday. Until then, don't bring this up to your mother. Promise?"

"I promise." My heart sinks a bit because these words come from my lips automatically. I never intended to talk to my mother. I told the truth, not worrying about the consequences it would bring either of them. At least he's admitted to what happened. I envision a psychiatrist curing him, and he will tell my mother, and one day we will join in a circle, hugging and crying together.

He asks if he can come to New York to see me so that we can talk in person and work this whole thing out. He says he's never been to New York; he's driven by it but never stopped. I tell him I'm not ready to see him so soon, but maybe he can call after his first therapy session, and we can talk more then.

"Sure, I'll call you then," he says. "I promise."

"Don't wait too long, Dad. You don't have forever."

That night at home, I watch myself dancing in the mirror, feeling like a whole woman. I tell Michael my father called again and promised to call me after his therapy session on Monday.

Monday afternoon, the phone rings. I'm impressed my father has kept his promise. I answer, expecting to hear Dad's voice reporting how his therapy session went.

"Hello?"

"Hi, Sis. It's me—Rebecca."

I know from the wobbly tone in her voice that something is terribly wrong. "Hi, Becky. What's wrong? Why do you sound so sad?"

"Dad's gone," she says.

"Did he run away?"

"He's dead!" she cries.

"Dead?" I repeat. "What happened?" I ask, breaking down and crumbling inward, as if someone has punched me in the chest.

"He killed himself!" she wails.

"No! How did it happen?"

"He pulled over on the side of the road—" She stops, unable to get the words out.

"Go on," I say.

She finishes. "The police found his car on the side of the road, and they found him hung from a tree in the woods." Her voice breaks down.

"I'll be there as soon as I can." I drop the phone without saying good-bye and sit on the floor in shock.

It's the shock of Papa Non's death all over again, and I think there is nothing he could have done to hurt my mother more than this. To have a father and then a husband end their lives in suicide must be unbearable. I could not have imagined in a million years his life would end like this.

I remember believing as a child that once the secret was out, it would end in tragedy and that someone would die. There can never be a circle of us all crying together; our family will always remain a triangle. As long as he was alive, he carried his own burden, but he couldn't bear the weight of it.

I thought I'd feel relief at his death, but I don't. I sob uncontrollably.

He never said good-bye. He never said, "I'm sorry." My last words to him were "Don't wait too long, Dad. You don't have forever." Now he will wait forever.

I feel my wild orange cat nudging his nose into my face and curling his way into my lap. I hug myself and find his warm fur comforting. I ask him, in tears and rocking, "Why now? You're always so wild. You never sit on my lap, especially when I want you to."

I cry until I have no more tears. My head is numb and

empty of thought. I don't question who, what, when, or why; I just calmly walk out the door and go through the motions of getting through the rest of the day.

I stop at the jewelry shop to pick up some pieces being gold plated for one of the props due today.

"I'm here to pick up the job for the model-making studio," I say.

"Sure." The man behind the counter smiles at me as if I'm on drugs.

I think it is ironic to be in this shop, waiting for the gold-plated pieces, because it reminds me of the factories my father worked in when I was small.

The counter person comes out with the job wrapped in special tissue. Holding it delicately, he tells me to be careful with the package because it could scratch the finish on the gold-plated pieces. I'm a zombie looking into space.

"You know," he says, "your husband called, asking if you had gotten here yet."

"Oh." My words come out slowly. "He worries about me. I get lost."

The man looks at me strangely. I don't understand what I just said either.

When I get to the studio, Mike is obviously upset. "What happened to you? You were supposed to meet me here first thing this morning right after the meeting; the client has been calling every fifteen minutes for the prop. It's holding up the photo shoot, and they are billing us for the time."

I sit down and look at the clock. Hours have passed. I drop the carefully wrapped gold pieces onto the table.

"What's the matter?" Michael asks.

I look at him and stammer out, “My father's dead!”

“No! Oh no,” he says, sitting down beside me. “When? How?”

“He hung himself,” I say, staring into space. We cry together, hugging each other. I whisper, “I thought I'd feel happy when he died. Instead, I can't stop crying. If I had gone down to see him, maybe this wouldn't have happened. Maybe I could have helped him. Now, with hindsight, I see he tried to give me clues that he was thinking of suicide. When I was confronting him, he interrupted me about the scarves hanging in his closet. 'You know those scarves you made me?' he said. 'Well, I've been thinking of—' and I cut him off, yelling at him for trying to change the subject.”

Michael looks at me, saying, “Don't even think that way. Don't blame yourself for coincidence, for unlucky timing. There was probably a lot going on in his life that you don't even know about.”

23

?

The screen door opens into my mother's parlor. The first person I see is Melissa, who is sitting alone on the couch, staring at the wall. She is now twelve.

"Hi, Melissa," I say.

"Hello," she says, looking sad and embarrassed. We don't hug or cry; we just sit next to each other on the couch, looking at the wall together.

My mother comes out from the kitchen. It's the first time we've looked into each other's eyes since I heard the news. "I came as soon as I could, Mom," I say.

She grabs my hand and pulls me to her, whispering, "I'm glad you came, but I wouldn't blame you even if you didn't. I'm so glad you're here."

From the kitchen, I hear the familiar voices of my aunts Leah and Sophie. When I walk in to see them, everyone pretends we aren't here for a funeral, making small talk. My mother looks at them and says to me, "I knew my sisters would be here."

We make more small talk. "Look how you have grown,

but you're so thin. All you girls are so thin these days—toothpicks, you are," Aunt Sophie says wistfully.

Seeing all of their faces at my mother's table brings back memories of long ago. I see them in bikinis with their rear ends to the sun, laughing the days away as young mothers, with Nonie screaming at them from the top window about the shame of letting the neighbors see their bodies. I remember Papa Non's tomatoes and cigars hidden in the doghouse. I have no memories of my father's family, although I'm sure they remember me as a baby. I have no past here in Ohio and am about to see all his family at the funeral.

We stop talking, becoming uncomfortably still and contemplative. It's as if we've all realized at the same time that we are here for a funeral.

I think about my final conversation with my father and recall him saying, "We won't tell your mother just yet." I look at my mother, and it's as if she is trying to read my mind. To escape the still silence around the table, I excuse myself to the bathroom. I pass my mother's bedroom, and her door is open. There is a perfectly starched white lace dress on her bed. Someone has pressed and ironed it and laid it out for her. It looks like a child's confirmation dress. My mother comes up behind me, having followed me into the hall, and whispers, "My sisters brought me a dress and got all my clothes ready for me for the wake and funeral tomorrow. I knew they'd be here." She holds on to my arm, asking, "Are you okay?"

"Yes, Mom," I assure her.

"Thank God you are here; thank God my sisters are here," she says. "You know, Dad had a lot on his mind, and

Ray's illness took a toll on him. I don't want you to blame yourself for anything."

I nod. I think she must know about the phone conversation my father and I had before he died. I excuse myself again.

I quietly click the bathroom door shut. I wash my hands, comb my hair, put some lipstick on, and wash my hands again to buy time because I feel uncomfortable at the table. There's a light tapping on the door. Then my mother's voice says, "Mary Ellen, are you all right? You've been in there for a while."

"I'm fine, Ma," I say. She probably thinks I'm in here trying to slit my wrists or something. "I'll be right out. Please don't worry, Mom. I love you. I'll be right out."

The night before the wake, my sister Rebecca comes into my bedroom, and we hug. I tell her about my confrontation with Dad the day before he committed suicide. She looks into my eyes, saying, "I believe you. I have no memories of anything like you went through, but I'm not shocked. It's like I always knew something was wrong."

We all go to the home of a young minister, who counsels the immediate family. "Does anyone have any questions?" he asks sensitively, yet he is cheerful enough to make us feel comfortable in case we want to talk about mourning Dad's death.

We are all dressed up and looking strong and stoic as we sit in our nylons and high heels with our legs crossed in the same direction. My aunt Leah wants to know what he thinks about the act of suicide. I put my head down, ashamed, wondering why there is always shame tied to my father, not only in life but also in death. I hoped no one would mention the word, yet it's the first thing out of my aunt's mouth—*suicide*. The minister responds wisely by saying we should not judge another man; only my father knew what it was like to walk in his shoes. The rest is between him and God. "Let us not judge him. God rest his soul."

"I think you have to be brave," my aunt says, putting her head down and crying. I know she is thinking of Papa Non. It is the first time anyone from my mother's family has said anything positive about my father. "Brave!" she cries out, breaking down in tears again. "Courageous."

I've never thought of suicide as an act of courage, least of all bravery. I see him as a coward, running away and unable to face life.

The next morning, Michael and I go to see Ray at the institution to tell him of my father's death and see if he wants to go to the funeral. His psychiatrist already knows why we are here and greets us at the door. He asks us to sign in, saying he will talk with all of us afterward. When I sign in, I see my father's name at the top of the sheet. I look at his signatures from past visits. There are red checks above his name and a notation next to each one that says, "Limited visitation."

Ray is waiting for us outside on a bench in the sun. It's a restful place that looks like a park, with landscaping and birds chirping. He looks up at us, expecting bad news. I try to speak but can't. Mike says, "It's about your father."

"What?" Ray asks, looking scared.

"Your father died," Michael says. I wish he said it more kindly, but how else can you say it?

Ray looks at me for an explanation of how it happened. I lie to him, saying, "Heart attack."

He wants to know where it happened.

My lie grows. "He was driving."

Ray says, "Driving and just had a heart attack?"

"Yes," I say. "The police found him in the car."

I know Ray has to spend the night alone in the institution with no one to comfort him, and I can't leave him with the thought that our father committed suicide. I want him to think my father's death was of natural causes. I want him to think that there was nothing anyone could have done and that there's no one to blame, not Raymond, me, or Mom. Ironically, Ray cannot get out of the institution because he attempted suicide. My father found Ray with his throat slashed and saved him.

"Do you want to go to his funeral tomorrow?" I ask.

"I don't even know if I have a suit to wear," he says.

"Mom's got one ready for you from your closet."

He nods that he will go.

We return the next morning to pick up Ray. He is in a waiting room with his psychiatrist. When I greet the doctor, the first thing he asks is my age. "Thirty-one," I say as I wonder why psychiatrists always ask your age even before they say hello.

He brings out a bottle of pills for Ray, saying, "If you think you need these, take them." Ray looks at him and nods, putting the container of pills in his pocket. "Do you think you can make it through the funeral?" the doctor asks, concerned about taking on the responsibility of releasing him for these two days. Ray nods.

During the drive to the house, Ray seems like his old

self. I realize how much I've missed him. We don't say a word about our father. Once we're home, my mother brings out one of his suits, which he hasn't worn in five years. He's gained a bit of weight, and it's a tight fit.

"It will have to do," my mother says. "We gotta get there."

He looks uncomfortably stuffed and is still fumbling with his tie noosed around his neck. My mother helps him unravel his shirt collar and presses it flat around his neck. The collar is still too loose, revealing the scar on his neck, so my mother pulls the tie to tighten his shirt collar and hide his scar.

I worry that when Ray sees my father in the casket, he might have an episode, but as we walk into the funeral home, he stares ahead, completely calm. So far, he has not shed a tear. Then I worry someone might mention the word *suicide*. I meant to tell him before we got there, but I never found the right time to bring it up.

The large room, lined with folding chairs, begins to fill up with friends and family. My mother and our immediate family are in the front row. My father's coffin is no more than eight feet away from me. My mother sits to my left and whispers, "The undertaker asked me for a suit, so I gave them his best blue one that he always looked so good in. It was his favorite suit. They didn't do his hair right, though. They combed it funny; it's not the way Dad combed his hair. I guess they did the best they could from the picture. I sent shoes too, but they said he wouldn't need them."

It's quiet except for the sound of people filtering in. We turn around, and my mother points out his brothers and sisters. "There's Uncle Art, his oldest brother. He practically raised your father." He is barely able to walk without the help of his cane. "There's Uncle Daniel, Doris's twin, and Aunt Esther." I am struck by their sameness as one after another comes in. They all look like younger and older twins of the same demeanor, height, hair color, and eye color. They are masculine and feminine versions of each other. My mother whispers that the Sinclairs are a good-looking family. "They have a distinct look. Don't they?"

My father always told me I look like his mother, and I wonder if his family sees the resemblance, because they look at me as if they are reminiscing—maybe because the last time they saw me, I was a six-month-old.

The organ begins playing, and a voice sings "Amazing Grace." I hear the words "that saved a wretch like me." I see his still, soulless body and truly understand the human body as a vehicle for one's soul. Now it is an empty vehicle like an old Chevy polished with dignity, deserving of people paying their final respects and saying good-bye. I think about his tattoo with the eagle and the words in a heart: "Mother and Muffy, the Only Tow I Love." The word *two* is misspelled for eternity.

I'm surprised at my thoughts and how unemotional I am.

Occasionally, my mother cries and sobs out, "We had so many dreams! Why, God? Why?"

When the service is over, people talk in small groups. After everyone gets up and walks away, I'm still sitting in the front row, looking at the casket. There's no one left in the room, and it's quiet. I hear footsteps walking from behind; they are my father's footsteps. They are the good father's footsteps, one after the other, echoing through my heart. Then I feel the touch of my father's hand on my back. "I'm sorry," I hear him say. I look back into sad ice-blue eyes exactly the color of Dad's. It's his brother. The weight of his hand comforts me exactly the way my father would have. I finally cry as I say, "You look so much like him."

He pats my shoulder, saying, "I'm so sorry," and then he leaves. His footsteps sound just like my father's as he walks away.

I feel as if Dad found a way to say, "Good-bye. I'm so sorry."

Strong young cousins and uncles carry his casket. Ray can't bring himself to do it.

There is a final sermon on the grass, and my mother receives an American flag folded into a triangle for Dad's service to his country in the Navy; she cries when they hand it to her. At the gravesite, I hear the words "ashes to ashes, dust to dust." Melissa places a violet orchid on his coffin.

We all leave for home. I'm emotionally drained by tears of sorrow. He has been laid to rest.

Everyone brings food to my mother's, and we talk until late.

My aunts Rosie and Doris ask me to go for a ride with them to take Uncle Don home. I think it will be good to get out for a while, and it's time to make amends with Uncle Don. He looks like a much heavier version of my father and has a more amusing personality. When we reach his apartment, he invites us up for a cup of coffee.

Aunt Doris and Aunt Rosie both look at each other and laugh. Doris says, "If it's on you, sure, Don."

Before we leave, he wants to show us a new invention. He pulls his jacket's zipper up and down until it jams saying, "See? It's stuck." He pulls out a spray can and sprays a magic ingredient along the zipper, which immediately zips smoothly up and down.

Aunt Doris takes the wrapper off the can and says, "Why, that's nothing but Pam cooking spray."

"I know," Don says, still zippering happily up and down, "but we can repackage it, make a label, and call it Zipper Quick. What d'ya think, girls? Want in on it? It's gonna be big—in every household in America!"

24
Monday's Mother

When I open the door to my studio, I see the red light on my answering machine blinking like a throbbing heart. I wonder who is calling me so early. I listen to a familiar voice that sounds like an old friend, but I don't recognize who it is.

"Hi. I'm home. It feels great to be back. Call me when you get in. I love ya."

I think someone left a message for someone else by mistake. I don't know anyone who's been away, especially a man with such a charming voice.

Suddenly, I realize who it is. It's Ray. My brother is home after spending years in an institution, and he sounds as if he's back from a trip to Paris. My father spent years working with him, visiting him, and wishing for this day, and now, after his funeral, Raymond has been released. I have my brother back, the brother who used to have long hair and John Lennon sunglasses. My brother's back.

I call home right away. A woman's voice practically sings the word *hello* into the phone.

I say, "Hello. Is Mrs. Sinclair there?" wondering who this woman is at my mother's house.

"This is she," the singing voice chimes. "Is that you, Mary Ellen?"

"Yes," I say. "I didn't recognize your voice."

We talk and talk, not once mentioning my father; it's as if he never existed and nothing ever happened. We talk about Ray and the message he left on my machine. She tells me it is true that he is out of the hospital for good. He was released today, but she doesn't want to get anyone's hopes up. If he continues to see a psychiatrist and doesn't skip his medication, he probably won't ever have to go back. "Can you believe it? We thought this day would never come," my mother says, her voice full of hope.

Eventually, I get used to my mother's new voice on the phone. I remember when we lived on the first floor of Papa Non and Nonie's house. When my father wasn't home, she would put on the stereo and waltz around the parlor with our new sister, Becky, in her arms, singing and swirling her around. That happiness doesn't even match what I hear in her now. I can only describe it as an inner happiness. I don't know what freedom sounds like, but if it has a sound, it is the new melody in my mother's "Hello."

There's a knock at my studio door. "I gotta go, Ma. My appointment is here."

"Good-bye, Mary Ellen. I love you." It's been a long time since I can remember her saying this.

I open the door to greet Jane, a gallery dealer, and her assistant. They reek of perfection in suits with matching accessories. Jane has a dark blue suit and a wonderful swirling silver pin on her lapel. She looks over my work, excited. She asks if she can take two pieces to sell on consignment at their gallery in Florida until we schedule a show for next year.

As we go over ideas for my exhibition, the industrial sewing machines on the floor above me start humming, causing my ceiling to vibrate. I previously hung a large cotton sheet across the ceiling, fastened by ropes at the corners like a hammock, to catch crumbling plaster loosened by the vibrations. I realize that quite a heavy mountain of plaster has been accumulating, and it's hanging in a lump directly over our heads. They don't notice, as the machines buzz and vibrate, that more plaster is falling; I can see the sheet stretching to its limit. I try not to look up, and I decide to get them out before plaster and boards land all over their perfect suits.

"Yes," I say, "so good to talk to you. Take these pieces, and I'll send the paperwork." I rush them out the door. After waiting and being excited for so long to see them, I am unable to enjoy the studio review.

They seem a little upset at getting rushed out as I walk them downstairs. Within moments, a loud crash emanates from my studio. They look up, asking me if I should go see what's happened.

"Oh no, I know what that is. Nothing to worry about," I say, trying to sound nonchalant. I show them out and then run back upstairs to find that the whole ceiling is just slat boards. The makeshift hammock has fallen, and there's plaster dust everywhere.

Most everyone is afraid to complain to the landlady, because it's a commercial building, and some people live here. Her attitude is "This is what you get for three hundred dollars a month." There's no heat on Sundays, the hallway lights shut off at midnight, and the stairways slant so badly that it's only a matter of time before they collapse. There's a writer down the hall from my studio who wears gloves with the fingertips cut off so he can type. I hear his voice in the hall as he bangs on Mrs. Babel's office door. It starts in a low tone but ends in a scream because she won't open the door.

"I can't type! Would it kill you to put the heat on for at least an hour on Sunday or leave the damn hallway lights on? Someone's going to end up dead." He continues to bang, but she won't come out. I swear I hear her giggling inside. Yet it's still a luxury to have my own work space in New York City.

By the time I clean up the mess and replace the hammock, it is dark and raining out. Michael waits for me with a smile under a big umbrella. We walk home in the rain, and I tell him that Edna's ceiling finally came down and then relay the wonderful news about my family. Saving the best for last, I tell him the gallery took two pieces back with them to sell. He's so happy for me.

"Someday people will go out of their way to meet you," he says.

"Yes." I laugh. "When we are old and gray."

He always says things like that to warm my heart and help me believe in myself.

Dr. Hansk's waiting room is quiet except for the white noise cranked from a machine in the corner. I wait for his door to open and for him to invite me in with his kind smile, thick black glasses, and tall, lanky swagger. His leather easy chair creaks back. I wonder why I ever came here in the first place and what his degrees on the wall really stand for. Perhaps I should have left my memories alone. Since our last session only ten days ago, my life has been a whirlwind—I've called my father, gone to his funeral, seen my two aunts from long ago, heard my mother's new voice, and gotten news of my brother's release from the hospital he's been stuck in for five years.

I tell Dr. Hansk about my father's suicide. "I am so sorry, truly sorry," he says. It is comforting the way he says it. He's shocked and sad. I can tell by the way he pauses and looks deep into my heart that he's sorry for me and not at all for my father.

I tell him how discouraged I feel after standing up to my father and then, only a couple of days later, having to deal with the shame of his death. I tell him how difficult it's been when people give their condolences and then ask what he died of. I say, "Heart attack," covering up the truth, and I change the subject. How can I answer, "He killed himself"?

Death is an embarrassment.

Dr. Hansk lets me talk everything out before he comments: "I am sorry about his death and that he won't be here for you to work on things further. But he did one thing for you at least before he died: he acknowledged that it happened, which brought it into reality for you. He validated the truth."

Weeks later, at another session with Dr. Hansk, I say, "I never take for granted what I have. Sometimes I look down at myself and wonder if it's really me walking in these feet, going to plays and restaurants, and buying silk blouses. I have kept my promises to myself. My house is quiet and peaceful. Michael and I say to each other, 'How was your day?' I enjoy cooking, and we eat dinner by candlelight; sometimes he brings me roses for no special occasion, and we never intrude on each other while in the bathroom.

"It's not always this perfect. Sometimes we clash. I don't like something he said. He doesn't like something I did. When we get into a fight of words and lash out in anger, I see my mother and father in my head. I stop dead in my tracks and feel sick inside. The way they argued never got them anywhere; it just cut deep scars into their love. They attacked each other because they were unhappy. Fighting for the sake of fighting is like two children pulling at a toy that no one ends up with. I'm learning to fight—for my point of view and for what I believe in—with fairness and respect. It's fair to battle with words to get across something important to me but not to use cruel words in revenge."

"Good for you," Dr. Hansk says proudly, clenching his fists as if cheering for a boxer in the ring. "Good for you."

I tell him that I talked to my two sisters about what happened to me, expecting them to confide in me. Instead, they said they have no memories of abuse. It's a puzzle for all of us, especially since they believe and support me without a doubt. Sometimes I think that just because I was ready to face my abuse doesn't mean they have to be ready, and all I can do is believe them as they believe me.

Dr. Hansk says maybe someday they will want to tell

their stories, which might be different from mine, or they might truly have escaped his abuse. By the end of our forty-five minutes, he looks exhausted as he says, "Once again, I'm so truly sorry for your loss. Let's talk more next week."

Dr. Hansk always makes me feel as if I'm his only patient. Today I see by the way he takes my check that he's done this over and over—today and all week, session after session. It makes me feel more normal, as if I'm not alone. The world is full of people who have problems they struggle to understand.

Creating my work and going to therapy keep my world together. I've come to trust Dr. Hansk, although in the beginning, I secretly blamed him for my father's death. It's a family trait to believe that when something goes wrong, someone else is to blame.

I've come to see that my father was responsible for his own life. If I had to do it over again, I would do it a bit differently. I wish I had gone there in person instead of confronting him on the phone, but I didn't, so there's no point in looking back.

As I work, I can hear a saxophone playing in the distance in the corridor. That's a clue not to open the door. I can't go out now. Whenever the mood strikes him, the musician on the third floor roams the corridors mostly naked, playing his saxophone. Once the music stops, I'll go out for coffee, but not until then. I bumped into this man behind the music once, and it wasn't a pretty sight. From the front, everything's covered, but from the rear—that's another story.

Mrs. Babel's building is like a fun house. Everything is at different angles, so I feel off center while walking down the stairs. The plaster is falling from the walls and ceilings. A contractor demolished a row of buildings on Twenty-Third Street to build a new high-rise as housing for the blind. They offered our landlady lots of money for her building so that they could knock it down along with the other rows of buildings, but because of her promise to her husband, Irving, it remains standing like the Leaning Tower of Pisa attached to the new megastructure on its west side. On its east side is an alley and the Church of St. Vincent.

During another therapy session, I tell Dr. Hansk how well my brother's been doing since he left the institution. He's practically his old self, as if he's returned from a long trip. I describe the melody in my mother's voice. Excited, I tell him I've been scheduled for an art exhibit, something I've worked toward for three years. After the tragedy of my father's suicide, there's nothing but good news.

Sometimes I feel like Rip Van Winkle after awakening from twenty years of sleep. Dr. Hansk looks at me kindly, crossing his lanky legs to get comfortable and slowly bobbing his head up and down, as if he knows something. I'm not sure what, but he is sure of it.

"Let's talk about your mother," he says.

"My mother—you mean about her doing so well now that he's gone?"

"No." He shakes his head.

I say, "She tells me she won't go to his grave, and she's

cleaned out all the rooms and gotten rid of his stuff, and she's painted everything white."

"No," he says, interrupting. "Tell me about when you went to your father's funeral and had a feeling that she knew about the conversations you had been having with your father before he died."

"Well, yes," I say. "It's not something I feel ready to talk to her about right away."

He says, "We can talk here, and in time, you might feel strong enough to talk to her, especially about the fact that she might have known all along what was going on between you and your father throughout your childhood."

I question the possibility that she might have known. "He was always careful to hide it from her by doing things to me when she wasn't home or by taking me in the car or somewhere else or—"

He interrupts. "But in your early memories, there were so many clues she should have picked up on and acted on. She may have chosen not to see. But with so many red flags up, it's hard to think she didn't know something wasn't right with him. It's a statistic: most mothers know." His tone is matter-of-fact. I expected more compassion to help the words sink in.

She might have known. *She knew!* The words echo in my brain.

The realization that she might have known drags my feelings down like a lead weight. It's like the last piece of a puzzle put into place that I would never have thought to put in that spot, because it didn't look as if it fit there. Could my mother have known all along?

Until Dr. Hansk said this, I never thought for a

moment she knew. I thought I was protecting her all those years by keeping our family together and saving face for her, for us, for the family. If I'd ever told, there would have been no family without my father. We could barely make it with him. Papa Non and Nonie would have had him killed without thinking twice. I remember being scared and seeing the story of my uncle Ruby in all the newspapers. Nonie's sister, Aunt Lena, found her son in the hallway, shot dead. The picture in the papers was of Aunt Lena's hallway, with Uncle Ruby's body lying in a pool of blood with a newspaper covering his head. When somebody hurt their family, they took the law into their own hands with the Mafia. I know for sure they would never have seen my father as a man who needed help.

The thought that my mother knew what a sick man he was and didn't find a way to stop the abuse is almost as humiliating for me as having been abused by my father. *Is there no end to the Pandora's box of emotional bugs that continue to fly?* I thought that confronting my father, even though he committed suicide, would bring closure and that his funeral was the end of my healing process.

"This changes everything, Dr. Hansk. If she knew, my whole childhood was a lie." I think that this is how people must feel when they find out they are adopted.

"How do you feel about your mother?" he asks me in that deep, penetrating tone.

"I feel betrayed," I say. "I was drowning all those years, barely keeping my head above water, and she had a life raft but didn't throw it to me. How could she know and not help me? I thought by not telling the secret, her husband wouldn't go to jail; she wouldn't be forced on the street with us. But now, her knowing sounds so obvious. How could she not have known? It was her job as a mother to know. This changes everything. Now I feel like a victim of my mother and my father."

Dr. Hansk says, "It is complex, this process of discovering truth yet not wanting to discover the truth. Denial is a very powerful force. When what might be true cannot be coped with, a person lives in a constant state of denial. The difference in your denial is that you were a child who trusted your father. You were always suspicious until you figured things out for yourself as your knowledge grew. You discovered the truth and dealt with it. You are a survivor of a terrible trauma; your mother was a victim too."

I look at him as if to say, "Will I ever be able to close the jar?" I shrug and want to give up.

He says in a serious, realistic tone, "You have done hard work, yet there's more to do. You must talk this out with your mother. Tell her what went on before the funeral. Tell her about your phone conversations with your father, and talk more about when you were growing up. She's probably too afraid to bring it up herself." He pauses, looks deep into me, and uncrosses his cramped legs. "That's all the time we have today."

He's right. I should talk to my mother, but I don't want to hear it, do it, or think any more about it. As I walk toward the subway, depression takes hold of me. The feeling I have now is different from the feeling of facing what I always knew about my father, because I lived through it. I never thought my mother knew.

Dr. Hansk is a great thinker and an expert on the

psychology of the human mind, but there are some things he cannot help me with. Without his answers and insight, moving forward is frustrating. I listen to my inner child, nurturing her, giving her what she wants. One day she wants me to scorn my mother and make her responsible, and then she cries to me, "I want my mommy!" I feel alone, with only my gut feelings, courage, and love to help me make a decision.

I'm going to visit my mother in person to talk to her about the phone conversations between my father and me before he died.

When I call her on the phone, she is excited that we will spend time together. She goes on about how she is getting by. "I'm so much calmer now; life is too short to holler and get nervous. I used to watch every dime because I grew up poor with so little, and your father and I could never seem to get ahead. Anyway, money can't buy happiness, and it sure as hell can't bring someone back from the grave.

"I was always a good money manager. And it's ironic that I'm doing better now financially than I ever did clinging on to your father for support all those years. He left me in debt when he died. There were no insurance policies—nothing. It's strange that my mom, your nonie, died not long after Dad and managed to leave us sisters a nice chunk of money. I don't know what I would have done without that. It got me back on my feet, and I'm ahead financially. Here I am, managing for myself. It's so easy; I can't believe how afraid of this I was."

After I hang up the phone, I wonder if that is all life is about—facing fear.

25

Where the Grass Is Greener

Getting ready for my trip to Ohio, I try not to pack anything that might look suspicious or set off that annoying beeper at the airport. I can't stand watching a stranger's hands rummaging through my underwear in front of a whole line of people who are all looking and inspecting as well. I pick a small, lightweight bag to carry on board. I pack precisely and efficiently, determined to take the greatest amount of stuff with the least amount of weight, since I'll be carrying it around with me. I pick clothes by the weight of the fabric—two pairs of silk panties instead of a single pair of cotton panties, light khaki pants instead of heavy denim jeans. I pack no shampoo or deodorant (my mother has all that) and no slippers, as socks will do. I'm proud of myself for keeping my bag as light as a feather.

I whiz through security at the airport, not setting off any beepers.

When I arrive at the airport in Columbus, Ohio, I see Uncle Darrell, Aunt Doris, and Mom waiting at the gate with open arms. I reach to hug my mother and scratch my hand on the buckle of my bag's strap. Aunt Doris slaps a Band-Aid on it before the blood has a chance to drip.

"Shoot, let me take that bag; it must be heavy," Uncle Darrell says. He comments on how light it is as he hangs it over his shoulder, and then he asks, "Do we have to stop by the baggage claim?"

I smile. "Oh no, I've got everything."

We walk in circles in the parking lot. No one can remember what section the car is in. We walk and talk, hoping something will look familiar. Finally, Uncle Darrell tells us to wait with the bag while he finds the car and drives it around to pick us up. "Shoot," we hear him saying. "I could have sworn it was row G—an orange G. Shoot."

On our drive along the highway, I appreciate Ohio's endless flatness. From the car window, I watch rows of trees, in limitless space, whiz down the highway. I listen to Aunt Doris and my mother talk about who got married, is growing, gave birth, moved, died, and so on.

I hear a click. It's Uncle Darrell slipping a tape into the player. He looks back at me, announcing, "This is my sister and me singing. It is the best one of about twenty tapes we did together." I wonder why my mother is making a face, until I hear the nasally, high-pitched duet screech out a religious song about finding a new home with the Lord, over and over, as if we don't get it the first time. Occasionally, an organ hits a few notes, and I think I hear a washboard as well.

My mother whispers, "He thinks he can sing, but he can't carry a tune in a bucket." On and on the music goes, with Uncle Darrell proudly describing the words they're singing. There's no need to describe them, but he wants to make sure we get the religious message. I open the window to let some of the screeching escape. Just as I'm thinking to myself, *Thank God the ride is only fifteen minutes*, bam—Uncle Darrell slams on his brakes.

He hits his hand on the steering wheel and yells, "Shoot! Can you believe this? Have you ever seen a traffic jam here? When was the last time you remember a backup on this highway at this hour?"

Aunt Doris, in a melodic, calming voice, replies, "Now, you just calm down, Darrell." She emphasizes his name sternly. "We are going to get there."

Uncle Darrell asks her to look up ahead to see what's holding us up. Aunt Doris's melodious voice continues. "You just don't pay any mind to it; that is what you're going to do. Have some patience." She looks back at my mother and me. "Well, this is just a lesson in patience, I tell you—a lesson in patience."

The shrill voices continue to sing from Uncle Darrell's tape: "I have a new home in the house of Jesus." My mother and I look at each other, gritting our teeth and rolling our eyes. Uncle Darrell decides to sing along with the nasally, shrill duet, penetrating our eardrums: "I have a new home in the house of Jesus."

In my mother's kitchen, we sit at her round colonial table in the simple chairs, leaving the captain's chair empty. The kitchen window looks out onto a small garden of flowers in a circle and a yard with trees. I have my hair tied in a ponytail because it's hot. My mother's hand reaches for my hair and combs through my ponytail from the elastic to the ends, saying, "God, your hair is thick."

I don't know why I'm so aware of the times when she touches me. It's because they are so few, I guess.

My mother lights a cigarette. The smoke she exhales fills the room with gray vapors. She reminisces sorrowfully. "Sometimes I think of what could have been; we had so many dreams. I wish I could go back to when my babies were all in diapers again. I remember the day I brought you home as if it was yesterday. The air was filled with the smell of the lilies of the valley, which had just come up.

"Your father and I promised each other we would give you children a better life than we had. He was so handsome, like a movie star. All he had, Mary Ellen, was his good looks. He could have had any woman he wanted—any woman. Instead, he hid under my skirt. I should have left him years ago, but I kept thinking things would change. Hanging on to dreams, I guess."

Streaks of sun through the window illuminate the dead silence, intensifying the aroma of smoke and sweat. I try to think of something funny to talk about to lighten the mood. I ask, "Ma, remember how much fun we had with me as the beautician, doing Aunt Sophie's makeup before her big party?"

"Oh yes," my mother says, puffing out smoke through her lips. "She had on a blue satin gown; her blonde hair was done up in French curls, piled on her head. You attached the false lashes, gluing her eyes shut, and her dusted eyelids and black eyeliner turned into tears running down her cheeks as she laughed!"

After a pause, she says, "Speaking of makeup, I got a new shade of nail polish—gold."

"Let's try it on," I say. "Come on. I'll put it on for you."

My mother stretches her hands out flat on the table, and we both look at them. I begin brushing the paint on her nails, and they become shiny, gold, and wet. I study her hands; already they are starting to look like Nonie's. Once young like Snow White's, they are beginning to swell at the joints. I see what my hands will look like at her age.

Her voice breaks my thoughts. "Dad hated the smell of nail polish. I could never put polish on when he was around."

"Michael's the same way," I say, continuing to polish her nails.

I know my mother wants to bring something up, but she can't. I look at her, leaving only one hand polished, and say, "Mom, you know, Dad did some terrible things to me when I was growing up."

"I know, Mary Ellen. He told me," she says, reaching her arms out to me. We hug each other. "Through no fault of your own," she says. She puts her arms around me. This is a moment I used to dream of as a child, when the abuse was going on, wanting so much to go to her and have her stop him and say it wasn't my fault. Now it doesn't matter that I didn't get it then. At this moment, age doesn't matter.

I listen to her confess what happened between them during my phone calls with him.

"I kept hearing him on the phone, and I couldn't understand what was going on, because he told me he was talking to you about a little problem. I began to worry, asking him why he couldn't tell me what it was about. 'What is it, Larry? What's wrong with her?' I asked. And then he said the strangest thing: 'I made an appointment with Ray's psychiatrist.' I asked him again, 'What's wrong with Mary Ellen?'

"'Oh, nothing,' he said. He kept saying it as if I was bothering him. I kept on him, asking, 'Nothing? What, Larry? It must be something.' He broke down and cried like a baby in my arms. I thought he was going to tell me you were dead. Instead, he told me what he did. I pushed him away from me and said, 'My only concern right now is Mary Ellen. I don't care about you!' I was so angry! I screamed at him, 'You kept me from my daughter all those years!' When he told me, I wanted to run to you, but I couldn't. I had to stay and love you from a distance. We were always so far away; he saw to that."

We stop hugging. Finished crying, she looks at me. I see the hurt in her eyes as she tells me more. "There were others, Mary Ellen. The walls were closing in on him, and he was running scared. Months before you called, his own niece accused him of abusing her. Like a fool, I stood by him. I couldn't believe it was true. But this time, when he told me about you, I said he wasn't going to hide under my skirt anymore and that I was going to divorce him.

"After all that went down, I couldn't believe seeing him out the window the next day, just lying on top of the picnic table, watching the clouds roll by, as if he hadn't a care in the world, and he already knew what he was going to do. We argued that afternoon, and I told him to go away and never come back. That's exactly what he did—got in his truck and drove away.

"When he wasn't back by the next morning, I called the police and told them we'd had an argument and that he was despondent and missing. I got the call telling me that they found his truck on the side of the road, and they went into the woods and found him hung. I blame myself for not figuring it out. With hindsight, I see that all the clues were there. I watched him throw a rope in the back of the truck before he sped away."

"Don't blame yourself. He did it to himself," I say, interrupting her from reliving the scene. I look at her hands. "Look, Ma; your nails are all smudged."

"It's all right, Mary Ellen," she says. "I feel beautiful inside for the first time in a long time. We should get some sleep now."

I call out from the bedroom, "Good night, Ma."

I hear her voice in the hallway: "Good night, Mary Ellen. I love you."

While I'm packing, my mother comes into the room with a gift for me wrapped in tissue. "It's a little something I got you for your birthday," she says. "I thought I'd give it to you now because it is too heavy to send by mail, and you can carry it back in your bag."

I remove the tissue from the package, exposing a heavy crystal paperweight with a cat's face etched in it. "Oh, Ma, what a thoughtful gift," I say. I hold it up to the light, saying, "You know how much I love cats! And it's made of such heavy crystal." I pack it in my bag with mixed emotions.

At the airport, Uncle Darrell lugs my bag to the gate and then hands it to me, saying, "Shoot. Am I getting old, or did this bag get heavier?"

I hug everyone and wave good-bye. I plop my bag onto the conveyer belt at airline security, and they ask me to step aside to identify an object in my bag. They zip open the bag, paw through my underwear in front of everyone, and then pull out the paperweight. Holding it to the light, one officer says to the other, "Nice crystal. Isn't it?"

"What's that—a cat's face?" the other says.

"Yep, it's a cat. Do you think it could be used as a weapon?"

"Nah, it's only a paperweight. Let her through."

26

Group Conscience

I decide my work is complete with Dr. Hansk, as I've devoured all aspects of the triangle between my mother, father, and me. What else could he possibly want from me? I tell him the whole story about being with my mother and tell him that she didn't know. I say that the rest is up to me. I can carry myself from here.

He looks at me as if to say there's still more work to be done, but I tell myself that therapy is expensive, and secretly, I resent going through so much and paying such a high price for the cure.

Dr. Hansk reminds me that his door is always open, and he's only a phone call away. He hands me a slip of paper, telling me that it is a list of Survivors of Incest Anonymous groups in my area. It's a twelve-step program that can be helpful. It is free, and it is competition for him, he admits. He makes me promise to call the number and sit in on a few meetings.

I keep the paper, call for a list of meeting places, and find one in Greenwich Village near where I live. I am afraid a male pervert might sit next to me, so I make sure the list specifies "Women only."

I find the number of the building and walk right past the entrance, battling with my old friend fear, which is immobilizing me. Eventually, courage wins, and I walk in. I expect to see three old women sitting at a table and staring at me, singling me out and asking what I want. Instead, once inside the room, I feel immediately anonymous. I study the meeting room. It's a school hall with a rehearsal stage complete with a curtain and a piano off to one side. Fresh flowers in a vase sit atop the piano, making the room warm and inviting. The women seem like any group of women in the city, on the bus, at the post office, or at a lecture. They are mixed races, young and old, and dressed in various clothing, from suits to jeans. Some women are unfolding chairs, and they place them in a big circle. I pick a chair near the exit door. I whisper to the woman I'm sitting next to, "Is this an SIA meeting?"

She looks up and nods in a kind way, as if to say, "Yes, you are safe here."

I ask if I have to speak, and she says, "No, you can just listen." I feel comfortable and decide to stay for a while.

The meeting begins with the attendees passing around a sheet of paper that lists the twelve steps of the program. Each person reads a step. Anyone who doesn't want to speak passes the sheet along. After the twelve steps, it is quiet, and some women raise their hands. The moderator points to someone, and a timer keeps track of three minutes as she tells her memories of abuse. It's called a share, or sharing. I can't believe women trust each other enough to tell their most inner secrets and feelings to a room full of strangers with only one thing in common: we have all been victims of incest. Everyone's trust in the room is referred to as a group conscience, which is like a group feeling. It's hard to describe, but it's there, and it works. No one is allowed to ask questions or comment on what another person has just shared. It might be insightful, good, or bad, but it is what it is. One of the slogans is "Take what you need, and leave the rest." If anyone can identify with another's share, it will give her knowledge, helping her heal. If others don't agree or it's just a horrible story, we can listen to the next share, and maybe there will be something helpful there. The most important rules of all are the following: (1) survivors only, (2) no perpetrators, (3) women only, and (4) what's said here stays here.

Seeing incest through the eyes of other victims and identifying with a part of humanity that has been through similar abuse makes me realize that it's not only my problem but also society's problem. The victims are artists, writers, lawyers, cab drivers, secretaries, and more. They come from many different walks of life. There are homeless, poor, middle-class, and wealthy women here. I thought everyone would be shy like me, but I observe different personalities, from aggressive to timid, extroverts as well as introverts.

I'm astounded as I listen to many stories of sexual cruelty to children. The image of a perpetrator changes as well. The abuser can be a father or a mother. I also hear stories of nuns abusing girls and priests abusing boys. In the beginning, it is overwhelming to comprehend, but over time, I am no longer shocked.

A woman tells a story similar to mine, of finding the

courage to say no, but her story has a different ending. She was beaten and then raped for saying no. She tells her story in our circle of at least fifty women sitting in chairs. We have only our collective sighs to give her as comfort. However, when magnified fifty times, our sighs resonate into a powerful healing force—like tiny fish swarming together in the ocean to create the illusion of a fierce sea creature to scare away a predator.

I watch an amazing healing process unfold in others through their shares, yet I still don't have the courage to raise my hand and tell my story. There is a writing workshop afterward, in which the women are broken down into smaller clusters, and I join them. The workshop involves writing in a journal, and we take turns reading aloud segments of our writing.

I read, "I went to one-on-one talk therapy for many years, discussing my memories of abuse. My father committed suicide after I confronted him, and I sobbed. I cried for him at his funeral. No more. I cry for my inner child. From her earliest memories, she had to endure his selfishness and cope with his threat of rape disguised as lessons in love, warmth, and affection."

At the end of our meeting, we hold hands in a circle and say the Serenity Prayer. I feel a power of healing passing through our circle of clasped hands.

Maybe it is because the group is all women that I think more about my mother and the effects of what my father did to us. Many women whose fathers hurt them have come to terms with their fathers but can't forgive their mothers for not being there or protecting them.

"Where was my mother?" I hear that question time and again. I begin to ask it myself. *What about me? Where was my mother?* I start to doubt her story that she didn't know.

At night, the Serenity Prayer replaces the Our Father and Hail Mary before I fall asleep: "God, grant me the serenity to accept the things I cannot change, the courage to change the things I can, and the wisdom to know the difference."

I pick up the phone and call her. In the middle of a conversation about nothing, I say, "Mom, I can't believe you didn't know. You knew all along I was being abused, and you didn't do anything to protect me."

She's shaken and says, "As God is my witness, Mary Ellen, I never knew such a thing was going on under my own roof. You have a right to be angry but not at me."

"I can't believe you didn't know," I say angrily. "Unless you admit you knew, I'm never speaking to you again."

I don't know why I decided to call and say this, why dreams keep me up at night, or why all of a sudden I blasted her with my anger.

We are at a standstill. Time passes with neither of us willing to call the other. On Mother's Day, she calls me, crying because she got a card from every one of her children except me; she put all the cards on top of the television and then found a card she saved that I made her when I was thirteen and put it up there with everyone else's.

My heart is cold. I say, "You knew."

She says, "I can't believe you didn't send me a card. Are you trying to say I wasn't a good mother? You are wrong; I was a good mother. This card you made me when you were thirteen proves it. You did love me then. I am a good person who helps people. I hurt too, but no one seems to care about me. I was selected Outstanding Officer of the Year in 1985, and I was getting ahead, but instead, I had a husband who told me what he did and a son in a psychiatric hospital. When he told me what he did, I wanted to kill him and run to you. I couldn't do it—just couldn't."

"You didn't protect me," I say, and I hang the phone up. The standoff continues.

I'm an angry, raging, stubborn Taurus bull. Michael can't believe the way I'm acting. I expect him to be supportive of whatever I decide, just as he was with my father. He puts his hand on my shoulder, saying, "Mary, you only have one mother. You can't just write her off. She's not dead."

I tell him to mind his own business. Still angry, I say, "She's my mother, and I'll be mad at her if I want. Just mind your own business. It's between her and me."

My brother and sisters try to help me. I'm not used to this because I'm the oldest. They call me, trying to help, but I don't care anymore. I know my brother and sisters have a right to their memories and feelings about my mother and father. They don't want me to be angry with my mother, so they try their best to patch things up.

I am grateful that all my family members believe me. At SIA groups, many survivors say that once the secret of abuse is out, the survivors become outcasts—liars—and it's devastating to them. Letting the secret out causes havoc and devastation to families just as a volcano does to the earth, but it's not the victim's fault. I see my father as the core of the fire. His abusive acts, like molten lava, erupted and blasted through the surface. Eventually, the truth comes out.

That's what I feel my family is experiencing now. We are all trying to recover from a devastating explosion of the truth. Raymond firmly believes my mother never knew; however, even he never knew or suspected my father and was shocked when I told him everything. Melissa wisely says, "I love you both and hope you can work something out."

Rebecca makes me think by saying, "Just remember, she isn't the one who did it to you. When you were a girl, it was different for women then. There weren't that many places or alternatives to get away from their husbands. Today things are different, and you might look at it from the times we are in now."

Their comments hit a brick wall. "Well, thanks," I say, "but the fact that I missed the boat doesn't make me feel any better. As a mother, she should have protected her children."

I love Raymond, Rebecca, and Melissa, even with many years between us. We all want to be a family, now more than ever, since my father is gone. My anger toward my mother is stopping that, which somehow keeps my father in control of us—he is still keeping us apart from the grave. Yet anger toward my mom has taken over me, and it won't let go. I'm closed.

My mother calls me; her voice is a little shaky on

the phone. I think that she's finally coming around to admit that she knew and say she's sorry, but she doesn't. "I wanted to let you know, Mary Ellen, I'll be going to the hospital for an operation to have a gallstone removed. I haven't heard from you, 'cause I know you are mad at me, but I just wanted you to know I'm going into the hospital for my operation."

I think she is trying to soften me by playing the death card, and I say, "You know, Ma, this doesn't change anything. I'm still mad at you."

Her voice is quivering as she says, "Well, I'll be going now. Just wanted to let you know."

A memory surfaces in my mind of helping my mother make a bed. We are fluffing clean sheets over the mattress, and she tells me Nonie's belief about marriage: "You made your bed; now lie in it." There was no divorce. A husband was a husband for life; if he was a mistake, she had to live with him.

I weaken before she hangs up, and I say, "You know, being mad at you doesn't mean I don't love you."

"Really?" she says with a cheerful voice.

Hearing her voice and spirits lift, I soften. "Let's have a truce until you come back from your operation."

"Okay, Mary Ellen," she says happily.

I wish her good luck. She says good-bye. We both hurry to hang up, not wanting to start an argument.

Neither of us says, "I love you."

Rebecca calls me in the morning to report that my mother went in for the operation at eight o'clock and that the operation is still going on. She says she will call me as soon as the operation is over. She gives me the telephone number of Mom's hospital room in case I want to call her while she recuperates.

As the day goes on, I begin to worry. *What if she dies?* It could happen. People never come out of the anesthesia sometimes. I know she smokes and is getting older. Now I am sure she is going to die, and I won't get a chance to say, "I love you." She will go away and never come back, as my father did.

I think, *Why can't I be angry for once without death as a consequence?*

At the end of the day, all my anger dissolves. I can't take the uncertainty anymore and dial the number to my mother's hospital room. Despite all the anger and hate and all that's come and gone between us, I love my mother and want to tell her so. I listen to each ring of the phone, waiting for her voice, and my heart races.

I hear the phone being picked up, a hand fumbling with it. I cry out, "I love you, Ma!"

"Hello?" an old man's quivering, anesthetized voice squawks. "Hello? Hello?"

"Oh, um, is Muffy Sinclair there?" I ask, feeling my face get red hot from embarrassment. I hear the receiver being put down and someone picking it up. A woman identifies herself as a nurse and wants to know who I'm looking for. "Muffy Sinclair," I say quietly. The nurse tells me she was released half an hour ago. I should have remembered that my mother, just like Nonie, hates hospitals because she can't stand the uncomfortable beds, so she will get her clothes on and sneak out if they don't release her.

Becky calls me no more than ten minutes later to tell me Mom is home and fine. She goes over all the gory details of how the doctor came out after the operation with a glass jar filled with clear liquid and the stone bouncing up and down and showed it to her. "Oh man, what an ugly thing it is! It looks like a greasy black peach pit," she says.

"Shit. She isn't going to keep it, is she?" I ask, appalled at the thought.

"Hell yeah, she is!" Becky laughs. "Old people love that stuff. They keep it on the mantel to show their friends."

"Shit," I say again. We laugh nervously, relieved that she's fine.

"Want to say hi to Melissa? She's here," Becky says.

"Hi, Missy," I say.

Missy repeats the news. "Mom's fine! Good news! Love ya."

My sisters keep me informed about my mother. She thinks I didn't call, and I don't care, but I know she's alive and kicking, sneaking out of the hospital early because those beds are so damn uncomfortable.

I was mad at her, and she took it. Her operation is over, and she's sprung back to life and taken her mantelpiece home.

Our truce is over. We are at a strange standstill about who, if anyone, will break down and call first.

27

Winter Chestnuts

Thanksgiving comes, and we still haven't spoken. Christmas approaches, when everyone wants to be part of a family, especially with snow falling and Christmas songs in the air. We have fallen into our old pattern of loving each other from a distance.

I tell myself to go ahead and call. *Yes, maybe.* Then I get mad. *No, why should I? I am always the first to break the ice; it's all been up to me in the past.* My *father couldn't have brought things up to me first, could he? Maybe gotten help and then helped me? No! My mother couldn't have come to me first, could she?* It's an endless cycle, a bottomless pit that I'm tired of. *What's the use?*

She calls me.

I hear, "Mary Ellen, I miss you."

I say, "I miss you too, Ma. So much anger got a hold of me from when I was growing up; I had to put it on someone. I'm not mad anymore."

I hear her crying on the other end of the phone as she says, "Christmas is only a few weeks away, and I had to call you. A young woman was admitted to prison for life for killing her husband. She shot him dead when she found him in bed, abusing their little girl. She told me about it in the intake room at the prison. I was supposed to search her the way I do everyone when they first come in. I have done it a thousand times. But there she was, shivering and naked and sobbing when she finished telling me her story. She knew she killed him with the first shot but just kept pumping the bullets into him, not able to stop. I'm supposed to be tough and not get involved, but I didn't care; I hugged her anyway." My mother's still sobbing. "Mary Ellen, I hugged her the way I wanted to hug you, the way I wanted to say I'm sorry to you. I pretended she was you, Mary Ellen. I had to call you. Please don't stay mad at me forever. You can't be mad at me forever."

I'm crying now. Christmas music is playing on the radio, and snow is falling outside the window. I tell her, "It's just that with all the hurt I suffered, neither you nor Dad ever said, 'I'm sorry.' That's all. Just 'I'm sorry'—not you or Dad."

"Well, I am sorry, Mary Ellen," she sobs, catching her breath before continuing strongly. "If I didn't know, I should have known; it was my responsibility as your mother. Please know that I am sorry. That's all I have to give."

There is genuine anger in her voice at herself when she says, "I should have known."

I tell her, "It's all right, Mom. Apology accepted," as I watch the snow fall silently out my window.

"I want to see you, Mary Ellen," she says. "When can I see you?"

"As soon as you want," I say. "How about spending Christmas in New York with Michael and me?"

Her voice sounds happy as she says, "I will be there."

At the airport, I worry, watching each person come through the door, wondering where my mother is. I'm sure she's nervous about being in the middle of a big airport and not being able to find a familiar face waiting for her. Finally, I spot her. She's the last one off the plane. "There she is!" I call out. "Mom, here we are." She stands still, surrounded by an aura of accomplishment, having traveled alone for the first time. She is holding two packages wrapped in brown paper with twine wrapped around them. She hands one to each of us, saying, "One for you and one for Michael—a little something."

I notice right away that she is a new woman who looks beautiful from head to toe. "Mom, you lost weight," I say, excited for her.

She spins around, twirling her skirt. "It's a Liz Claiborne, size eight."

Michael gives her a wolf whistle, and she gets embarrassed. We walk, giggling like two schoolgirls, down the airport corridor. Her green eyes meet mine. *Green?* I ask, "Ma, don't you have brown eyes like me?"

"Contacts," she says with a wink. "They're aqua. Do you like the color?"

"Like them? I love them!" I say. When she says the word *contacts*, I notice big white movie-star teeth. "Mom, your teeth aren't tiny anymore."

"Bonding," she says through a wide smile, as if posing for a toothpaste commercial.

Her nails are manicured and polished pink. I am proud

of her. I haven't seen my mother this full of life and energy or care so much about her appearance since I was a little girl.

Michael tells her that we are going to a great little Italian restaurant later on. "But first, let's go to Rockefeller Center and see the tree and the lights and the ice skaters. It wouldn't be Christmas without that. Are you too tired to go?"

My mother bubbles with excitement. "I'm ready to go! I just love the hustle and bustle of the city."

It is snowing as we weave our way through the crowd, holding hands, forming a human chain so that we can't get separated from each other. We settle into a good spot with a view of the skaters below and marvel at the Christmas tree towering above. My mother says, "It must cost a fortune for the city to keep that lit. I hope it's not the system where when one bulb blows out, they all go out. Can you imagine?"

On our walk back to the car, I notice my mother rubbing her hands to stay warm. "Mom, where are your gloves?"

"Oh, I forgot them," she says, shrugging.

We walk by rows of vendors until my mother stops in front of an old man roasting chestnuts. His dark eyes twinkle as he shakes a basket of nuts over charcoal embers. Mom reminisces out loud. "Do you know how long it's been since I had a roasted chestnut? Let's get some to keep our hands warm on the walk home." My mother holds out cupped hands, and he places a bag of warm chestnuts into them, wearing worn wool gloves with the fingertips cut away.

Walking to the car, we take turns cracking them open—one for her and one for me. They taste delicious dissolving on my tongue.

We have a good time together. We both realize we can't make up for lost time in one visit, but we are free from the hold my father had on us. Now that he is gone, we try hard to be close and get to know each other. It's odd because it's like what happens when a mother gives her daughter up for adoption and doesn't see her for twenty years, yet we were in the same house every day.

We both gave each other up emotionally long ago, held under the thumb of an illusion of a man—my father and her husband.

When the illusion disappeared, we were free to love each other.

28
Autumn

My mother and I have come to know each other and put the past behind us. She still lives in Marysville, Ohio. At age seventy-four, she enjoys the luxury of decorating her home and paying attention to all the details she didn't have time for while she was working. She doesn't date much and plays cards with friends and relatives on the weekends.

It's been sixteen years since my father's funeral. We never talk about him or mention his name. It's as if he never existed. She called me once, on his birthday, to tell me she went to his grave to stomp on it.

She's finally stopped smoking after a lifetime of trying to quit. "I'm on a fixed income now, you know. I just couldn't stand spending the damn money on those cancer sticks anymore," she says. It's long overdue because her health is deteriorating. She can't breathe after walking up a few steps. Whenever there's a family crisis, her heart beats irregularly. She gets chest pains and is rushed to the hospital. They give her a series of tests and send her home with medicine to regulate her heartbeat. Family problems still come and go, and she survives.

This morning, we talk about her upcoming visit, and she tells me she's been bragging to all her friends about coming to New York and has bought new outfits for the trip, but she can't do as much running around as she used to.

My mother has a romanticized notion of what I do. She thinks I'm dedicated to my work, but it's more of a compulsion to create. If I stop making art, I feel as if a part of me is missing.

I used to think that the epitome of being a successful artist would be being like Picasso, who scribbled on a napkin in a café and got an absurd amount of money for it. I've matured. While commanding a lot of money for one's work is evidence of fame, this alone does not define what art is. It's like the debate about what came first, the chicken or the egg. I follow my heart, knowing one thing about art: it's not instant gratification. Over the years, several people have become collectors of my artwork. While it's happening, it doesn't seem like much, but with hindsight, making art becomes a rewarding personal accomplishment, and then getting paid happens. It becomes my job.

It's challenging to answer people's questions.

"What do you do?"

"I'm an artist."

"Are you a painter?"

"No, my medium is fabric and thread."

"Like sculpture? Soft shapes?"

"Not exactly."

"Then what do they look like?"

"I stitch thread and layer fabric, recreating illusions of ordinary objects, like a paper coffee cup, a lunch bag, a box of pencils, a cigar box, or a matchbook."

"Why?"

"Because it makes the viewer take a second look at the simplest things in life, which are the ones we most often overlook."

"How much time does it take for each piece?"

"That varies. I never keep track of time, except for commissions with a deadline. Otherwise, I will put a work away for six months and work on something else, completing it in a few days, a week, or a month or two."

"Your stuff sounds interesting. Where's your next exhibit?"

"OK Harris on West Broadway."

"And your work—does it sell? Do you make money at it?"

"Yes," I can answer proudly, catching people off guard.

"Rough life, eh? No health insurance, I suppose."

"I pay for it on my own."

"Any retirement—401(k)?"

"Cashed it in for a down payment on our loft in the city."

I've watched our neighborhood change dramatically. It seems as if every square inch of space has been renovated over the last twenty years. When we first moved here, the streets were dark and deserted at night. I remember a cabbie dropping me off and warning me not to walk too close to the vacant corner lot. I asked him why, because I know only harmless winos and mentally ill people unable to take their medication are there. He looked me in the eye, pointed his finger at me, and said in a serious tone, "A wino will never hurt you, but a junkie will kill you for a dime."

There was a dilapidated gray building that looked vacant, except at night, when red lights from inside illuminated through drawn curtains. Lo and behold, it got raided and became a McDonald's. A lot of SoHo art galleries moved here to the West Side. There was scaffolding around two corner buildings—for forever, it seemed—creating a great mystery as to what was going to be there. A huge Barnes and Noble appeared, complete with a coffee shop and big, fluffy couches to sit on. The new store made the streets much safer in the evenings. Now many people walk on the street, and the store is open until eleven o'clock every night. The windows shed light on the deserted corner lot. It is still overgrown with weeds and scrub trees, and the homeless still sleep there on makeshift beds of cardboard under the stars.

One spring morning, just as the ground thawed, a bulldozer arrived in the lot with a surprise attack on the residents, breaking up their cardboard homes and disposing of their meager belongings in a Dumpster. The noises of digging, dump trucks, and jackhammers shook the neighborhood for months as construction crews created a luxury high-rise building. Now successful people with jobs and money live there, and they pay extra for the penthouses that guarantee a view the homeless people once enjoyed for free. Our six-story building stands among a few others as a quaint remnant of an older New York, with each floor a loft. We are surrounded by new higher buildings, big-name department stores, restaurants, specialty shops, cafés, parking garages, and health clubs complete with decks and swimming pools. Toward Fifth Avenue, where Galaxy Pizza used to be, there is now a diamond store.

My mother is visiting, and she is no trouble at all. Bless her heart. I do love her.

She comes into the room. "Boy, it was hot and noisy last night."

"Sorry, Mom. Didn't the sound machine help you sleep? It emits white noise to mask other sounds."

"So that's what that noise was that sounded like wind blowing all night? I was having nightmares about freezing to death, so I pulled the covers up over me even though I was sweating. The wind, or white noise or whatever you call it, did not cover up the fire truck siren or the dog next door howling to it. Then a motorcycle went by with the muffler so loud that the vibrations set off the alarms on all the parked cars on the street. Did you two sleep through all that?"

Mike laughs, saying, "That wasn't a bad night. We've heard worse. Once, I heard gun shots, and I looked out the window and saw a person dead on the street with ambulances and police around him."

"Oh my God!" My mother gasps. "Is it safe to walk the streets?"

"Of course. You've seen what the day is like, but it's different at three o'clock in the morning, when the clubs are getting out."

It's only day two.

Are there inseparable mothers and daughters with perfect pasts who completely enjoy their time together? It's always a work in progress for my mother and me. She's only been here for two days and has developed a habit of following me around the house everywhere I go, tiptoeing in an effort to be quiet and not disturb me. It's as if she's sneaking up on me. I turn around, and there is my shadow, saying, "I love you, Mary Ellen," hoping for an "I love you" in return.

Instead, I'm struck by how much shorter she's getting—she's shrinking. I wonder if this is what I have to look forward to. I can't afford it, not even half an inch. I'd better start doubling up on my calcium pills. My thoughts consume me, and the moment is gone. It's too late to hug her and say, "I love you." My face is red. *Why am I such a jerk?* I realize that's why I've come to love her—because she'll give me another chance again and again.

I take her to the flea market, and we browse for treasures in a lot full of junk. It's obvious we don't know what we are looking for, because everything's a possible candidate. We have no criteria for putting anything back on the table except for my mother's constant complaint: "Everything is so expensive in New York, even junk."

There's so much activity on the streets that it's always an interesting day. We laugh together. Mom is amazed at the get-ups some people have the guts to wear. By now, I'm used to it, but for her, it's like watching a parade. In front of us, a man is walking a tiny dog that prances proudly down the street with a fluffy tail. I tell my mother I think it's a Pomeranian, when, before our eyes, the little dog quickly lifts its leg and pees on an oil painting that is for sale and leaning on a fence. It happens so fast that no one else sees it except my mother and me. We are aghast with our mouths open, until our eyes meet, and we laugh uncontrollably. She laughs so hard that she starts gasping for breath, as if she's choking. I pat her on the back, and she leans more into her walker for balance. She doesn't have much stamina. I make light of it, saying, "I guess the dog doesn't like the painting. I pity the person who buys it, takes it home, and puts it on the wall. Do you think you can make it to the Bed, Bath, and Beyond store? We can sit and have lunch in their cafeteria." She nods, smiling.

While we eat, she says she wishes she could walk around more, because there's so much interesting stuff in the store. "Look, Ma, at all those motorized shopping carts stacked in a row for just such an occasion." She tries one out and loves it. Before I know it, she's buzzing up and down the aisles with people dashing out of her way. There is only one scary incident, when she doesn't realize the cart is in reverse. Luckily, nothing is broken.

In the evening, we unload our shopping bags and begin preparing an Italian dinner together. The TV's on, and I can hear the laugh track from a sitcom. My mother tells Michael about the flea market we've been to and the painting a dog squirted with pee. We talk while organizing cooking ingredients, and I show off my new pans, holding one up to reflect the light. “Michael and I treated ourselves to these for our wedding anniversary.”

My mother smiles for us. “Oh, those must have been expensive, but what the hell? You’ve gotten your money’s worth out of your old pots. You’ve had them ever since you got married. I hope the new ones have a lifetime guarantee, especially with the glass tops.”

I laugh. “A lifetime is an arbitrary guarantee, don’t you think? What if I got hit by a bus a year from now?”

Her lips form a crooked grin while she contemplates what I said as she stirs the bubbling sauce and breathes in the vapors as the onions brown. “You can’t get this pure olive oil in Ohio. Mmm, mmm, good,” my mother says as she tastes from one pot to the next.

I read the instructions out loud on how to break in the pans. “It says not to stir with a metal spoon, because it scratches the bottom of the pans.”

She stops stirring with the metal spoon and says guiltily, “I hope I didn’t scratch it too badly.”

“Oh, we had to break them in,” I say. I think to myself that long after she’s gone, the scratches will be a reminder of this time in the kitchen with smells of tomato sauce, salami, garlic, cheese, and percolating coffee.

Mike is working on the computer, and the cat is asleep on his lap. I feel as if we’re a scene of a happy family portrayed in a dollhouse.

Midweek—Wednesday

I've forgotten what a snooper she is. After leaving her alone in my studio, I catch her. I come in, and she quickly shoves my green notebook into the desk drawer and slams it shut. What a guilty smile she has. She begins talking up a storm and shuffling papers around as subterfuge. The words *secret ingredients* on the notebook cover probably aroused her curiosity. The notebook is a collection of my favorite recipes. It is an old habit of hers, searching for clues. This knowledge must have been in my subconscious while I was cleaning and preparing for her visit, because I hid all my personal things from her. I hid the manuscript that developed from my writing workshops at Survivors of Incest Anonymous, with secrets of our family from my life growing up. When I look up at it amid my books in a stationery box with scotch-taped edges, I remember losing sleep over whether or not to let her read it. I thought about hiding it someplace obvious, such as where she found my notebook. That way, she would discover it on her own and decide whether or not to read on or talk about it.

It's ironic because early on, when we were getting to know each other, I thought we were never going to find common ground. Nothing seemed to click when we talked. We stuck with small talk about our family, her house, and what's going on in the world. Then I mentioned a book I was reading that she got excited about, so I sent it to her. Then she sent me a book of hers that she loved. After that, we were into each other's thoughts. I remembered all the books she read to me as a child and recalled that she read the whole newspaper from front to back every day. Reading stories is a long-forgotten thread to happy memories between us—of quiet times alone when my father wasn't home.

I find myself wondering if she would feel proud or ashamed of the way I told our family's innermost secrets and what we did with the cards we were dealt. Would she find what my father did to me not as bad as or worse than what she's imagined all these years? She's never asked about what she never knew but says she should have known. My intuition says to let it be. It's all cried out, and our relationship moves forward. I'm not looking back. I can't take the chance it would make her heart start to palpitate.

She asks me what I'm thinking, but I don't tell her. Now she is like the child, and I'm the adult, hiding things from her for her own good—way up on top, where she can never climb in her condition. I begin to wonder if she has already found my manuscript, read it, and put it back.

Thinking fast, I reach for a book with a red cover and say, "Oh, I was just looking for a good book for you to read while you're here. This one is really good; it's *Phantom of the Opera*."

"We just saw that last night. Weren't the costumes and the music great? Let's buy the sound track tomorrow," she says.

"Then you will like this book, Mom, because there are so many versions of how his face got that way. In this one—"

"Stop! Don't tell me any more," she says. "I can't stand knowing the end until I read the whole book. If I don't finish it here, I'll bring it back with me, and then I'll have something to read on the plane. I'll call you when I get to the end."

The end of the week arrives.

Last night, the clubs were closed, so the streets were quiet, and we got a good night's sleep. My cat sticks his paws in the printer and pushes the cartridge, jamming it so that it continually beeps. With one eye open, I read the clock; it's seven in the morning. I'm up, and everyone else is asleep except for the cat munching at his bowl of food. I decide to go out and get some fresh bagels for breakfast. The street is quiet, and the air is damp. A homeless person on the corner talks to himself about the theory of relativity. Vendors are setting up their carts for the day. I pass the familiar fruit vendor. He's a plump Indian man with a red beard whose head bobs up and down as he says, "Taste the sweetness. The oranges are the best today. I give you extra—throw in two extra—if you buy a dozen." He holds out his hand with red fingernails, offering me a slice of orange to taste. I cringe, shaking my head, because I see the rusty razor blade he's slicing into the fruit.

Walking toward the diner, I pass the home for the blind, and I overhear two men talking.

"It sure smells like rain today."

"Yep, smells like it's gonna rain."

Their simple conversation touches me, giving the rain a whole new dimension.

Monday

"Today is Monday, isn't it, Mike?" my mother asks with a sigh. "It seems like I just got here, and it's time to go home. I'll miss you both. I had such a good time."

She holds both of our hands, sending a prayer to God, asking him to bless us with children. She still believes in miracles.

Mike says he always loves having her and insists she's no trouble at all. It's true, although old habits and annoyances add up by the end of the week, and as much as my mother and I have come to enjoy each other's company, we both look forward to getting back to our own private lives. She heads back to Ohio with plenty of bragging ammunition—in the form of stories and photographs—about her stay in New York City with her daughter, the artist.

Autumn isn't far away, and we agree that fall will be a good time for me to visit her. It will be a nice change of scenery from the city, especially with the foliage and all.

Walking through the airport was too hard for her, and I had to get her a wheelchair. I wonder how many more trips she will be able to make.

29 Wing and a Prayer

"What is going on?" I ask myself, half asleep. I'm awakened in the dark by our lights going on and off. "Is that you, Michael?"

"I'm right here next to you," he says. "Someone must be in the house."

Scared, we look toward the doorway—and are shocked to see our cat atop a chair under the light switch, using his paw to push the dimmer up and down. We laugh in relief. Our cat never stops inventing new ways to get us up when he's hungry.

We slip comfortably into our Sunday morning routine: feed the cat (immediately), put the water on to boil, and relax in front of the television. I sip tea and watch a blonde woman with a tan body exercise, lifting her thighs effortlessly in the air, smiling all the while.

"Good cup of coffee this morning," Mike says.

"Come on. That's right. You can do it. Lift! Lift!" The woman on TV beckons us to get up and join in. Her teeth sparkle through a perky grin. We are mesmerized by her body movements and the tropical surroundings of palm trees and a vast ocean.

Mike wraps his housecoat around him. "It's getting chilly, isn't it? Is she gaining weight, or has she just got big hips?"

I sip and analyze. "They are kind of big for a physical fitness instructor, but they are probably solid muscle. I'm going to join a gym, get in shape, and take a yoga class or swim."

On Sunday mornings, I call my mom to say hello. The phone rings for a long time, but I know it takes her a while to walk to it.

"Hi, Mom. It's me."

My mother answers, out of breath. "Hello, my darling daughter. It's a beautiful day here."

I tell her about a teapot I bought at the flea market and then ask how her doctor's appointment went last week. It takes her awhile to answer, and she doesn't have good news.

"It's my heart. The walls in my heart have always been thicker than an average heart. It's a birth defect. Well, now it turns out I have some kind of deposit making the walls even thicker, so my heart is hardly pumping any blood. It's why I have no energy and trouble breathing."

"What kind of deposits? Where are they? Can't they clean them out?"

"My doctor says I should have an operation, but I only have a forty-five percent chance of surviving. Without the operation, he gives me about six months to two years. I'm not gonna let them cut me up no more. I'm tired of it. I want to live with my heart the way it is and enjoy whatever time I have left without suffering in pain, recovering from surgery. I just want to sit in the yard with my children and grandchildren, watching the leaves fall."

"Is there any other less invasive treatment that can be done, Mom?"

"Yes, I'm going in for a procedure to inject liquid into my veins that should unblock some of the deposits clogging them."

"Let me call your doctor and have him explain what's going on. Something is getting lost in the translation of you telling me what the doctor said. How can he give you a time frame like that? Six months to two years? What does that mean? No one can predict how many more beats are left in anyone's heart. You know, Mom, just by quitting smoking, you've added years to your life. Aren't you glad you quit?"

"Oh God, I can't stand the smell of cigarette smoke anymore. For that matter, I can't stand the taste of food. I'm losing weight, which I wanted to do, but not this way."

I suspect no one wants to say what my mother has already decided. There's nothing more that can be done; they'll leave her alone and let her heart beat as long as it can.

I change the subject and ask about her new house. "How do you like everything all on one level?"

Her voice gets excited now. "Oh, I love this place. It's just what I wanted, with plenty of space and no stairs to climb anymore. It's working out great with Melissa, Josh, and Beth. With four bedrooms, we all have our privacy. I try not to burden Melissa too much. God, it's like she has another kid here, but she never complains about taking care of me. She started a new job working for 911 in the police department on the third shift. At least I can be of some help by being here with the kids at night. I hope this isn't all too much pressure on her with a stressful job and all. I qualify for Meals on Wheels, and they deliver meals right to my door. It's a big help for everyone. I worked hard my whole life, and I don't feel guilty about this benefit."

"As soon as I get a flight number, I'll call. Love you, Mom."

"Love you too, Mary Ellen. Good-bye."

I find a million little things to do before I dial the airlines to order my ticket to Ohio. Subconsciously, I must be putting my visit off. When the clerk asks me for time slots, I pick dates toward the end of September and then decide to go two weeks earlier.

The airplane is packed, and I'm assigned a seat near the window overlooking the wing. I stare down its long, lonely expanse, thinking of the episode of the television program *The Twilight Zone* in which a passenger sees a monster on the wing and no one else does.

Partway into the flight, we hear loud popping sounds coming from the belly of the airplane. I think it must be turbulence, but where is the captain's cool, calm voice? He should be telling the passengers what we are experiencing, saying there is nothing to worry about, and advising us to fasten our seat belts strictly for precaution. There it goes again, louder. *Plop. Putt. Sputter.* It sounds like noisy pans clanging. We all stare at each other while waiting for the cool voice of the captain. The man next to me looks up from his laptop, saying, "I fly a lot and have never heard anything like that before."

Our captain's voice finally breaks the silence: "Ladies and gentlemen, you may have heard some noise a few minutes ago; there's no need for alarm. We lost our right engine, and we will make an emergency landing in Cincinnati. The left engine is running fine. You should feel no difference in the landing, although emergency vehicles will be standing by at the edges of the runway as a precautionary measure."

People begin buckling up before the captain gets a chance to request it. I think, *We are coming in on a wing and a prayer*, as if I'm on a warplane in the movie *Memphis Belle*.

We land with everyone jerking forward sharply. Just like that, all the anticipation is over. Sitting at the airport, we all fill out cards with our opinions on what happened. A new airplane arrives to take us to Columbus, Ohio.

When I reach the airport, Melissa is there waiting. On the drive home, we talk about her new job and her children, and we have a good laugh over the wing-and-a-prayer story.

When I first see my mother, I realize she hasn't been out of bed much. Her room looks new and has a frilly, feminine feel. The walls are pale lavender with a border of lilacs, but the air has a medicinal smell, like a hospital.

I tell her how much I love the new house. "It's hot in here, though, Mom. Would you like me to open the windows a crack for a little cross breeze?"

"Oh no," she says. "I'm ice cold, and I have to be careful not to catch pneumonia again. I got so sick last time."

"Sure, Mom, you rest now. I'll see you in the morning."

Beth shows me her room, where I will be sleeping. She reminds me of Melissa as a little girl. She even has the same haircut Mom gave us: shoulder-length curls with little bangs clipped short in the front. She shows me her snake in an aquarium. "Don't worry," she says, speaking as articulately as an adult. "The snake can't escape because I put a rock on the lid." I notice plastic dinosaurs everywhere, and we move on to her box of live crickets. She says, "I have the most crickets of anyone in the neighborhood. They are in this box with the holes punched on top for air."

Falling asleep to silence is a luxury. I relax, breathing in deeply and savoring the quiet. Subconsciously, I wait for a sound, such as a screen door closing or a car passing, to disturb me, but there is nothing. Faintly, the sound of a cricket begins to lull me to sleep. I breathe in softly and then exhale, relaxing into sleep. I hear another cricket and then another and another. The sound is becoming unbearably louder as a horde of angry crickets rub their legs together all at once, trapped in the box on Beth's bureau. Their screeching sounds like the background music in a science fiction movie that warns everyone that the monster is approaching. I'll go insane if I have to listen to this all night. I grab the box, take it down to the end of the hall, and put it next to their dog, Grommet, who is snoring.

In the morning, my mother makes an effort to be more active. She gets dressed, puts her makeup on, and comes into the parlor with the help of a walker. Exhausted from these small movements, she sits to catch her breath. She shows me her driver's license, proudly saying, "It's been renewed. It took every ounce of energy I had to stand in line at the registry with just my cane. They would never have renewed it if they saw my walker. Even though I'll probably never drive again, I didn't want to lose my license. It's my independence."

We go over a list of projects to do that she's written on the back of a brown paper lunch bag in wobbly handprint:

1) Get a handicapped sticker for the car at the registry.
2) Get the car to Bob Chapman Ford to be winterized—the tires need to be balanced; the left tire keeps going flat.
3) Hank is coming to cut the grass—remind him of weeds and where the bulbs are.
4) Hang pictures in the living room and bedroom.
5) Fix the broken handle on the toilet.
6) Check the gutters for clogs.

"Look at how crooked those drapes are; I wish we could hang them straight."

I tell her we will start knocking things off the list when I get back from driving Josh and Beth to school. To my surprise, she wants to come with us for the drive, saying she can show me how to get there.

We all sit in the car in the school parking lot, waiting for eight o'clock, when the doors open. I look above to my left and notice that the sun and moon are out at the same time. "Look, everyone. Look at that!" We are astonished. I say that it probably happens a lot, but I have never noticed it.

"Me either," Beth says, causing my mother and me to laugh.

I notice my mother's cheeks are pink. Her color is coming back. She seems happier when she gets out of the house a bit.

At night, we get a lot of company: nieces, nephews, and cousins. Uncle Darrell and Aunt Doris stop by. It hasn't been easy for Aunt Doris to take care of Uncle Darrell, who is developing Alzheimer's disease. She pulls me aside and tells me to say to him, "Later on, Darrell," when he asks if anyone wants to hear him sing an old country church song. The minute she finishes speaking, Uncle Darrell pulls out a paper from his pocket, sings, and then sits down. He stands up to start the whole thing over again, and Aunt Doris winks to us while saying to him, "Later on, Darrell."

"God bless her little heart" is what everyone says about my aunt Doris. "She's got the patience of a saint." It's true. I feel bad for Uncle Darrell because he doesn't know what's happening to him. It's sad to see him clinging to the last thing that meant so much to him: singing.

By the end of the week, we have finished most of our projects, and we enjoy just sitting in the yard, watching Beth capture grasshoppers.

My mother asks me to get a black briefcase from her bedroom closet, on the third shelf to the left. I bring it out, and she tells me it contains all her important papers. She shuffles through the plastic tab dividers, reading what's filed behind them: the house papers, her birth certificate, her Social Security card, and her will. She tells me to keep the folder in case anything happens to her. She tells me

I'm the executor because I'm the oldest. "Not because I love you more than the rest. I love all you kids exactly the same. Don't fight over anything; just divide everything equally four ways. What could be fairer than that?" The last tab is marked "Burial plots." She says, "Your father and I bought four plots a long time ago, and they are already paid for. The receipt is in there."

I know my father is in one plot and wonder if she wants to be buried next to him after all that's gone down. She's been mad at him all these years. Embarrassed, I ask her, "Do you want to be buried next to Dad?" I don't know what to expect, tears or a long silence.

She doesn't hesitate. "Hell yeah, I paid for it." She's nonchalant about it, waving her hand in the air, saying, "It doesn't matter." But I catch a glimpse of "It does matter, but I don't want you to know" in her eyes.

We sit in the living room, waiting for my ride to take me to the airport. "I hope I didn't wear you out with all the running around and shopping, Mom," I say.

"Hell no," she says. "I needed to get out. I had a good time." We both look at the crooked curtains.

"We just ran out of time," I say, "but we got a lot crossed off our list. Didn't that handicapped sticker come in handy at the supermarket?" She nods, smiling.

We watch a van pull into the driveway, and my mother says, "That must be your ride. Don't forget anything. Have you got your ticket? Your cell phone? Money? Don't forget to call me when you get home so I'll know you're safe." She promises to take it easy, eat more, and not worry about anything.

As I begin to rush out, I hear her say, "What does worrying change anyway?" and then "I love you, Mary Ellen."

I turn around, reach for her outstretched arms for the first time without hesitation, and hug her until she lets go. I look into her eyes, which are magnified by her glasses. She looks worried. "I love you, Mom. Good-bye."

Walking through the Columbus airport, I wonder why traveling isn't more futuristic. People are using cell phones and sitting with laptop computers, but it seems gray and ordinary without the ambiance of what I imagined the twenty-first century to be. People should be dressed in slick fabrics and sparkling hats, clicking their heels on polished acrylic floors that expand into long white corridors and zipping in and out of time zones.

We are flying above the storm clouds in a cool blue atmosphere that would be serene if not for the pressure in my ears, which makes floating conversations sound like bees buzzing. Tired of studying the sky through the small, circular window, I begin to read my book. Half asleep, I mark my place with my airline ticket stub before closing the book. I imagine more things that should have happened by now, since we are here in the future. *They should have had the cabin-pressure problem solved by now so that my ears wouldn't hurt, and the plane should be able to travel faster, shouldn't it?* A stewardess's disgruntled voice interrupts my thoughts, asking what I want to drink. An assistant follows behind her, throwing packages of peanuts onto our trays. It's a far cry from the film *2001: A Space Odyssey*, in which the stewardesses float around in white suits with egg-shaped hats and place space-age pills marked "Turkey sandwich," "Broccoli," and "Ice cream" daintily on trays.

I feel the pressure in my ears as the airplane descends.

I watch the wing slice through the clouds as the skyline of New York City appears below. The captain announces, "Ladies and gentlemen, we would like to thank you for flying with us. The weather in New York is partly cloudy or partly sunny, depending on how you look at life." He chuckles. "On behalf of myself and the flight crew, I would like to thank you for flying with Continental Airlines. Have a safe and pleasant trip."

On the bus ride home, I see my stop through the foggy window. The front of the deli appears to be filled with dots of colors glowing in the mist, but as I get closer, they come into focus as flowers filling the storefront. I wait under the awning of the deli amid the flowers, in a temporary oasis from the rain. A man's song of "Umbreylahs! Umbreylahs!" cuts through the wet air. His rough hand appears in front of me, popping an umbrella open above my head. I look into the salesman's face, and he says, "Three dollah." Once paid, he grins and disappears down the street, singing his umbrella song.

There's no better feeling than coming home to Michael's hug, our cat waiting at the door, and the smell of soup bubbling on the stove. We talk about my trip and my mother.

I fall asleep listening to the sounds of cars passing on the wet road, but soon I wake to what sounds like the cat making the printer beep. I realize it's the phone ringing. *God, it's early. It's got to be Ohio. Only my family calls this early*. I forgot to call Mom to let her know I got home safely, so I figure it must be her, worrying.

"Hello?"

"Hi, Sis. It's me—Melissa. Mom was rushed to the

hospital early this morning. She can't breathe. I'm driving there as soon as our neighbor arrives to watch the kids."

"Oh God, I was just there. Why didn't this happen yesterday? I could have been there. I'll call the hospital and keep track of her condition until you get there."

I call the hospital, explaining to the nurse that my sister will be there as soon as she gets someone to watch the kids. The nurse tries to let me know that it is urgent and that it might be too late, but her words don't sink in. I think this is like every other time—they will send her home with medicine once they get her heart beat regular again.

"Can I talk to my mother?"

"All right," the nurse says, "but someone should get here as soon as possible."

The nurse puts the phone to my mother's lips. She tries to talk and starts to tell me something funny Beth said after I left, but a nurse takes the phone away.

"Her lungs are filled to only sixty percent capacity," I hear someone say in the background.

A nurse speaks into the phone. "Your sister is here. We will put her on the phone."

Melissa and I try to comfort each other, convinced they will regulate her heartbeat and send her home. Raymond is there, and Mom's friend May is on the way. I tell her I'll call Mom's sister Leah in Rhode Island and Rebecca in Florida to update them on Mom's condition.

Melissa promises to call me as soon as she has any news.

It is a long day. Each hour, when my sister calls, the background noises are worse, not better. The situation is touch and go. I hear her doctor in the room now.

My sister calls at two o'clock in the afternoon. What

the doctors and nurses want from us is all a blur because we don't understand exactly what "no heroics" entails.

They try not to say what they can't say: "Remove the tubes."

Melissa cries. "It's hard to stay in the room right now. She can't even breathe with the respirator and tubes."

The nurse in the background picks up the phone. "Her doctor says your family must make a decision now."

We all know Mom's stance on not wanting to be kept artificially alive, and we agree to remove the tubes, hoping she will breathe without them.

I hear a machine beeping, and the doctor's voice says in the background, "Forty percent capacity." *Beep, beep.* "Thirty percent capacity." *Beep, beep.*

Melissa says she will call me as soon as she has any news.

I wait, expecting a call in an hour or at the end of the day, but the phone rings again within minutes, and I hear crying on the other end.

"Is she gone?" I ask.

"Yes."

"It can't be true. It isn't. Is it?"

"It is."

At the funeral, I wonder if my mother is looking down at us looking at her, but I don't feel her presence, only the memory of her, which makes me miss her.

Who could have known that day when Mom and I drove Josh and Beth to school and cut through this funeral home parking lot that it would be only three days until she passed away? That it would be our last time together and that we would be here at her funeral so soon afterward?

Melissa, Rebecca, and I hold hands as we enter the funeral home. Mom looks beautiful in a black dress with red roses that match the roses on top of the coffin. Her hair is perfect, but we all notice that the makeup artist penciled in her eyebrows, making one arched unusually higher than the other. None of us can think of what to do about this, when her best friend, May, standing in line at the coffin, pulls an eyebrow pencil out of her purse and fixes the problem on the spot while talking to my mother. "Don't worry, Muff; I'm going to make you look beautiful." And she does. She perfectly copies the way my mother used to pencil in her left brow to compensate for the right one, which rested naturally higher, just as mine does.

May tells me that she and my mother checked each other's makeup on the way to work every day for twenty-five years.

The funeral home is filled with people, flowers, and condolences. Melissa begins the services with the eulogy, and May's daughter speaks for her because she is too upset. I notice an odd-looking man at the service; he is wearing a wrinkled red polyester suit, dog-eared shoes, and a beat-up camera hanging from his neck. Rebecca tells me that he is a homeless man my mother invited to Thanksgiving dinner one year. Rebecca's son, Logan, places a touching note next to Mom on her pillow, saying, "We will meet again, Grandma."

Aunt Doris, who is sitting behind me, touches my shoulder, whispering, "You girls did right by your mother."

Uncle Darrell, sitting next to her, begins fidgeting,

and I think he is about to stand and sing his old country church song about having a home with Jesus, which would be appropriate, but instead, he says out loud, "Gee, I sure wish I could get out of here."

The next morning is sunny as we enter the funeral home for the last time. By the time the service is over and we are heading to the gravesite, rain is pouring. Everyone sloshes through the mud with colorful umbrellas and finds a place to sit in the rows of chairs under an awning.

In front of me is the inevitable sight of my mother's coffin before her tombstone. My father's grave is to the left, and my parents are now side by side once again.

When I read her name etched into the solid, cold granite, the reality of death—not just my parents' but also mine and everyone's—strikes me as peculiar. We don't know why we are on Earth or what happens to us when we die, yet we carry on in good faith, living with the mystery. Then, when we are face-to-face with the end, it's normal. It's expected. It's a ritual that we are taught.

Closing my eyes, I feel both sad and happy as images from a long time ago float through my head. I remember the smell of dusty erasers, the sound of chalk writing on the blackboard, and lessons about our souls, which are ours and only ours—which no one can touch.

30
To Thine Own Self Be True

The air is brisk, and the sun reflects blue-gold hues upon everything. It's a picture-perfect summer day as I walk to Madison Park with a book to read. When I pass the Flatiron Building, an old picture of this skyscraper comes to mind: the corner of Fifth Avenue and Broadway in the early 1900s. The snow is falling upon gas streetlights, horse-drawn carriages, and people dressed in Victorian-style clothes. I marvel at the idea that I am walking their same path more than a hundred years later.

Once inside the park, I hear the sounds of children laughing and water splashing from the fountain. I stop to enjoy the flowers at the base of a bronze statue about fifteen feet high. The plaque reads, "Chester A. Arthur, the twenty-first president of the United States." He is standing up from his chair, frozen in speech, and a homeless man wrapped tightly in a white blanket is asleep on President Arthur's empty chair. It looks surreal like a game of musical chairs between a mummy and a statue.

I pick a bench to sit on under a tree. A round-bellied

squirrel appears at my feet, waiting for a handout, until someone throws a scrap of food, and the squirrel runs to catch it, along with an onslaught of other squirrels. The winner disappears under the gnarled roots of an oak tree, where a young couple is kissing passionately.

Two men carrying briefcases walk past me in shiny black shoes, dressed in nice suits. I notice a woman in red high heels walking a black Doberman that wears a rhinestone collar and has her purse clenched between his teeth.

A woman wheeling a baby carriage stops and sits next to me. We smile at each other as she rocks a baby in the carriage, and I settle in to read. The pages of my book fall open to an airline ticket stub used as a bookmark. The logo on top is a drawing of the earth in blue lines. Below it are my name, the date of the flight, the seat number, times of arrival and departure, and the final destination.

The fine print reads, "This portion of the boarding pass should be retained as evidence of your journey."

CPSIA information can be obtained
at www.ICGtesting.com
Printed in the USA
FSOW02n0031230217
31130FS